Team Spirit

R J Gould writes contemporary fiction about relationships using a mix of wry humour and pathos to describe the life journeys of his protagonists. *Team Spirit* is his tenth novel and the fourth in the 'at the Dream Café' series. He has been published by Lume Books and Headline Accent and is also self-published. He is a member of Cambridge Writers, Society of Authors and the Romantic Novelists' Association UK. Before becoming a full-time author he worked in the education and charity sectors.

R J Gould lives in Cambridge, England.

www.rjgould.info

To Sharon

Team Spirit

R J Gould

Best wishes

R. Gould

Acknowledgements

There are several people I would like to thank for their help with the publication of this novel.

Joss Alexander, Thure Etzold and Angela Wray, fellow members of the Cambridge Writers Commercial Editing Group, provide generous advice, ranging from a broad consideration of plot and characterisation to meticulous proof reading.

My launch team readers – Alex Elbro, Dr Karen Jost, Gwen Nunn, Helen Appleby, Katy Dowling and Mary Robinson – offer enthusiasm and encouragement in addition to giving valuable feedback on my draft.

Ken Dawson at Creative Covers has once again done a great job in designing the cover which is a perfect fit for the series.

Although all characters are fictional, my thanks go to the members of my tennis club whose antics have sparked some of the ideas for this novel.

Finally, a thank you to Terry Chance for her patience and support together with perceptive, tough judgement of my wilder ideas.

1

Oliver Kilroy strides through Dream Café offering token nods of acknowledgement to tennis club members, aware that civility might prove invaluable when the vote is taken. He reaches the toilets, now unisex of course, urinals having been removed. Entering a cubicle, he closes the seat lid and slumps down. At last, a moment of peace and quiet. He takes out his hip flask and swigs some more whisky.

He knows that he has a drink problem. His working life is centred on the acquisition of proof and there is plenty of it to verify this fact. Blue recycling bins are full to the brim ahead of each fortnightly collection. If he is at home when the refuse van arrives, he can hear the crash as wine and spirit bottles tumble into the container. Of course, some will be from his wife Stephanie, but most are his. Then there are the intimidating entries on his credit card statements, the soaring upward expenditure for purchases from the high-priced wine merchant just off Muswell Hill Broadway.

There is little doubt that his performance is suffering of late – impatience with clients, poor decision-making in court. There have been slip-ups at home too; he used to be such a good liar. Often he's exhausted which has never been the case in the past.

Kilroy the Killer is his nickname at the Old Bailey criminal law courts, with a reputation for twisting and turning evidence until the jury are ready to dismiss every truth a witness utters. Over the years he's received adulation for the way he destroys his victims, but lately he's picked up murmurings about having lost the plot.

Oliver lifts the hip flask to his lips again and takes a drink, savouring the warmth and the kick as the liquid slides down his throat. This flask is the single remaining memento of his father's existence, kept because it must be worth a bit rather than for sentimental reasons. There was no love lost between him and his father. The flask is a work of art, solid silver with fine inlay, crafted in the 1820s and verified with a hallmark. A bonus is that it's perfect to conceal in the inside pocket of his jacket for surreptitious use when seeking Dutch courage during a tricky court appearance. Increasingly he's needing a drink or two or more to steady his nerves.

There's no need for nerves tonight though, a doddle compared to the challenge of standing up in court to fight a case. It's merely the tennis club annual general meeting and he is bound to be voted in as Chairman for a fourth year. However, it will be the first time during his tenure that there is a contest and the need for an election, the rival candidate being Stephanie. He anticipates a furious onslaught from his wife because of what happened and her quest for revenge. She will be a determined adversary, but her skill set is rather limited and he's well-prepared to counter any claim she might make. Yes, no need for nerves, he'll put her in her place, to be followed by a landslide victory.

He is about to make his way to the meeting when a couple of women enter the facility. There are two clicks as cubicle doors are closed and the women start shouting across to each other.

'Tonight is going to be so much fun; I can't wait.'

'You bet. There'll be fireworks alright, hopefully with Oliver being humiliated. The arrogant shit.'

'Too right. He thinks he's Adonis but he should take a look at himself in the mirror. I will be voting for Stephanie but I don't think much of her either.'

'Agreed, it'll be a vote for the lesser of two evils.'

Two cisterns are flushed and two cubicle doors are opened. For obvious reasons, Oliver will stay put until they have left. But they're lingering, chatting away.

'I haven't seen either of them yet.'

'No worry, they'll be here.'

'Do you think most people are on Stephanie's side?'

'We'll soon find out; Oliver will have some supporters. How's your little one getting on?'

'Do you mean Charlie or the baby?'

'Very funny!'

How much longer, Oliver is thinking. He takes out his phone to check on the time. He needs to be out there soon but the women are still gossiping. He can't bear being idle so googles to kill the time.

Adonis. *In Greek mythology the god of beauty and desire.*

He already knows that; he did Classics at school.

Present-day usage: a very handsome young man.

Fair enough, he might not be young, but plenty of women would testify to his good looks.

The women are rabbiting on.

'God, look at my new hairdo, Abi. I hate it. I might go back tomorrow and kill the stylist.'

'It's nice, Jas. Though why so heavy on the blusher tonight?'

'Men's team captains. Male coaches. They'll all be here.'

'Sometimes I think you only play tennis so you can get near them.'

'Sometimes I think you're right!'

'Here, give me some of that, I'm not going to let you have all the fun. Take a spray of this if you'd like.'

'Ta, darling.'

There is laughter.

Oliver is googling on.

Dutch courage. *Foolish courage and misplaced confidence as a result of intoxication. Origin: the British mocking Dutch sailors by accusing them of only being willing to fight when they were drunk.*

'I reckon there's more chance of finding someone at the club than through online dating.'

'Still no luck with that then?'

'Hopeless.'

'Come on, let's go. The meeting's starting in a couple of minutes.'

The door opens and shuts and there is silence.

Oliver has recognised one of the voices, Abigail, or Abi as she likes to call herself. He's played with her during social tennis mornings. She's a pretty young thing and it's a struggle to concentrate on the game when she's crouching down by the net. When they chat between points she laughs at his jokes, so wildly that he's even wondered whether she fancies him. So what's going on between her and her friend with their nasty comments?

He lifts the hip flask to his lips to discover that it's empty. He'd swigged once or twice on the short walk from home to the café, the whisky chasing a few glasses of red wine he'd had with dinner.

Leaving the cubicle, he glances at the mirror above the washbasin. OK, perhaps no longer an Adonis but he's still got a lot going for him for a man in his mid-fifties. A nicely balanced face with everything exactly in the right place and the right proportions. Best features? Definitely his enticing ice-blue eyes that can heighten an impish grin at the drop of a hat. Possibly his hair too, peppered with grey but mostly as jet black as when he was a youngster.

He fails to note that the face in the mirror looking back at him is a tired one with a sallow complexion.

Folds of skin hang from his cheeks and there are serious bags under his eyes. A bald patch runs from his forehead up to his crown. Eyebrow, nose and ear hair could all do with a good trim.

Only one of these versions enters the room to chair the annual general meeting of the tennis club and it isn't the one with the face he has admired when looking in the mirror.

~

Stephanie Kilroy looks at her watch. Nine minutes to go. She is still sitting in her BMW having decided on a last minute entrance to avoid socialising ahead of her involvement in the first item on the agenda. She peers down at her phone, flicking through the text at speed. Her notes are meticulous, a skill developed while working as a barrister at the Old Bailey. It's an unnecessary check though because she's fully prepared to present the evidence – a long list of misdemeanours her husband has been guilty of over the past year of his chairmanship of the tennis club.

Only once have she and Ollie been on opposite sides in the courtroom. This was soon after they had started dating and she was ruthlessly defeated by her future husband. No, more than that, humiliated, with Ollie having manipulated witnesses' accounts and twisted evidence to sway the jury. Stephanie had laughed it off, admiring and allured by the man's power. However, a deep down subliminal resentment must have lingered for all these years because she is out for revenge this evening. If necessary, if it gets

6

nasty, her assault will include reference to her husband's marital indiscretions.

Six minutes to go.

She picks up the thermos flask on the passenger's seat, purchased long ago in the children's department at Selfridges. It is lime green, patterned with dinosaurs, and whenever she takes it into the courtroom it brings smiles to the faces of the jurors. No bad thing in the battle to win them over. Is it filled with water they could well be wondering? Or maybe tea. Or even coffee. Wrong, wrong and wrong again because it's vodka mixed with tonic water and a teaspoonful of lime juice.

Stephanie pours a sizeable quantity into the beaker and gulps it down as if it were lemonade. Still thirsty, at least this is what she tells herself, she pours out another cupful and drinks.

That's helped quell nerves and she is raring to go.

Four minutes.

Time to enter the café.

2

This is all my fault, Jennifer Kroll is thinking as she regards the boisterous tennis club members, fuelled by alcohol, who have piled into Dream Café. She fears the worst. On catching sight of David, the café owner, she offers a half-hearted wave and manufactures an unconvincing smile. David smiles back; he has no idea what might follow.

Jennifer considers her options. There aren't many. Two in fact. The first is to climb onto the rostrum and unilaterally declare that the meeting has been cancelled. The second is to flee. She will do neither; she'll just stay put and hope for the best.

Helen is by her side. She's her closest friend at the club and a sharp cookie if ever there was one. Not for the first time she seems to possess a sixth sense when it comes to reading Jennifer's mind. 'It'll be fine, stop worrying.'

Jennifer is sure that it won't be fine and it's because of her that this annual general meeting is taking place at the café. 'Hardly,' she replies. 'Not after everything that's been flying around on WhatsApp this week.'

'You're wrong. I've spoken to Laurie and he intends to step in if things start getting nasty.'

Laurie, the deputy chairman, is a softly spoken, gentle soul. Jennifer has little confidence in his ability to calm things down. If Helen were deputy it might be different.

~

Jennifer, a relatively new member of the club, had only been trying to help. Oliver, the chairman, had posted an S.O.S. on WhatsApp asking for suggestions of where to hold meetings while the clubhouse was closed for refurbishment. Dream Café seemed the obvious choice. Over the past eighteen months the café had become a popular meeting place in the affluent London suburb of Muswell Hill and was already hosting all sorts of events for local groups, including the amateur dramatics nights that Jennifer organised.

Jennifer was deputy manager at On the Hill, the boutique hotel part-owned by Bridget and David, who were also the café proprietors. At the end of their Monday catch up meeting at the hotel, Jennifer had asked David if there was a possibility of using the café as the venue for the monthly tennis club committee meetings. All that would be needed, she told him, was to push a couple of tables together and reserve them for the small group. She'd added, based on what she'd read in the WhatsApp post, that it would be great if the café could also provide the teas for eight players after weekend matches during the winter months. Definitely only over the winter she stressed; the work on the clubhouse would be completed ahead of the busy summer season.

'Of course,' David had said, happy to oblige with this relatively small addition to the café schedule.

However, soon after reaching their tentative agreement, Jennifer received a text from David informing her that Bridget had concerns about over-committing. She wanted a meeting to get further details ahead of a definite yes.

Jennifer texted back. *No problem. I can't provide all the info myself so I'll get someone to join me.*

Great. Can you make it tomorrow early evening, say around six? I'm assuming we won't need more than half an hour to firm up the arrangement because I need time to get ready for a guest speaker at eight.

The club chairman would have been the obvious person for Jennifer to bring along, but Oliver was away on a cruise so it would need to be Laurie, his deputy. Jennifer was happy with that because Oliver, arrogant and a snob, would be expecting something for nothing and could possibly end up antagonising Bridget. Laurie on the other hand was thoughtful and a good listener. This modest man was oblivious to the fact that women at the club were either in love with him or intent on mothering him. I guess I'm stuck somewhere in the middle, Jennifer was thinking as the pair of them made their way to the café. Too old to swoon but too young to be maternal.

'Are you sure this is only a formality?' Laurie asked.

'Absolutely. Bridget wants to know exactly what's required which is fair enough. She's really nice so there's nothing to worry about.'

She led Laurie to the small office where Bridget and David were waiting, seated behind a desk.

'Thanks for coming over to chat about this,' Bridget began. 'Look, I am worried about taking on another commitment. We have so much going on I'm struggling to keep track of everything. And an added concern is that when an outside group comes in to run an event, however small, it changes the atmosphere for the other customers.'

'I can appreciate what you mean, Bridget, though I really don't think that our occasional presence would do that. Let me outline our exact requirement and then it's up to you to decide. If you feel it's too much of a burden, no problem. We can look elsewhere.'

Wow, this was Laurie speaking, his clarity and polite assertiveness taking Jennifer by surprise. How could Bridget possibly say no?

'Go on then,' Bridget suggested, her tone yet to soften.

'There's a committee meeting for eight of us on the first Monday of each month, although it's unusual for everyone to turn up. The average session is no more than an hour long.'

'Mondays would work for us; it's the one night of the week when we never have anything planned,' David said, his comment encouraging.

'Exactly, David. It's nice to have an evening with nothing to worry about.'

What's going on, Jennifer wondered? She'd always regarded Bridget as a can-do person.

'If I could just add,' Laurie continued, 'that there really would be nothing for you to arrange other than putting a reserved note on our table. We'd go to the bar to get drinks and then be out of everyone's way in a quiet corner. Actually, I have an idea. If it helps I could get to the café early and reserve the table simply by sitting at it – so no need for any signage.'

'Wasn't there something else you wanted to run here?'

'Yes, Bridget. There is a winter league. We play matches against other clubs, though nowhere near as many as in summer. Afterwards the home team provides tea for themselves and their opponents. We're talking about eight people coming in at about four o'clock on some Saturdays and Sundays, starting the week after next and running on until Easter. We'd be in the café for half an hour or so, no more because in winter everyone seems keen to get home. When we were on our way here I was thinking about how that might work. You have a lovely venue, I'm a regular customer, and we could simply do the same as everyone else, place our orders for tea, sandwiches and cakes as we arrive.'

'But there might not be much left by late afternoon, particularly on Sundays,' David said.

'So is another option that we order a week in advance and pay upfront?'

'Yes, that would fit.'

'OK, here's a proposal. What about giving it a go for a month to see how it works, followed by a review?' Bridget suggested.

'I'm sorry, but that's no good for us. We wouldn't want to have to search for another venue midway through the closure of the clubhouse if you decided not to continue.'

Laurie let his statement sink in before continuing.

'So it's all or nothing really.' There was another pause. 'You're known for supporting the local community and this would be a great addition.'

'And you're talking about using the café for six months, definitely no longer?'

'Absolutely. The builders are hired and ready to start and they'll be providing us with a schedule.'

'We all know what builders' schedules are like.'

'I'll make sure they deliver on time; the clubhouse has to be open for the start of the summer season. There is one more event to mention, our AGM next month. Based on past experience it will be as uneventful as the committee meetings, though sometimes we get a few additional members turning up to ask questions. So we'd need to reserve the café for exclusive use for part of that evening. Naturally we'd pay whatever you feel is fair since it means no other customers for a couple of hours.'

At last there was a smile from Bridget. 'There's a job for you out there in public relations or even the diplomatic service, Laurie. Or do you already work in that field?'

'No. Actually I'm a chemist. I'm stuck in a laboratory with no one else around most of the time.'

'OK, all good. We're happy to host the tennis club at the café over the winter. Perhaps for the sake of clarity we should formalise things with a contract. Can you sort that out with Laurie and Jennifer, David?'

'Of course.'

'Thanks. I'm going to head off then. We've had a hectic few days and I'm shattered. A pity though because I was looking forward to listening to tonight's speaker.'

'A local artist; I've seen your advert,' Laurie said.

'Bridget's also an artist,' Jennifer got in. 'The paintings in the café are hers.'

'I know – and they're wonderful. I admire them whenever I'm here.'

'Definitely the diplomatic service awaits you, Laurie!' Bridget stood up. 'I appreciate you taking the time to explain things.'

David turned to face Laurie as Bridget was leaving. 'I'll have the contract ready to pass on to Jennifer tomorrow afternoon. If you're happy with everything, sign and return it via her. Now, if you don't mind, I need to set things up for tonight.'

'That was mighty impressive,' Jennifer said as she and Laurie were leaving the café. 'It was much tougher than I expected; I don't know what came over Bridget. I guess she's feeling the strain.'

'Well, the important thing is that all is sorted thanks to you finding the perfect place. It would have been useful for Oliver to check the contract given his expertise, but I'm not expecting to see any surprise clauses.'

'I'm sure not. After all, it's hardly complicated. All the club wants is somewhere to run those boring meetings and we'll be bringing in customers for teas. There's absolutely nothing that can go wrong.'

~

Jennifer is thinking about those words of reassurance she had uttered to Laurie – there's absolutely nothing that can go wrong – as more and more members squeeze into the café. Laurie had reassured Bridget that the AGM would be as low key as the committee meetings with perhaps a few additional members turning up. The place is packed. Judging by the comments she's overhearing, the participants are baying for blood rather than ready to offer polite applause at the appropriate times.

The noise is deafening, with laughter, shouting and the clinking of glasses. Tables are being pushed to the sides without permission and Jennifer can see David looking at her with an expression suggesting concern.

'Where's Oliver?' someone calls out, the demand echoed by others.

'And where's Stephanie?' others are asking.

And then it's as if a person is slowly turning down the volume dial on a radio, from deafeningly loud, to tolerable, to faint, to a hushed silence as first Oliver emerges from the toilet area and then Stephanie appears at the café entrance.

Oliver walks towards the stage unsteadily, stumbling as he steps onto the platform. Laurie dashes to his side to help him up. Laughter erupts as somebody shouts, 'What have you been drinking, Oliver?'

Meanwhile, Stephanie is staggering through the crowd, ricocheting against those she passes as she makes her way to the front. She slumps onto the chair that has been reserved for her at the side of the stage and pours a drink from a children's thermos flask.

The two stars of the night are in place and Oliver is ready to speak.

Looking up at Oliver on stage and then at an over-excited audience, Laurie is worried.

3

It was Oliver who had decided on a cruise to celebrate their twenty-fifth wedding anniversary, but it couldn't be a surprise trip because the holiday had to fit in with their busy work schedules. "It's a once in a lifetime event, Stephanie," Oliver said when his wife questioned the cost of an exclusive trip with every optional extra going, "and you're worth every penny."

They were high earners, so why not?

Stephanie smiled, hugged her husband and planted a kiss on his flabby right cheek, as much of a play-act as her husband's false warmth. Their marriage was a sham. Stephanie was aware of her husband's philandering. At least in the past Oliver had planned his indiscretions with as much respect for Stephanie's feelings as possible given their nature, but recently he'd been careless or indifferent. Despite this, Stephanie stuck with it, recognising that their marriage was convenient, or more to the point, divorce would be an inconvenience for a barrister specialising in family law. Anyway, when it came to extra-marital relationships she was hardly guilt-free.

She'd gone on a shopping spree as soon as their booking was confirmed and as departure day approached was quite looking forward to a Mediterranean cruise. Her suitcase was stuffed with designer clothes and her holdall was weighed down with guidebooks, purchased as a pleasant respite from reading everything online. She put together a list of the must-see places at the ports of call – Venice, Athens, Barcelona, Casablanca – cities she'd previously visited, of course, but still loved. She made a resolution not to over indulge, despite Oliver selecting the eat-and-drink-as-much-as-you-want option. She reserved daily places on the yoga and aqua aerobics classes. She even pledged to be nice to her husband.

It did not go to plan.

However easy it might be to conceal womanising within the vast city of London, in the confines of a cruise ship, even a giant one, the task was beyond Oliver.

"Just going for a stroll on deck" or "I fancy a play in the casino" were the tired explanations in advance of his absence. The idiot would return to their luxury cabin in the early hours of the morning, slumping down onto their bed in a drunken stupor, reeking of a mix of alcohol and the fragrance of the day. Stephanie could recognise the brands – Dior, Chanel, Gucci.

One morning, still half asleep, he greeted Stephanie with, "*Bonjour ma chérie*" and the following morning with, "*Buon giorno Tesoro mio*". It didn't take a genius to work out what that was about.

Stephanie sought hard facts. She was practised at accumulating evidence of sexual misdemeanours for court cases but now, for the first time, it was she who was doing the shadowing and snooping on a husband. It was enjoyable this private detective work, in fact rather more fun than being a barrister. Oliver appeared to be working his way through the Women of the Mediterranean Lands, although a liaison with an American dented that theory. Cruises, Stephanie knew, were notorious upmarket dating opportunities and these ageing, loose women were doing the rounds with her husband an easy catch. Actually, she began to feel sorry for them with their highly transparent desperation – over made-up to conceal wrinkles, mutton dressed up as lamb designer wear, spending money like there was no tomorrow.

Oliver had always regarded himself as God's gift to women, making this cruise nirvana as far as he was concerned. Fogged by alcohol, he had no idea that his wife was recording the goings on. Stephanie was happy to let the drama roll on because finally she had decided to file for divorce. The portfolio of evidence that she was building up over the three weeks would be used to take as much money from him as possible in the settlement. Revenge was round the corner.

As soon as she returned home Stephanie set to work. She opened a Twitter account (or must everyone have to call it X nowadays?) named *@OKilroy_social*. Using the hashtags *#olliekilroy* and *#myfemalefriends*, she posted salacious one-liners like

Thanks Ruby, you were SO hot last night. It hardly went viral but it was fun making up the posts.

She informed friends that she was leaving Oliver, explaining that his appalling infidelity on their anniversary cruise was the final straw. She added photos to her messages, knowing that her female friends were likely to show them to their husbands and partners. She wouldn't need to tell Oliver that she was leaving him; those male friends of his would do the job for her.

The tennis club WhatsApp group was barely used of late, members preferring to text an individual directly, for instance to arrange a game. Occasionally one of the team captains would put up something like *Need an extra player for Sunday's match for the Men's C Team. Please get in touch if available.* But that was pretty well it.

Things were about to change.

Several of the Kilroy friendship group were members of the tennis club and Stephanie got the ball rolling with a dignified WhatsApp statement.

Stephanie
Sad to announce that Oliver and I are separating. 13.57

Flo
Sad indeed, you're such a lovely couple. 14.02

Stephanie

Thanks Flo. You know how it is, things change.
14.04

Dee
But you've only just got back from that wonderful cruise. 14.07

Stephanie
I know, Dee. It just didn't work out. 14.11

Ursula
Have you tried mediation? It helped us. 14.20

Stephanie
I fear it's too late but thanks for the suggestion.
14.26

Oliver
Could I please ask everyone, including my wife, to refrain from posting about this personal matter? Thank you. 14.27

Stephanie
Obviously my husband doesn't want everyone to know that he has been unfaithful. 14.31

Jane
Really? How could you, Oliver? Stephanie is a star. 14.32

Julie

Agree. Disgraceful. Never trusted him. 14.38

Abi
Too right. Whenever we're playing together he's leching. 14.46

Oliver
I totally reject that accusation and demand an apology. 14.48

Abi
I won't apologise because it's true. 14.50

John
Excuse this interruption but I'm short of a player for tomorrow's match. Please respond ASAP if able to play for Men's B Team. First come first served selection. 14.52

Stephanie
Abi, if Oliver's behaviour on our anniversary cruise is anything to go by, you're spot on. 14.55

Frank
Why? What happened on this cruise of yours? 15.07

Stephanie
Oh, only that Oliver ignored me but not those from countries across the Mediterranean. 15.09

Tim
Hi John. I'm around so happy to play if you're still looking.

Frank
Meaning? 15.11

Stephanie
Work it out, Frank. 15.16

Oliver
Stephanie, this is disgraceful and indeed slanderous. You know the consequences and I WILL take action unless you cease now. 15.17

Stephanie
OK, I will stop apart from announcing that I intend to stand as Chair at the forthcoming AGM. 15.13

Oliver
That's ridiculous. Why would you want to do that? 15.18

Stephanie
To make the club dealings more ethical than is currently the case. 15.19

Oliver [Private reply]
Stephanie, I'm warning you! 15.21

Stephanie

I'm logging off now. But – VOTE FOR ME, EVERYONE! 15.24

Enough was enough because Stephanie had a full understanding of the risk of litigation even if Oliver was unlikely to go down that route. A court case involving two top lawyers would be a godsend to the tabloids.

Warned by Helen, Laurie had seen the WhatsApp posts before his meeting with Oliver to discuss the agenda for the AGM. When questioned about the likelihood of potential conflict, Oliver assured Laurie that all would be fine. He was dismissive of his wife's challenge to run for chairman, confident that the members would appreciate what a good position the club was in thanks to his hard work. Apparently, there were further initiatives he had in mind to ensure that the club continued to thrive.

Laurie had no choice but to trust Oliver's judgement despite failing to discover what Stephanie was planning. Since announcing her intention to stand she had kept away from the tennis club and hadn't responded to Laurie's texts and emails. If nothing was contentious why was she avoiding him?

During the days leading up to the AGM there was a further wave of malicious gossip on the WhatsApp group. People were taking sides, those who had never liked Oliver, who didn't think he was fit to represent the club, who felt that his immoral behaviour should rule him out of such a role, against those who considered Oliver's personal behaviour to be irrelevant. Members of this latter group were inclined to express a dislike of Stephanie.

'Which group is in the majority?' Laurie had asked Helen on the day before the meeting after they'd finished playing tennis together.

'Based on the WhatsApp posts I'd say Stephanie is in the lead, though perhaps not by much.'

'Who will you vote for?'

'Neither of them because I know someone who'd be a much better choice.'

Laurie reddened when she said this and he looked away. 'I'll see you tomorrow evening then,' he uttered, his eyes fixed on his racket.

~

Beaming at the audience, Oliver raises his arm in acknowledgement of their adulation as if they are disciples of a religious guru or fans of an ageing rock star. There is an astounding lack of awareness that the crowd are laughing at him, not with him.

Laurie considers his responsibility as Deputy Chair. Should he be up on the platform cancelling the event? He spots Helen pointing towards Oliver. What does that mean? A signal for him to intervene? He decides to wait and see what transpires, a small part of him hoping to see Oliver humiliated. He sits down next to Stephanie whose vacant look suggests that she, too, is intoxicated. What's in that kid's flask she's clutching?

Laurie is the note-taker for this meeting. He opens his iPad and skim reads the previous year's minutes. They record a sedate affair with just seventeen participants, including eight committee members, two team captains and three coaches. Clearly, back then interest in the management of the tennis club wasn't a concern for its members, and why should it have been with everything running so smoothly? Club finances were in fine shape. Membership was high with a waiting list to join. The teams had enjoyed a successful season. The popular coaches were being kept busy. It was unsurprising that no one challenged Oliver's chairmanship last year. Although not well-liked, he was doing the job competently with members aware that this volunteer post required considerable time and expertise.

Since last year's AGM, Oliver has kickstarted the rebuilding of the clubhouse. Laurie, now in his second year as deputy, respects Oliver's tenacity in managing the project – working with the architects, gaining planning permission, tendering for builders.

If it hadn't been for the WhatsApp posts, this would be another poorly attended, rather dull annual meeting, just as they had promised the café owners.

That promise is at risk. The place is packed and it threatens to be anything but dull.

He types *AGM Monday 4 October* on a new Word document.

Last year he could count the number of attendees. This year he's hoping that everyone has signed in by the door as requested.

He judges that there are seventy or so crammed into the café. *Number of participants* he types, followed by *???*

He looks up in the hope of spotting Helen. Yes, there she is, edging closer to the front. He likes her. She's practical, down to earth and a good tennis player. He's kidding himself that these are the things he most likes about her. She's stunning and he's awestruck. A couple of times she's told him that she's single. Maybe this slipped out in passing but he reckons they were deliberate hints. He'd love to … but it isn't possible the way things are.

Laurie looks up at the stage to see Oliver glancing down at the sheet of paper he has placed on the podium. Oliver looks across at his audience and there's a weak 'Ahem', his call for silence. He raises an arm in an attempt to quell the chatter.

'Ahem. Ahem.'

Laurie stands up and shouts. 'Can we have quiet please everybody? It's time to begin the meeting. So, over to you, Oliver.'

4

'Good evening, ladies and gentlemen. How wonderful to see such a large turnout.

'Ahead of carrying out the usual business matters, the first item on the agenda is to select your chairman. As most of you will be aware, in the recent past this has been a formality because there has been no contestation. But this year, for reasons unknown to anyone but herself, my wife Stephanie has decided to stand against me. Consequently, and in discussion with Laurie, we have each been allocated five minutes of your time, a wasted five minutes I believe, to present our cases.'

'You're the fuckin' wasted one, matey,' a man calls out and there is a tittering from those leaning against the counter at the back of the room, matched by the tut-tuts from those seated towards the front. Oliver ignores the comment and presses on.

'Allow me to outline the successes of the past year and, if I may, outline my role in facilitating such tremendous progress.'

'Speak plain English,' someone shouts as Oliver glances down at the sheet of paper. There are five headings with a brief note underneath each of them.

'Firstly. Membership.' He pauses for dramatic effect. 'We have a record number of members this year and a substantial waiting list. My interview for the local newspaper together with a hard-hitting advertising campaign have raised our profile no end, as have my Facebook, Instagram and Twitter posts. I am delighted to announce this evening that one of our youth members has volunteered to take on the by no means straightforward task of establishing a TikTok presence.

'On to my second success –'

'Bullshitting!' a member cries out and laughter drowns any tut-tutting.

'Income,' Oliver proclaims when the laughter subsides. 'Our balance sheet has never been healthier, in part due to membership fees, but in addition through our programme of social events which has raised a considerable amount. I must take some credit for this financial success, having used personal contacts to acquire generous donations to add to the pot.

'Teams.' Once again Oliver pauses to enable the audience to focus. His gravitas replicates the courtroom performances when he declares "Motive?" and provides time for the jury to recognise the innocence of the seemingly motiveless defendant.

He continues. 'In all my time as a member, and that goes back over thirty years, we have never had such success. A special mention must go to the men's fourth and the women's second teams for winning promotions.' He pauses. 'Perhaps that men's success is because I am no longer in the team!'

Oliver's loud guffaw in an attempt to induce audience laughter falls flat. A stoney silence descends beyond the clink of glasses and the ongoing chatter by the bar.

'Coaching. Using my influence with senior members at the LTA, we have been able to recruit Dan Wilkins. You may not be aware that Dan is the former British Number Seven and for us to acquire him is a tremendous achievement.

'Finally, the clubhouse rebuild. Planning, designing, funding, project managing – these are the considerable tasks that have been required in recent months and indeed will be ongoing now that the building work is about to start. To reach this point, I have held numerous meetings with local council officials, architects, residents' committees and builders.

While I am honoured to hold the position as chairman of this tennis club, I must remind you that it is a voluntary post taking up an inordinate amount of time and effort to ensure that everything runs smoothly. I continue to be willing to carry out this service.

'My friends, our club is going from strength to strength and over the past four years under my leadership there has been nothing but success, success and still more success.'

Oliver pauses in expectation of applause but there is none, so he continues. 'May I suggest a short break to refill our glasses and give you the opportunity to reflect on what I have said, after which time the second nominee can put forward her case if she so wishes.

'Thank you.'

The ovation is little more than a gentle ripple, drowned by the chatter amongst members.

'What do you reckon?' Helen asks Jennifer. 'A worthy leader?'

Having only recently joined the club, Jennifer doesn't feel in a position to have an opinion on the accuracy of Oliver's claims. What she is overhearing though are complaints about a boring speech and disappointment that the predicted fireworks are so far absent.

'Let's see what Stephanie has to say,' she replies as they watch Oliver barge his way towards the bar.

~

Stephanie steps up onto the Dream Café stage. In the past it has been used for poetry and literature readings, for concerts and drama performances. This is a first for political hustings. Oliver has returned to the stage uninvited. Noisily, he slides a chair adjacent to his wife, his close proximity intended to be intimidating. Stephanie is used to such tactics at home and in the courtroom. She ignores him and turns to face the audience.

'Hi everyone,' she begins, her voice firm, her balance less so. 'I will base my candidate's statement on the current chairman's five claims of success. Membership. Income. Teams. Coaching. The clubhouse. I intend to dismantle each claim with a sledgehammer, exposing exaggeration, lies and corruption.'

'Hang on, Stephanie. How come you've seen what I was going to cover in my speech? Have you hacked into my laptop?'

'I saw handwritten notes when the chairman left them for all to see on the kitchen table at home. Might I remind him that we do still live together, though hopefully not for long, and I have as much right to be in the kitchen as he does.'

'Stephanie, there is no need to raise personal matters tonight. And you still have to explain why you think it's acceptable to use my notes, even if catching sight of them was unplanned.'

'Which hardly constitutes theft.'

'If not theft, it certainly is highly unethical. Immoral.'

'I suggest the current chairman refrains from using words associated with ethics and morality in the light of the points I am about to raise. Assuming he will now allow me to proceed.'

'No, Stephanie, I will not allow you to proceed.'

'Let 'er speak will ya,' someone in the audience calls out, followed by cheering from those at the back of the room. There are even calls of "Here, here," from the less raucous attendees sitting towards the front.

Stephanie raises her hand for silence. 'Thank you, everyone. Let us begin with Membership. The current chairman stated that we have a record number of members. Indeed this is correct, the increase this year being a single person. Sadly, Maisie Longhurst passed away and when the first person on the waiting list was approached he implored us to allow his partner to join with him. We agreed to this request and as a result, instead of five hundred members we now have five hundred and one, an increase of 0.2%. Bearing this in mind, the local newspaper advertising campaign, costing £486, seems a total waste of money. To avoid any danger of litigation I will not be suggesting that paying for unnecessary advertising has anything to do with the fact that our current chairman is having an affair with the newspaper editor –'

'Stephanie, stop at once!'

'Keep quiet, you've 'ad yer turn,' another member shouts.

'One final point about membership concerns the TikTok account that a youth member has volunteered to set up. This happens to be our son and he is being paid £250 for doing so. I was opposed to any payment going to a family member but was overruled.

'On to Income. I don't intend to dwell on this other than to make one point. A sizable donation has been received from Stan Smithers. Last February Stan was in the dock charged with fraud and theft. The current chairman was his defence counsel and he got him acquitted due to a prosecution irregularity. The donation followed. Perhaps everything in life is coincidental – I leave it for you to decide.'

There is silence as Stephanie pauses. Even the crowd by the drinks counter are quiet, sensing that things are hotting up. Maybe there will be fireworks after all.

Bridget has joined David on duty behind the bar and a lull in sales is giving them the opportunity to collect glasses and tidy up. They do this quietly, as keen as anyone to hear what Stephanie has to say.

'Next, Teams. Yes, a huge well done to everyone, win or lose. You have done our club proud.

'Coaching. Acquiring Dan Wilkins is a major scoop and we are lucky to have him. However, I should point out that recruiting Dan has nothing to do with the current chairman's imagined connections with the LTA. In fact, it was Dan who approached us. Having retired from the circuit he is taking a sports science degree at the University of London and was looking for work at a nearby club. I was in the clubhouse when he came to enquire and it was me who convinced the current chairman to hire him.'

'I do have a name. What's all this "current chairman" rubbish?'

'Very well, Oliver. Ollie. Or Olé as the Spanish woman on our cruise, the one you dabbled with one night, called you.'

'Don't you dare get personal!'

'Oh, just you wait until I get really personal, Olé. So we move on to Olé's final success in this list of his – the refurbishment of the clubhouse. I feel obliged to let you know that the builder selected to carry out the work has kindly rewarded the decision maker with a Rolex watch. You even have an opportunity to see the item because the foolish Olé has decided to wear it this evening. It costs £1,200 according to my Google search which makes it a rather expensive thank you gift. Were I not in fear of litigation, I might be inclined to call this a bribe.'

'Come on, show us your watch, Oliver,' someone calls out.

'Yeah, come on, Olé.'

'Come on Olé,' a female member with a gruff voice belts out to the tune of Dexys Midnight Runners' *Come on Eileen*. There is an abrupt halt to the proceedings as others join in the singing.

Jennifer is alarmed. As she feared, things are getting out of hand. She should never have suggested using Dream Café to host events while the clubhouse was out of use. She'd encouraged David to allow it, coerced Bridget into agreeing. At the time, the risk of poor behaviour as she was now witnessing hadn't entered her head. Next to her, Helen is singing along as she sways her arms. Looking behind her she sees Bridget laughing and David singing. It's a tune her partner Gareth had got her listening to when they were in the States and it became one of her all-time favourites. She joins in with the *ta-loo-rye-ays* as a red-faced Oliver looks on.

Stephanie calls a halt to the joviality, her raising of an arm having the magical effect of restoring order. 'Exposing the current chairman as corrupt and unethical,' she continues, 'is the relatively painless part of my speech this evening, but now I would like to turn to the broader issue of common decency.' She's clearly drunk, holding on to the rostrum for dear life and slurring her speech. 'Tell me, how can a man take his wife on a Mediterranean cruise to celebrate their twenty-fifth wedding anniversary and then proceed to you know what with women from a variety of countries that border the Mediterranean Sea? What puzzles me is why these women would succumb to a man with a penis the size of a stick of chalk, a rather small stick of chalk.'

All hell breaks loose as Oliver takes a lunge towards Stephanie, grabbing hold around her neck. There is a cacophony of gasps, cheers and jeers and a fight breaks out in the left hand corner of the room. Jennifer sees one of Bridget's lovely paintings tumble to the floor and someone engaged in the melee treads on it. She looks across to see if Bridget has noticed. She has and Jennifer dashes across to apologise and to suggest they call the police.

'I'm so sorry,' she shouts as she reaches the café owners.

'No David, do not!' she hears Bridget say as she grabs hold of her partner. 'Remember what happened the last times you tried to intervene?'

Bridget is holding onto David's arm. 'I'm not letting go of you. Help me, Jennifer, tell David he's not to interfere.'

What is she talking about? This is madness!

Jennifer is unaware that David has been floored while trying to restore justice twice in the past. The first time was while being robbed in a London alleyway. David's attempt to ridicule the assailant earned him a trip to A&E with a broken jaw. More recently at the café, his attempt to placate an aggressive local had ended with David being felled by a hefty punch.

David has conceded and Bridget relaxes her grip.

'I feel awful. What can I do?' Jennifer cries out as the three of them watch Laurie and two others on the stage separating the Kilroys in a scene worthy of a Muswell Hill Amateur Dramatics Society performance during a Dream Café theatre night. She is relieved to see that the fight by Bridget's smashed canvas has ended, the protagonists laughing and shaking hands.

'I think the melee is drawing to a close,' David suggests and his assessment seems true as Oliver stops struggling and steps off the stage.

Oliver turns back to face Stephanie. 'I'll see you in court!'

Turning again, he heads towards the door but his path is blocked by a woman who slaps him hard across his cheek.

'And fuck you, too!' the woman yells as she points towards Stephanie.

'Who's that?' Jennifer asks David.

'I believe she's the editor of the local newspaper. She won't be happy that Stephanie's announced her affair to the world. She's married, I think her husband is here tonight …'

There's another commotion around Oliver. Two middle-aged women of slender build are trying to restrain a beefy man who has grabbed hold of the current chairman and is shaking him vigorously. The women have no chance and are brushed aside before a crunching blow sends Oliver crashing to the floor.

'Yes, I'm right, that's the newspaper editor's husband,' David confirms. They watch the man storm out.

'Wait, let me explain!' his wife shouts as she races after him.

Oliver pauses, perhaps wary of a second assault were he to leave the building too quickly. Finally he departs, ignored by everyone.

The shocked silence is broken as Laurie steps up onto the stage. 'I suggest we cancel the meeting.'

5

Stephanie is clambering onto the stage. She pushes Laurie aside and grabs hold of the microphone.

'There's no need to cancel. Apologies for my husband's appalling behaviour this evening, but since I'm left as the sole candidate for the post of chair, allow me to reassure you that I remain happy to take it on.'

'Excuse me,' a voice calls out, quietly but insistent.

Stephanie ignores the interruption. 'It will be an honour to serve you and I promise to do my utmost to make this club a success and bring joy to all its members.'

'I said excuse me!' All eyes turn to Helen, her voice now raised and challenging.

'I'll take questions later, Helen.'

'It's not a question. I don't think that you being chair is a good idea.'

'Well, I disagree,' Stephanie says dismissively. 'And anyway, may I remind you that I am the single remaining candidate.'

'You *were* the only candidate, but to be honest, after what's happened this evening, I don't think you're fit to run the club. It's only fair to allow others to come forward.'

'How dare you? Who do you think you …' Stephanie pauses, aware of a growing murmuring around the room.

'The girl's right,' someone calls out. 'You're not fit to wear the shirt.'

There is an outbreak of the "You're not fit to wear the shirt" football anthem, last sung by several in the room during a shocking Chelsea display the previous weekend.

'Enough!' Stephanie calls out, but her plea together with her raised arm fails to quell the refrain. 'If you don't stop this nonsense immediately I'll be walking out and then you'd be stuck without anybody to take control.'

There is a waning of frivolities as the more practical members reflect on Stephanie's warning. But then another infamous chant erupts – 'Lock her up! Lock her up!' – this mingled with laughter from those not singing.

Stephanie is on her way out, accompanied by a mix of chants, laughter and boos. A fretful Laurie looks up to the empty stage then across to the rowdy audience. In the hope of telepathic advice from Helen about how to restore order, he spots her smiling broadly as she chants.

Jennifer is alarmed that this meeting, at the venue she procured as a favour, is an utter fiasco. However, on spotting Bridget and David still smiling and seemingly relaxed about the whole affair, she is happy to dismiss any thoughts about the consequences for now.

Not for the first time, Jennifer is in awe of the British comfort with parody, irony and farce. She wonders what next because, fuelled by alcohol and the surrealism of the evening so far, the meeting has become a comedy club event.

She links arms with Helen and joins in. 'Lock her up! Lock her up!'

Laurie is on the stage calling for order and finally there is quiet. 'Well,' he starts. 'Well …' he continues.

'Well what?'

'Well, I suppose all we can do is postpone this meeting until the committee has convened to decide on next steps.'

'Excuse me.'

'Yes, Helen.'

'Isn't there an obvious thing we can do now?'

'Is there?'

'You've done a great job as deputy chair, including managing the club during Oliver's frequent absences. I nominate you as our new chair.'

'He looks more like a human than a chair to me!' a would-be comedian calls out, causing indignation with accusations of sexism, misogyny and a pathetic attempt to be humorous. 'I know it's not PC to use chairman; it was a joke,' he pleads. He will not be welcome to play mixed doubles for a while in this genteel London suburb.

'Back to the issue,' Helen continues. 'What do you think, Laurie?'

'I'm not sure.'

'You can decide whether to accept or not after a vote. So, I nominate Laurie Wilberforce. We need a seconder.'

Several arms are raised.

'Thank you,' she says having jotted down a name chosen at random. 'Hands up if you would like to have Laurie as chair.'

It looks like all hands have gone up.

'We need to record the result scrupulously. Are there any opposers or abstentions?'

No hands are raised.

'Great, a unanimous view which leaves it up to you to accept or not.'

Laurie has reddened as all watch him, hushed in anticipation of his decision. 'To be frank, I'm still unsure. I know how much time is needed to do the job properly and I have a huge commitment at work. And I definitely don't have the connections like Oliver has.'

'According to Stephanie, Oliver's so-called connections were only used for personal gain. But apart from that, bear in mind that you wouldn't have to do everything. That's why we have a committee.'

'OK, I will give it a go, but on one condition. That we elect a deputy this evening to share the workload.' He is looking at Helen. 'And I know who I'd like as deputy. You.'

'Let's vote on it then,' someone calls out.

'First of all we need a nominator and a seconder.'

The whole audience is offering to do so. Randomly, Laurie selects two members sitting near the front. The vote is immediate and unanimous.

'Good. Right,' Laurie says having thanked the members for their decisive action. 'So now ...'

Helen is by his side, the meeting agenda up on her phone screen. 'So now we can move through the other items on the agenda.'

'Yes, exactly. Item 2 is the team captains' reports.'

As the men and women's captains make their way to the front there are drifts, a smallish one towards the counter to get more drinks and a substantial one towards the exit. For most, with the excitement over, there is little reason to stay on.

Jennifer's belief that things have worked out fine despite the earlier chaos dwindles as she sees Bridget approach. She considers pretending she hasn't noticed her and sneaking out with the crowd of leavers. But that would only delay a necessary conversation, not avoid it altogether. The tennis club are using the café because of her so she has to take responsibility for what's happened.

'I'm sorry about tonight,' she says, hoping that the single sentence apology might be enough.

'It had its moments. I think we will need to talk it through. Could you arrange a meeting with both of us and those two up on the stage?'

'Do you need me? I'm not on the committee.'

'I think so since you're the one who set the whole thing up with the tennis club. I'm working at the hotel most of this week so perhaps we can meet there.'

'OK, I'll choose a day and see if Laurie and Helen can join us after work.'

'Sounds perfect. Just let me know when. It looks like your meeting is about to restart.'

Laurie is calling for order, easy to achieve because the room is almost empty. The small cluster of drinkers standing by the counter clearly have no interest in proceedings.

There are polite ripples of applause in appropriate places as Laurie races through the agenda. A tremendous season for the Women's B Team. A junior member selected to play for the county Under-13s. A record-breaking amount raised at the charity evening.

It had taken an hour to get past Item One on the agenda and less than that to cover the remaining seven points.

'Since there is no AOB, I call this meeting closed,' Laurie says. The few remaining members immediately make their way to the exit. 'If anyone would like to stay behind to help tidy up it would be appreciated,' he adds. The drift towards the exit continues.

Jennifer feels obliged to stay and help, but David indicates that his own staff will do the clearing up.

She can now dash home to tell Gareth about the evening's excitement.

Jennifer had met Gareth while waitressing in a Los Angeles diner, this the go-to employment for the many naive youngsters failing to reach Hollywood stardom. He was in America doing IT consultancy work. When the contracts dried up she followed him to England, but soon after the move the relationship deteriorated and she decided to leave him. When Gareth quit the corporate sector and started teaching, he was back to being the gentle soul she'd first met. She realised she still loved him and wanted him back.

Jennifer has reached the grand Victorian villa where the couple live. She has the top floor apartment and can only afford the rent because of a generous monthly contribution from her mother. Her deputy manager post at the On the Hill hotel is well-paid but she would never be able to afford to buy a property in affluent Muswell Hill.

'I'm back,' she calls out as she enters the flat.

'I thought you said it would be a quick meeting.'

'Stuff happened.'

Gareth is sitting at the dining table surrounded by piles of marking. He looks up. 'So it wasn't as boring as you expected.'

'Not boring. Wild.'

'How can a tennis club AGM be wild? That's an oxymoron.'

'You wait 'til I tell you what happened.' She pauses. 'I left you here hours ago, surrounded by books and papers. Have you been working all evening?'

'No. I took a break to watch a documentary about Welsh bands of the nineties. What a golden era. Manic Street Preachers. Catatonia. Stereophonics.'

'And manic is the word to describe my evening. Are you ready for a tale full of that twisted dark humour you Brits have?'

'Fire away.'

6

It is early evening and Helen and Laurie are standing outside On the Hill ahead of the meeting with Bridget and David. Jennifer rushes up to join them.

'Hi guys. Sorry I'm a bit late.'

'You aren't. We're early,' Helen says.

'And terrified,' Laurie adds.

'Why stand in the rain though?' Jennifer asks as she leads them into the foyer. She unbuttons a 1960s double-breasted raincoat, cream with silver buttons. It had cost a small fortune at Roll Back the Years, the recently opened vintage clothes store. Over a few weeks the place has become the star fashion apparel performer on The Broadway. There are queues out onto the street during weekends.

'We didn't want to start before you got here,' a serious looking Laurie explains.

'He's expecting a verbal onslaught and hopes you'll protect us,' Helen teases as she squeezes Laurie's arm.

He smiles. Jennifer senses that there's something going on between them. She's pleased; they seem well-suited.

'I wouldn't blame them after Monday's disaster. We need to convince them that nothing like that will ever happen again,' Laurie says, stating the obvious.

'Which it won't,' Helen adds. 'Not now that Oliver and Stephanie are out of it.'

'It'll be fine. Come on, let's go in,' Jennifer says. She isn't as confident as she proclaims. The meeting with Bridget to set up the agreement hadn't been as easy as expected. She'd put it down to Bridget being stressed out by work, so how would she react to the AGM shambles?

Helen and Laurie follow Jennifer into the small office located behind the reception area. There's no David, only Bridget. She's behind a desk and slides a computer screen to the side before gesturing for them to sit on the row of three chairs in front of her.

'Hi. Drink anyone? There's tea or coffee or a juice.'

'No, not for me,' is Laurie's abrupt reply. Jennifer wishes she could convey a telepathic message for him to lighten up.

'I'll have a tea, please,' Helen says.

'Me too,' Jennifer requests, relieved that Helen has gauged the right tone.

'Oh, well if everyone else is having a drink, I suppose I'll have a tea.'

'You don't have to, Laurie.'

'No, tea is good. Thanks, Bridget.'

Bridget texts the order to someone then looks up at Helen. She is smiling, a smile that seems to be implying, "Well, that was a carry on the other night, wasn't it!"' It's early to judge but the atmosphere doesn't appear to be threatening.

'We –' Helen begins.

Laurie cuts across her. 'On behalf of the tennis club I would like to apologise for what happened at our AGM. It was inexcusable and I can't tell you how embarrassed I am to be sitting here today.'

'We've certainly never had anything like that before. Our events are usually exceedingly calm, even dull by comparison.'

'Let me –' Helen starts.

'I can give you a cast iron guarantee that such behaviour will not be repeated,' Laurie declares.

Bridget looks down at the signed agreement. 'So, obviously no more AGMs but you have got your monthly committee meetings to come.'

'They're for a maximum of eight of us and I won't allow other members to attend. So that's eight rational adults sitting quietly in some corner …'

Laurie pauses as Melissa, the co-owner of the hotel, comes in with the tray of teas.

'Hi everyone. I heard you had one hell of a party the other night.'

'We're here to apologise,' Laurie says.

'Apologise? I just wish I was there with you!'

'Thanks, Melissa,' Bridget says as she starts to pour the drinks.

'I'll leave you to it then but do let me know ahead of the next tennis club event.'

Bridget is reading the agreement. Jennifer is wishing her party animal friend Melissa could take life a little more seriously.

'OK, that's the meetings covered. Then there are the post-match teas,' Bridget continues.

'Sedate affairs, Bridget, I can promise you that. It's just four club members and four opponents coming in after weekend matches for a quick cup of tea and refreshments. As agreed with David, we'll confirm our orders for food the day before a match. I will personally vouch that our members are aware of the code of conduct we expect and I'll be carrying out spot checks to ensure everything is running smoothly.'

'I imagine tennis players are usually well-behaved,' Bridget says with a twinkle in her eye, 'and that Monday evening was an exception.'

Jennifer reflects on the outrageous behaviour of some members earlier that week, fuelled by alcohol, but even so. She feels like a naughty kid being reprimanded by the college principal, but a tolerant principal who isn't going to dwell on it.

'Are you still on schedule for your clubhouse to be open by Easter?' Bridget is asking.

'Absolutely, the builders are going great guns. They've more or less demolished the old building and they'll be starting with the foundations this week.'

This isn't quite the case, but Jennifer isn't going to say anything. She looks across at Helen who avoids eye contact.

'OK, you can have your teas, too,' Bridget announces.

'Thank you so much,' Helen gets in before Laurie has time to speak.

'Monday was quite something. David and I haven't laughed so much for ages and we're still walking around humming *Come on Eileen.'*

Everyone except Laurie is chuckling; he remains serious. 'There's something else, Bridget. One of your paintings got damaged.'

'Yes. How did it end up getting trodden on?'

'From what I understand there was an argument in that corner between Oliver and Stephanie supporters. Someone had his kit bag with him and started to chuck balls at one of the opposing group. Apparently, and I've only picked this up second hand, the man under attack took hold of the nearest protection he could find.'

'Which happened to be my painting?'

'Unfortunately yes; he used it as a shield. I'm sure there was no intention to damage it but when it ended up on the floor somebody accidentally stepped on it.'

'Several people I imagine, judging by the collage of footprints.'

'Inexcusable. I took off the price tag when I was clearing up. £325. Of course the club will reimburse you for that amount and add £50 for the inconvenience.'

'Forget the £50, but I will take your payment for the painting.'

'Also, the club will pay for the time needed for your staff to clear up after our meeting.'

David and Bridget have discussed whether to charge for cleaning and the loss of revenue, the café having been left in such a mess that they couldn't reopen to the general public that night. Monday evenings were never busy though, perhaps a few customers after the cinema closed, but not many. They'd estimated a loss of around £200 which they decided to write off, joking that the comedy on the night had been worth it.

'No need, we've agreed not to charge you. However, we'd appreciate no repeat performance.'

'Absolutely not. We would expect you to cancel the agreement immediately if anything like that happened again,' Laurie says, failing to notice Helen and Jennifer's looks of incredulity. 'Can I also say that I absolutely love those paintings of yours at the café.'

'Thanks.'

'The lighthouse perched on the cliff is wonderful. I'd like to buy it.' Laurie takes his phone out of his back pocket. 'Can I use Google Pay?'

'If you really do want it you can take it when you're next in the café and pay then.'

'I'll do that. Soon.'

'Great. I think we're done unless you have anything else.'

'No, that's it. Thanks, Bridget,' Helen says as she stands up.

'I'll come out with you,' Jennifer says before turning to face Bridget. 'I'm here all evening if you wanna catch up on anything.'

'I've still got this awful cold so I'll be heading home soon.'

'Happy with that?' Jennifer asks Laurie when they've reached the hotel entrance.

'You bet. Thanks for setting it up.'

'Yes. Thanks Jennifer,' Helen adds.

Jennifer watches them walk off with matching nimble strides. Definitely a relationship waiting to happen if it isn't already the case. Maybe Helen could help Laurie to unwind, to ditch that frown as if he's got the weight of the world on his shoulders. Today he was like that guy in the Dickens novel, Uriah Heep.

As Helen marches along to keep up with Laurie, she is reflecting on his behaviour at the meeting. 'How do you think it went?' she asks.

'Objective achieved – we can carry on using the café. My tactic worked.'

'Are you saying your grovelling was a pretence?'

'It did work, though having said that, an apology was needed.'

'I wasn't happy when you kept cutting me short.'

'Sorry. When I realised I was doing that I stopped.'

'So, acting is one of your strengths then? Is wanting her lighthouse painting part of the act?'

'No, I like it.'

They have reached the junction of The Broadway and Laurie is looking along the line of shops. 'I'm going to pop into M&S and get something easy to cook for this evening.'

'I was thinking exactly the same. I'll be following you in there.'

'Helen?'

'Yes?'

'Would you like to eat out with me tonight? It would save both of us having to cook.'

'Good idea,' Helen replies, the good idea well beyond anything to do with food.

It might have been nice for Laurie to indicate that having dinner with her wasn't merely because he couldn't be bothered to cook, but at least this was a start.

7

They manage to grab a table at the popular pizzeria despite not booking. The aroma of the wood-fired dough hits Helen as she steps inside the restaurant.

'God! I'm immediately starving whenever I come here.'

The waiter appears, a tall, slim young man, his jet black hair swept back with a ponytail. He hands them the menus. 'Can I get you drinks?'

'What are you having, Laurie?'

'I think I might go for one of these microbrewery beers,' he says pointing. 'This one please.'

'OK, make that two. And I already know which pizza, the same as always even if it is a bit boring.'

'Which is?'

'Mushrooms with fungi,' she jokes and Laurie smiles.

'Give me a minute,' Laurie tells the waiter.

'No problem. I'll take your food order when I'm back with the drinks.'

Helen watches as Laurie edges his index finger down the menu, his expression intense. 'I'm not sure why I'm doing this,' he says, still peering down, 'because I also always go for the same one. I like to see what I'm missing though and whether there's anything new. Yep, same as usual. Pepperoni.'

The waiter is by their side with the drinks and he takes their orders.

'So …' they both begin enthusiastically when the waiter has moved on.

'Go on, you first.'

'No, you,' Helen insists.

'I was only going to say how well this place is doing. It must have been quite a gamble opening a new restaurant when there are already so many around here, but it looks like it's paid off.'

'I suppose it has,' Helen says, stuck for an inspirational comment relating to the topic. She changes tack. 'Should we consider how our relationship is going to work out?' her question deliberately ambiguous. She regards their new roles at the tennis club as the chance to take friendship with Laurie further.

So, over to you, Laurie, to grasp the hint and run with it. But no, he has reddened which makes Helen feel embarrassed for her insinuation about the other kind of relationship.

Since he isn't connecting she signals that she's on about the club. 'Obviously we'll have the committee meetings, but what with the new build and making sure things run smoothly at the café, I think we could do with some one-to-one catch ups in addition to the monthly meetings.'

'Yes, agreed. We could make contact as soon as something crops up or another option is to touch base regularly, say once a week.'

'That's what I was thinking.'

'What do you use? Teams or Zoom?'

'Don't you think it might be nicer in person? I'm fed up with virtual meetings.'

'I suppose we could meet,' Laurie states after a pause for reflection. 'But where? There's no clubhouse and I wouldn't want to use the café having just recapped on the terms with them.'

'I'd be happy for you ...' Helen begins.

The waiter arrives and sets two large wooden platters on the table.

'Happy for me ...?'

'I was going to say I'd be happy for you to come over to my place.' Specifically to meet in my bedroom is what she's thinking.

'Are you sure?'

'It's not a problem.' No problem at all said the spider to the fly.

'Let's take it in turns, you one week, me the next.'

'It's a deal,' is Helen's instant reply in the hope that this verbal agreement takes on full contractual weight. But is she showing too much enthusiasm? Should she at least wait for a sign of interest from Laurie because there is nothing yet?

Helen's attempt to get them to meet other than on a tennis court is apparent to Laurie, as are her poorly disguised hints about the other type of relationship. He'd love that but it can't happen, so it's best to

57

pretend that he isn't on the same wavelength. It hurts to see her keen and him acting disinterested.

'This is delicious. Want to try some?' he asks her.

'Thanks, but I don't eat meat.'

'I was thinking, should we invite Oliver to our meetings?' Laurie asks, shifting the focus back to work. 'He'd be useful when we cover the clubhouse rebuild.'

'N. O. Laurie! He's disgraced, and besides, if he did join us he'd be trying to take over.'

'You're right, it was a silly idea.' There is another awkward silence as he finishes his beer. 'Another one?'

'A drink definitely, but not beer. I'll have a glass of wine.'

'I will too. The house white?'

'I think I saw Vinho Verde on the menu. Maybe that.'

Laurie takes hold of the drinks menu. 'It isn't sold by the glass. Shall I get a bottle?'

'Sure.'

Helen is not enjoying their evening together. The conversation is stilted compared to when they chat freely before, during and after playing tennis together.

During a silence as they wait for their wine, they watch a group of young women enter the restaurant. There's screaming as they work out who is going to sit next to who at the nearby table. One of them has on a tiara, pink ballerina gear, and a sash with the words, *Last day of freedom.*

Laurie and Helen watch the drama and the comedy unfold in front of them until the waiter arrives. With over dramatic poise he pours two glasses and places the bottle in the ice bucket.

'Is it true though?' Helen shouts above the raucous din, suddenly feeling more grown up than she wants to.

'Is what true?'

'What's written on her sash. That marriage marks the end of freedom.'

'It depends on who's getting married. It's not a given.'

'No, I suppose not.' Enthusiasm about the prospect of a new relationship with this dishy man has faded. All the things that can go wrong are on Helen's mind, all the things that have gone wrong in her past affairs. 'I nearly got married once. Well, my boyfriend proposed, so that is pretty near.'

Laurie is surprised by this personal revelation. He notes that Helen is avoiding eye contact. Should he move on to a different topic or does she expect him to dig deeper?

It is Helen who makes the decision. 'I said no.'

The waiter is back by their side. He takes hold of the bottle of wine.

'It's OK, I can do it,' Laurie says. The waiter hands him the bottle and leaves them. 'Why did you say no?' he asks Helen as he pours.

'That sash is making me consider why not all over again. I suppose I didn't love him, at least not enough to want to spend forever together. I did like him loads at first though, so now I'm wondering whether it was the fear of losing my freedom that scared me off.'

'Maybe if you have kids and you're tied down with all that responsibility it might be true, but otherwise there's no reason why getting married should end freedom. I'd never stop a partner doing something she wanted to do.'

'I'm sure you wouldn't, but then you're not Ed. He didn't like me doing anything without him. I just about got away with playing tennis.'

'Then it's probably good that you did say no. Not all men are like him; I'm sure you'll find someone who's perfect for you.'

Fuck, fuck, fuck! Why am I talking about an ex, Helen is thinking. Rule Number One when on a first date: do NOT talk about an ex. Mind you, this is hardly a date. Why doesn't Laurie realise that that someone could be him? On the assumption that he isn't dense – which he isn't – this can only mean that he doesn't fancy me.

'Perhaps I will,' Helen says, now keen to drop the subject.

But Laurie is running with the topic despite having steered clear of anything remotely personal until then. 'Is your ex the reason why you never come to any social events at the club?' he asks.

'Back then yes and maybe it still is, even though we split over six months ago. I guess I'm stuck with the habit of not doing much by myself.'

'I'd go with you. I don't mean … I mean if you'd be happier coming to the next club event with someone, I'd happily do that.'

Helen smiles as she tops up their glasses. 'That's sweet of you.'

At last her lovely smile is back, but Laurie hopes Helen hasn't misinterpreted his offer as a chat up line. He returns to the theme of her boyfriend. 'It must have been difficult, him asking you to marry him and you saying no.'

Helen's smile disappears as quickly as it had returned as she thinks back to the disappointing relationship with Ed, quite possibly her worst ever. 'I suppose it was hard, though I think once I'd made the decision, relief was my strongest emotion.'

Ed had been such a charmer when they first met but it hadn't taken long for that leopard to show his spots. She'd clung on to the belief that things might improve, knowing – and not even that deep down – that this was wishful thinking. She'd only clung onto the relationship because she hated the thought of being alone again. Finally, when she turned down his proposal, he didn't seem particularly bothered.

This evening has become mired in gloom, Helen is thinking, the complete opposite to what she had hoped for. Now she's totally distracted and is thinking about her family.

Although there's never been competition between the four sisters to have a partner, there's unspoken pressure from her parents to "settle down", this their term for what they believe all young women should be doing. Her lack of success in sustaining a relationship is perceived as a failure, which hurts because pleasing parents is an embedded family trait. She is the second in line of four sisters. Her older sister is married with three children, another is in a long term relationship with one child and another on the way, and her youngest sister, six years her junior, has recently got engaged.

In an attempt to shake off gloom, she reminds herself that at the age of twenty-eight in twenty-first century Britain she is hardly unique in being single. Nevertheless, these thoughts have cast a dark shadow on this first evening alone with Laurie.

'God, I hate break-ups,' she hears Laurie declare.

'Have you had lots of them then?'

'Me? No, not at all. I just think it's sad when you can be so close to someone for a while and then it goes like it has never been real.'

'Are you in a relationship now?'

'No. Life's too complicated.'

'In what way? An ex?'

'Not that. I will explain but perhaps not this evening if you don't mind.' Laurie makes a point of looking at his watch. 'Maybe we'd better go soon, I've got a busy day at work tomorrow, an early start.'

Helen takes the hint; she also wants the evening to end. It's been such a disappointment. No, she isn't going to let it end like this. 'What work do you do?' she asks.

'I'm a molecular chemist.'

'Meaning?'

'The simple description is that we synthesise molecules to make new products.'

'I'm glad that's the easy version!'

'It's exciting – and important. We can alter molecules at the atomic level through skeletal editing. So for instance, we're experimenting with light to perform edits quintillions of times in a short space of time. If it works at scale we'll be able to do things like personalise medicines. Take cancer for instance. Did you know that everyone's tumour is different? Imagine a world where you can design exactly the right molecule to attack that specific tumour, where you have a synthesiser to draw it and the means to produce it. One click of a button and it's manufactured. Sorry, I'm rabbiting on.'

Helen loves Laurie's enthusiasm even though she has no idea what he's on about beyond it being "a good thing". Science was never her strong point at school.

'That sounds very complicated and very important too.'

'I suppose most people would find my work boring, repeating the same tests over and over again in a lab.' Laurie sighs, back to being serious, the buzz while explaining his work no longer evident. He glances at his watch again, calls the waiter over and asks for the bill. 'I'm paying by the way,' he tells Helen.

Helen considers contesting this, but it seems petty. 'Fair enough, but I'll get the next one.'

They pass the shrieking hen party on their way out. Helen notes the women eyeing Laurie; he doesn't seem to be aware of it.

'Look, I hope I didn't upset you asking about your relationship,' he says when they are by the restaurant exit.

'Of course not, in fact I think I was the one who started it. Relationships are such a big part of life it would be pretty odd not to have them as a major conversation topic.' As Helen speaks she realises that Laurie might be more tuned in to discussions about molecules than people. Mind you, he was as understanding as any of her girlfriends when she spoke about Ed and marriage. On an attempted first date though – honestly!

'We were supposed to be talking about the tennis club,' Laurie says as they step outside, confronted by a harsh wind whipping up and swirling the autumn leaves.

'We do have a plan though. Is next Monday good for our first meeting?'

'Nothing's likely to crop up over the weekend so let's leave it until the following week.'

'Fine by me.'

'Start at my place,' Laurie offers. 'I'll cook us something.'

'Are you sure?'

'Absolutely.'

'We can hold a weekly Masterchef competition!'

'Hardly. I live this way,' Laurie says, gesturing with his index finger.

Helen is taken aback by Laurie's abruptness and failure to recognise her tease. 'And I'm heading that way,' she says, pointing in the opposite direction.

They hover, Helen contemplating a hug. Or a kiss; she'd definitely like to kiss him.

'Bye then, Helen.'

'Bye, Laurie.'

Helen watches Laurie striding away, hoping that he might turn round for a farewell wave. She doesn't expect it but stays put just in case.

Is he going to?

No.

She heads home.

8

It is the first weekend in November and the winter league is underway.

Most members of the tennis club don't bother with competitive winter matches and as Jennifer sits in Douglas's car she can understand why. Douglas is her partner that day.

The eight players are in four cars facing the courts: all the windows are steaming up. They've been there for over half an hour watching slate grey clouds surge past, in the hope that the rain will cease and the game can restart. Under normal circumstances they would be waiting in the comfort of the clubhouse, but all that's left of it that day is a small amount of wall on one side ready to be demolished, with a cordoned off deep hole in front of it.

'It's improving,' Douglas suggests. 'Look, the clouds are breaking up. As soon as this mist eases we can carry on.'

It isn't mist, it's condensation, but Jennifer decides not to deflate Douglas's undying optimism. This is the second time they have halted play and dashed for shelter that afternoon.

She opens the door to check and it does appear to have stopped raining. A blast of cold air rushes through as Douglas opens the door on the driver's side.

Jennifer zips her fleece up to her neck and stuffs her hands into the pockets. 'It's not on,' she says, as much to herself as to Douglas. 'Even if it's stopped the courts are too wet.'

Douglas, who has a tendency to ignore what others might suggest, stretches out an arm. 'I disagree; the surfaces drain quickly here.'

'I can see puddles.'

'They'll soon be gone.'

His belief that the courts aren't saturated, with or without puddles, is bullshit but it's not worth debating the point with Douglas.

On days like this, English November ones with dampness, rain and sleet, Jennifer is pining for the bright blue skies on the bitterly cold days back home in Idaho or the mild, sunny winters in Los Angeles.

When Jennifer had told Gareth that she'd agreed to play for the Mixed C Team, he'd burst out laughing.

'In winter?'

'Yeah, but they're desperate.'

When the coach congratulated her on being selected, he called it an accolade in recognition of the considerable progress made since starting lessons over the summer. She knew it was false praise. Quite simply, no one else wanted to play.

Mind you, if she'd known that Douglas was to be her partner she would have quit before she started.

This rotund man in his mid-fifties, surprisingly nimble for his size, might be your typical English gentleman off court, but on it he's such a pain that no one wants to play with him on social tennis mornings. He tells his doubles partners what they're doing wrong and what's needed to improve as they play even though he's crap himself. It's infuriating.

Annoying though this is, Jennifer is usually able to laugh it off. However, competing against another team is different, upping the pressure compared to playing a friendly at the club. During the twenty minutes they've so far managed on court between the rainfall, he has been at his worst.

'Where are you going?' she asks as Douglas exits the car.

Ignoring her, he taps on the windows of the other vehicles. 'Come on, out. Let's get going again.'

Andras and Ying are the club's other pair. They do as instructed, leaving the unenthusiastic opponents in their cars, unwilling to continue.

'It's still drizzling and the courts are soaked. We should abandon,' the opposing team captain says.

'It's for the home team to decide,' Douglas declares. 'If you refuse to play you forfeit the match.'

'He is right,' Ying says. She is a slender, five-foot something Chinese woman of indeterminable age. In her thirties? Forties? Fifties? Jennifer finds it impossible to tell. Ying is probably the best player out of the four of them, someone who takes competitiveness to a new level. Andras, her partner, is a forty-something year old who thinks a lot of himself and is a flirt. Although a competent player, his effort on court is sporadic. Jennifer has noted that his enthusiasm and showmanship during mixed doubles games with younger women far exceeds that shown during men's doubles or matches with older women.

The four opponents are cajoled into returning to the courts to resume the match. They start, and Douglas is back to firing instructions at her which is pissing Jennifer off big time. She can hear arguing on the neighbouring court.

Down comes the rain again and they have no choice but to abandon without completing a single set.

Douglas outlines what is to happen next. 'As you can see, our clubhouse is being rebuilt, so we use a local café for teas. It's a charming place, about a ten minute walk from here. You can drive but it's never easy to find a spot to park.'

Something is not right with the opposing team, there's whispering and arguing going on. Jennifer picks up that a female player doesn't want to join the others for tea. Her captain's pat on the shoulder and hug seem to do the trick because she sets off with everyone else.

David is by the café door to greet the players. He leads them to their reserved table with a spread that looks amazing: a Dream Café tea to beat all teas. There are enough sandwiches to feed an army and a tray of delicious looking pastries and cakes. But the atmosphere remains frosty; the morose woman's gloominess has spread to the other opponents.

'What's going on?' Jennifer whispers to Andras.

'Tell you later,' he mouths.

In theory the post-match tea is a sociable and friendly get together, but that's not the case here. Jennifer's attempts to improve the mood with light conversation fall flat. In silence, the opposing four consume a small portion of the feast in front of them before announcing that they are leaving.

Since it is Jennifer who arranged to use Dream Café while the clubhouse was shut, she feels responsible for anything that goes wrong. Although she isn't the cause, she wants to get to the bottom of this unpleasant atmosphere.

She intercepts the woman with the attitude problem as she is making her way to the exit. 'Is something wrong?' she asks.

'Wanting to win is one thing but wanting to win at all costs isn't. I do not enjoy playing when there's cheating going on.'

'Cheating?'

'Ask your colleague,' she suggests, looking across at Ying. 'Enough said.'

The opponents head off, crossing paths with Laurie on his way in. 'Hello, I'm from the club. I hope you've …'

They ignore him. He pauses, frowning, before heading across to his own team.

Following the catastrophic AGM, Laurie has decided to pop into the café after some of the weekend matches to check all is going well.

'Hi guys. I set off as soon as you texted that you were here, Douglas, and that was less than fifteen minutes ago. I didn't expect to see the opposition leaving so quickly.'

No one replies.

'Has having tea here worked out?'

Still no replies.

Laurie lifts up a flapjack and takes a bite. 'Wow, delicious, though there's loads left.'

Silence.

'What's going on?'

'Our opponents didn't want to stay for long.'

'Why not?'

'I'll fill you in later,' Andras says, glancing across at Ying.

~

'Hi, Honey!' Jennifer calls out.

Gareth comes into the hallway to greet her. 'How did it go?'

'It didn't. We tried to play three times then gave up.'

'I knew you wouldn't be able to play; you only had to look at the forecast.'

'I think you still gotta turn up or else the other team gets the match.'

'You do realise that your end of season league table might read played six, won zero, lost zero, abandoned six.'

'Yeah, and that means six weekend days wasted when we could be doing something interesting together.'

'On the bright side I got all my lesson preparation for next week out of the way.'

'Cool. Me sitting in a car watching the rain all afternoon was hopeless but maybe better than having to play with Douglas.'

'Douglas?'

'My partner. I think I've already told you about him. He's the one who coaches as he plays, a running commentary about what I'm doing wrong. I'm stuck with him all season.'

'Pack it in then.'

'Nah, that ain't fair on Laurie and Helen. They've already got enough to worry about.'

'Well, it's up to you. It might not rain every time you're due to play.'

'You told me it will.'

'I was being flippant.'

'Or truthful. Anyway, I will go for it, despite Douglas.'

'Didn't you say you'd text me when you were at the café and I'd meet you there?'

'I was about to text, but when everyone left real quick I just wanted to get home. The vibes were bad; something was going on between the others.'

'Like what?'

'God knows, no-one said a word about it. Another experience of how you Brits do things, I suppose. Anyway, it's over, and I do have a surprise gift for you.'

Jennifer lifts a large irregular cube of silver foil out of her kit bag and hands it over.

Gareth peels back the top to reveal a stack of sandwiches and cakes.

~

Laurie leaves the café after a quick chat with David who seems unaware that there was any issue at the tennis club table. Why had the thoroughly miserable-looking opponents stormed out? They couldn't have been in the café for more than a few minutes. Why hadn't one of his own team members, including the usually dependable Jennifer, been willing to tell him what the problem was?

Another hassle to sort out.

Laurie isn't enjoying the responsibility of being in charge of the club, it's turning out to be more time consuming than he imagined. The Mixed C Team problem is minor compared to the slow progress with the clubhouse reconstruction – the builders are way behind schedule, not that there is a schedule in writing.

Helen has suggested sharing responsibilities with the other committee members but he's sceptical. Apart from her, no one shows interest beyond a light touch. And as far as Helen is concerned, he doesn't want to pile work and worries onto her. But is that wrong? He's never been good at delegating, a point made at his recent annual review at work. Maybe now is the time to address this, starting with getting Helen's help on club matters.

OK then, he'll share his concerns and get her to reflect on options ahead of their first meeting the next day. He calls her.

'Hi Laurie.'

'Hi Helen.'

He hears classical music playing in the background, sad strings reaching a crescendo then fading only to surge again. He knows it isn't *The Four Seasons*, this being close to his limit of knowledge when it comes to classical music. He listens to rock music, stuck with the indie bands of the early 2000s.

He could start the conversation by outlining that day's post-match drama or with an account of his unease about the builders' progress. But why do that? Neither is an insurmountable difficulty and he can sort both of them without Helen's involvement.

'Anything you want to say?' she asks, breaking the silence.

'Sorry. Yes. I was wondering what to cook tomorrow evening. You're a vegetarian, right?'

'Correct.'

'But not vegan.'

'No.'

'OK, I'm on the case.'

'Intriguing.'

'Don't raise your hopes.'

He hears her laugh. 'I definitely won't.'

'It's just that …'

'Laurie? Are you really worried about what to cook? I'll eat anything, a sandwich would do or even a takeaway.'

'It's not the food. A couple of things have cropped up at the club.'

'Like?'

'The clubhouse rebuild is one, and then something happened today with the Mixed C Team. I'm not sure exactly what but I'll try to find out before we meet tomorrow.'

'That's the team Jennifer plays for, isn't it? I'll ask her.'

'Let me investigate first, starting with Andras.'

'OK, if that's what you want.'

'It's probably best; he did offer to fill me in. I'll see you tomorrow then, around seven. Bye.'

Looking forward to it, Helen would have liked him to say as the profile photo of Laurie disappears from her screen.

9

As soon as he ends the call to Helen, Laurie googles *vegetarian meals to impress* and clicks into the *BBC Good Food* listing near the top. It's a safe bet that he's used before, the recipes within his capabilities as an enthusiastic though not particularly skilful cook.

He has no time to start his investigation because Andras is calling.

'Do you want me to tell you about today?' Andras asks.

'Fire away.'

'Well, let me say, Laurie, it was hugely embarrassing. Some of Ying's line calls were way off and when she was challenged she refused to replay the point. "It's my call and I've told you it's out," she said over and over again like a broken record. Having to stop because of the rain was lucky because our opponents were so fed up they were all set to concede and walk away.'

Laurie is aware of Ying's reputation when it comes to line calls. Members tend to laugh it off, but it's not the same when playing a match. But what can he do?

Accuse her of cheating? He has no enthusiasm to take that on.

Andras hasn't finished. 'She was as bad with scoring. At least twice she got it wrong but insisted she was correct and started arguing by the net. I didn't know what to do. I could hardly criticise my own team player, could I?'

'If she was wrong then yes, you should have. Politely of course.'

'Politely! This is Ying we're talking about. Remember I did that during the championships last summer and got a mouthful before she stormed off court.'

'Yes, I was there.'

'And I don't want to be attacked again.'

'It was obvious something was wrong as soon as I joined you this afternoon.'

'Our post-match tea was a disaster; I've never known anything like it.'

'I hope the opposition don't lodge a complaint to the league officials,' Laurie says, thinking out loud.

'If I was them I would.'

'Well, we can't have a repeat. I'll discuss what to do when I meet Helen tomorrow.'

Andras hasn't finished. 'There's a simple way out, Laurie. Ditch Ying and I'll partner Zadie.'

Zadie, a nineteen year old local girl, has just started a degree at the University of London. There's no denying that she is a rising star with bags of talent. She would definitely be ready to play at Mixed C Team level.

However, Laurie is uncomfortable with Andras's instant solution. It was only fair to speak with Ying first to get her side of the story, and he has a niggling suspicion about why Andras wants to play with Zadie.

'Mind you,' Andras says with a laugh, 'I'd struggle to concentrate on the tennis with that sexy gorgeous girl.'

Laurie's mistrust is confirmed; Andras has a certain reputation. He won't agree to the change until he's spoken to Helen and he's fairly certain what she'll think. 'OK Andras, thanks for filling me in. I'll discuss options with Helen tomorrow and let you know.'

Returning to the veggie choices on the *BBC Good Food* website, Laurie settles on the roasted carrot and whipped feta tart. Keeping the menu open on his phone he checks the ingredients in the kitchen. He's got many of them – olive oil, walnuts, parmesan, garlic, lemon, honey, eggs – leaving the carrots, feta and pastry to get at the supermarket. Would Helen notice if he used a readymade roll of puff pastry, he wonders.

The following day at work he runs his final set of laboratory tests earlier than usual to give himself plenty of time for the shopping and cooking. He buys the most expensive carrots, the ones with the foliage left on. He adds a couple of bottles of Vinho Verde to his basket, based on Helen's preference at the pizza restaurant.

Laurie is a competent cook provided he has a menu to follow. His strength is multi-tasking, perhaps unsurprising for a statistician and scientist. With all precisely on schedule for Helen's seven o'clock arrival, he turns his attention to Andras's proposal. Yes, Ying is a problem and yes, Zadie might be the solution, but he would put money on Helen opposing the pairing of Andras with the nineteen-year old. Zadie is a confident girl who wouldn't tolerate any nonsense, so why not put them together? Hang on though, having to tolerate something isn't good enough.

His thoughts turn to the clubhouse. He has no experience of judging such matters but senses that progress is wholly inadequate. What if the rebuild isn't complete by the start of the summer season? Might Helen have ideas about how to move things on?

All interest in tennis club matters disappears when Helen arrives. She hands him her jacket. He hasn't seen her in a dress before. She looks stunning and he struggles to shift his gaze from body to face. Her beautiful face. She instigates a hug, short, businesslike, and he's lured by the fragrance of her perfume.

If only he's thinking. If only it were possible.

He regrets not having made an effort himself. He's still in the work clothes worn at the laboratory, unfashionable trousers and a creased plain shirt. At least he'd whipped off the apron when the doorbell rang.

Helen has spent the day wondering what Laurie's feelings for her might be. There's a new optimism following their hit at the tennis club that weekend.

She'd won a point with a drop shot and he seemed to be sulking like a little boy; it was as if playing a drop shot was cheating. Then he'd burst out laughing and she joined in as they stood close together by the net.

She senses that he *is* interested in her. Perhaps the block is shyness. There's nothing wrong with being shy, it's better than Ed's arrogance and some of the others who came before him. But it does mean that if she wants a relationship with Laurie – and she does – then she'll need to be the one to take the lead. She dresses up for their meeting, putting on more make-up than usual and applying a generous spray of *Seduction* (a fitting name!).

As he stands passively at the door she takes hold of him for a hug. She's hoping a kiss might follow but Laurie steps away and leads her to the living area.

The kitchen and living room are open plan so she can watch him serve up while drinking the Vinho Verde that he has left by her side. The sweetie, he's got what she'd asked to drink at the pizza restaurant.

As pans and plates clatter she inspects the room. There's the cliché that scientists are more interested in the design of electronic gadgets than the design in their own homes. The interior of this room challenges that theory. It's tastefully furnished with pastel yellows and greys broken up by a turquoise splash wall on the fireplace side of the room.

'Did you choose this colour?' she calls out.

'Yeah. I used about twenty sample pots to get it right.'

There's a turquoise glass vase with an autumnal bouquet on a cabinet. She'd been thinking of bringing flowers but had brought a bottle of red wine instead.

'Ready. We can sit at the table,' Laurie says as he carries in two plates. It smells good and now that she can see the dish, she's impressed.

'So, you really did buy Bridget's lighthouse painting,' Helen says after a first taste of a puff pastry tart with a host of flavours coming through. The painting is hanging on a light grey wall. 'It suits the room.'

'Yes, I'm happy with it. Should we start with what to do about the Ying problem?'

Helen manages a smile, disappointed that Laurie has abruptly dismissed small talk. 'You mean that Mixed C match you mentioned?'

Laurie outlines his conversation with Andras, covering his reluctance to play with Ying again because of her cheating and his suggested solution to partner Zadie. 'So what do you think I should do?'

'By that I take it you mean what should *we* do.'

Laurie reddens. 'Sorry. Of course. I've only had Andras's side of the story,' he continues, 'and I'm uneasy about taking everything he says at face value. It's only fair to hear Ying's version of events.'

'Agreed. However I did chat with Jennifer and her account backs up what Andras says. Ying did annoy the opposition players with her line calls and scoring.'

'Which we know is an issue from past experience. We can't have a repeat of yesterday so that takes us to

Andras's solution, to ditch Ying and recruit Zadie as his partner.'

'For a start, I agree with what you've said. It's only fair to speak to Ying, to point out the complaint and get her take on it.'

'Would you do that?'

'It's better from you; you carry the authority.' Helen takes a final forkful of the flan. 'This is delicious. Give me the recipe, please.'

Laurie doesn't react; he's in task mode. 'But what's the follow up if Ying rejects the accusation? Get Zadie to partner Andras if she'll do it?'

'Andras is a lech so I vote no.'

'He did say something I didn't like during our phone call.'

'What?'

'Just a comment about her being a good-looker.' On being pressed, Laurie quotes what Andras said.

'That makes it a definite no; they mustn't play together.'

'Andras talks rubbish; I saw it as an attempt at humour. One thing he did say though was that the club should be championing ethnic minorities.'

'Bollocks! He doesn't care about that.'

'I suppose in the end it's up to Douglas. He's the captain.'

'No, it's your call, Laurie, because you're responsible for the safety and wellbeing of the members. We can't trust Andras, who has, by the way, made a pass at me.'

'I didn't know that.'

'You wouldn't unless you chat to young female club members.'

'I agree with you then, Andras can't play with Zadie. Let's hope Ying is willing to take some advice. More wine?'

'Best not. Work picks up tomorrow and I need to be on the ball.'

'Where do you work?'

'I play cello. We're rehearsing ahead of recording our first album.'

'Oh. Nice.'

Helen waits for something more, an inkling of interest, but nothing is forthcoming.

'Anything else on the agenda?' she asks.

'The clubhouse. The builders aren't turning up much. When I caught one man there he blamed the wet weather for the lack of progress.'

'That's ridiculous. It's only going to get worse as we hit winter.'

'Unfortunately I can't find anything in writing apart from a signed liabilities document and the cost of works. At committee meetings Oliver had assured us that everything was in order but he and the builder seem to have arranged everything verbally.'

'We all know why that is.'

'I've tried contacting Oliver to find out what has been agreed, is there a schedule for a start, but he isn't picking up my calls or replying to my emails.'

'So, what do you intend to do?'

'I can't see what we can do other than monitor progress. The person I saw on site said it'll be easy to make up for lost time.'

'OK.'

Laurie starts clearing the plates off the table, accepting Helen's offer of help. They load the dishwasher together.

'Next week at mine?' she says as Laurie presses the button to switch on the machine.

'Sure.'

He starts wiping the saucepans stacked on the draining board.

'I'll be off then,' Helen says. 'Thanks for dinner, it was delicious. The pressure is on me to match your quality.'

Again, there is no response to Helen's attempt to engage in friendly banter. In silence she puts on her jacket as Laurie stands by his open front door.

'Bye then.'

'Bye.'

On her walk home, Helen is wondering whether she's done something to put him off. She can't think what though.

10

Laurie remains by his front door, despondent about how the evening has gone.

In his mind he is replaying how it could have progressed. On arrival Helen had hugged him and he thought she was going to follow it up with a kiss. His response was to pull away when he should have kissed her, told her how gorgeous she looked, maybe firing off one of those slick chat up lines that friends used.

He'd never been good at flirting; it was always the would-be girlfriends who had taken the lead in starting a relationship. He remembers times when he'd had his phone in his hand, nervously dithering about what to text, when a message pinged through, something like, *Are you going to ask me out then?*

One thing is for sure, he's besotted by Helen, he can't stop thinking about her. After tonight, what must she be thinking of him? All he had to do was explain the situation then at least she would understand his detachment.

As a call comes through Laurie finds himself resenting this obstacle to a relationship with Helen. The sole barrier is this caller. Laurie had told his stepfather that he would be busy until around nine-thirty, that calling him any time after that should be fine. It is now nine thirty-three. He braces himself for another long and depressing conversation. Anger and guilt collide.

~

Helen has always been a rapid walker but now she's close to running, her thoughts racing as fast as her heart is beating. What's wrong with Laurie to be so incapable of showing emotion, of picking up signals? So much for spending ages deciding what to wear when Laurie looked like he'd been yanked out of a tumble drier. Being a scientist does NOT explain his detachment. The responsibility of running the tennis club does NOT justify his behaviour. Surely it's a straightforward case of him not fancying her and she has to get over it.

But is it only that because at times he looks so anguished, as if something traumatic is going on. What though?

Is it A (scientist), B (tennis club), C (fancying her) or D (personal problem), or all of the above? By the time she reaches home she's decided to put aside her multiple choice quiz. She'll avoid Laurie by keeping away from the tennis club all week. She'll wait until late Sunday evening to check by text that he is still on for the Monday meeting.

Come the Sunday, she keeps her message short and to the point. *You OK for tomorrow?*

Yes fine is his two-word answer.

Good she replies, her curtness an act of revenge.

It's a busy schedule of rehearsals for her string quartet but she takes Monday afternoon off to sort out what to cook, settling on pasta with roasted vegetables, hardly imaginative but a meal she does well.

She is slicing the vegetables when Laurie calls. It is five-thirty.

'Helen, I'm ever so sorry but I'm not going to be able to make it for seven this evening. It might be best to eat separately and I'll get to you as near to eight as I can.'

'Oh.'

There is silence as Helen waits for the reason for the change of plans at such short notice, in effect no notice, but it isn't being offered.

'Is everything alright?' she asks, perturbed because she doesn't associate Laurie with lack of consideration, quite the opposite.

'Yeah, it's just something that's cropped up. I'm sorry. I'll see you later, I must go.'

When he arrives at half-past eight Helen reckons he's wearing the same clothes as the previous Monday. She's just as slovenly, having dressed down with jeans, the oldest blouse she could find and a shapeless fleece.

It's not the Laurie she thought she knew. This version is distracted, barely communicative. 'What's on your list for us to discuss tonight?' he asks.

'Isn't it more a case of what's on *your* list? But never mind, I suppose we could start with Ying. Have you seen her?'

'No, we spoke on the phone. I was as polite as possible but we couldn't reach common ground. She reminded me that it's the person returning a ball who has the say about whether the opponent's shot is in or out. I know that, of course, and agreed with her, but suggested that for the sake of goodwill it might be sensible to replay a point if there is any doubt. I was told there can never be doubt because the one closest to the line when making calls is going to be right about them.'

'Then what?'

'I asked her to reflect on what I'd said about replaying points.'

'That hardly sounds promising. What do you suggest we do?'

'The Mixed C's have another home match next weekend. Let's see if she takes any notice of what I've asked. I've spoken with Andras and he's agreed to give it one more try, but after that he'd like me to invite Zadie to play.'

'Which means he'll be making sure it doesn't work out!'

'I only said maybe about Zadie.'

'The creep,' Helen says and she sees Laurie smile for the first time that evening.

'I've got some wine, the same as last time,' he says, lifting a bottle out of his backpack and holding it up.

'Thanks. I'll get glasses.'

She takes a deep breath in the kitchen. She's planning to push Laurie for answers, there's nothing to lose.

'When you called earlier I asked if everything was alright. Is it?'

'There is the clubhouse.'

'I didn't mean anything to do with tennis ...'

'Everything's fine. Thank you for asking.'

It isn't, she can see that in his eyes, but he's not going to say. 'OK, what's going on with the clubhouse?'

'I was there a couple of times last week to check and it does look like there's some progress, but no one is in charge on site. When I asked one of the builders he told me that their manager had quit the company. Apparently a new person has been hired.'

'Is that a good thing, a bad thing or neutral?'

'I can't say for sure, but I'm disappointed that we haven't been notified about the change.'

'Maybe you'll get to see the new person this week.'

'Maybe. That's all from me. Do you have anything?' Laurie asks.

'There's a committee meeting coming up. I'll email the agenda and let everyone know that this one is a closed meeting.'

'Good idea. I'll send you the agenda by Wednesday. We need an item covering the rebuild but there's no need to mention Ying.'

'Agreed,' Helen says.

'If that's all I'd better go. I've got loads to do.'

'There's nothing else from me. Since you're so busy let's skip meeting next week. We can deal with anything new after the following Monday's committee meeting.'

Laurie's nod in agreement as he stands up infuriates Helen even though it shouldn't. It's not as if there's anything between them other than a loose friendship at the tennis club coupled with their official responsibilities.

She can't let go though. 'So obviously things are not alright with you but you aren't going to tell me anything.'

'Things are difficult.'

Helen is waiting for more.

'Helen … thank you for caring.'

Standing there, arms to his side, head down, he looks like he's about to burst into tears. She takes hold of him and hugs and he responds by gripping her tightly as if he's hanging on for dear life. It's fleeting though; he's the one who breaks the embrace.

'I'd better go,' he says, edging towards the door.

'I'll see you at the committee meeting then,' Helen says. 'I'm here if you want someone to talk to.'

'Thanks, Helen.'

Helen sinks down onto the sofa after Laurie has cycled off. She pours herself a glass of wine from the near full bottle. One day she'll tell Laurie that Vinho Verde is not her favourite drink, she just fancied it that evening at the pizza restaurant.

She grabs a handful of crisps.

What an evening! At one point she was close to resigning as deputy.

Now she knows that something is wrong. She has no idea what but senses that it might not be long before he's prepared to tell her. She needs to lower her expectations. There isn't going to be a relationship but Laurie is a friend in need of help. Her concern is genuine.

11

The next Mixed C match is at home, so there'll be a post-game tea at Dream Café, and Laurie intends to join them to check on things. Ahead of the match he calls Jennifer, nominally to verify the pairings. As expected, Andras is with Ying again and Jennifer is stuck with Douglas.

'Could I ask you to report back on the atmosphere during the match, please?' he asks, this the real reason for making contact. 'I'll be at the café by the time you get there, but it would be useful to know whether all has gone well up 'til then.'

'So, you want me to be your spy?'

'I'm not sure I'd call it that.'

'I would,' she chuckles, 'and I'd be honoured to take it on.'

'Thanks,' Laurie says, leaving Jennifer unsure whether he's picked up the teasing in her response. He can be so earnest, almost to the point of appearing stern, but she likes him and is happy to help.

The match starts and Jennifer's light-hearted spying is turning out to be a distraction as she looks across to the neighbouring court.

'Concentrate!' Douglas snaps.

As she is about to serve she glances across to hear Ying calling an opponent's shot out. The ball was way inside the baseline.

'You cannot be serious,' she hears an opponent shout, all smiles as he replicates the John McInroe line.

Jennifer serves and the return flashes past her. Douglas is giving her a disapproving look.

She serves again.

The smiles on the adjacent court have been replaced by arguing.

It's too late to adjust her feet, the ball is too close to her body, and her return rolls into the bottom of the net.

She hears Andras tell the opponents on the other court that since he was facing the net, he couldn't possibly pass judgement on his partner's line call.

Jennifer serves. A double fault.

Douglas is reprimanding her.

She's seen enough to report back to Laurie but is unable to focus for the rest of the match and her play is dreadful.

Laurie is at the café well ahead of the expected arrival of the players. Bridget is on duty and the ever-polite Laurie praises her and her staff for the food on offer. 'They won't mind if I pinch one,' he says as he lifts up a cube of cheesecake topped with a berry coulis and takes a bite.

The players arrive and it's immediately apparent that all is not well. Laurie introduces himself and attempts to lighten the frosty atmosphere with banal conversation. It doesn't work; the two sets of players aren't communicating with each other, the opponents whispering, but loud enough for variations of the word "cheating" to be heard several times.

Ying leaps up and points towards one of the women. 'Don't you dare call me a cheat!'

'It's OK, Ying. Cool it,' Jennifer says in an attempt to defuse the situation.

Douglas comes up with, 'I say, steady on everyone.'

Ying has no intention of steadying on. 'I demand an apology!'

Andras is smiling inanely.

A cream cake is thrown, landing on Ying's midriff, and the four opponents are on their feet and storming out of the café.

Douglas sits in stoney silence as Jennifer helps Ying to wipe off the cream with a serviette. Andras is still smiling.

'I think we should go,' Laurie suggests, having looked towards the counter, aware that Bridget has seen the incident.

'Do you think it's still acceptable for us to take leftover food home?' Douglas asks Laurie.

'I'm sure that's fine.'

'Ying's already taking food home,' Andras quips, pointing towards the cake remains on her top.

'That's not funny!'

The four players leave but Laurie stays behind to offer to help with the tidying up.

'A bit of an argument was there?' Bridget says but doesn't seem particularly bothered.

'You know how it can be with over-competitive players.'

'I thought tennis was a courteous game. Anyway, there's nothing for you to do,' Bridget continues. 'I'll sort out the clearing up.'

Laurie's relieved because he needs to tell Helen what's happened as soon as possible. He calls her on the way home. 'More problems with Ying,' are his first words.

'Hello, Laurie.'

'Sorry, hello Helen. As I was saying –'

'Yes, I know. Jennifer has already called me.'

'What did she say?'

'The truth. I doubt whether anything will surprise you. Ying cheats. Andras laughs. Douglas tells Jennifer off, though today it was deserved because she was terrible. She reckons winter tennis is a miserable waste of a weekend day.'

'What can we do about Ying? We need to have a plan ahead of tomorrow's committee meeting in case some of them have heard what's happened. Could we meet this evening to sort it out? Maybe at a pub?'

'Possibly,' Helen says, her indecision apparent.

'Helen.'

'Yes?'

'I'm sorry about last week. Those things going on in my life that I mentioned, I will tell you what.'

'It's not an obligation. Only if you want to.'

'I do.'

'Well, I'm happy to listen. Where this evening? And what time?'

Laurie suggests the Red Lion which would have been Helen's choice. It's a comfortable place without blaring music or Sky Sports.

When she arrives she sees him sitting in a far corner of the room. She gestures holding up a drink. He nods and she assumes he's picked up her signal to depict a beer.

When she places the drinks on the table he lifts a bunch of flowers from a spare seat. 'An apology – for last Monday.'

'There's no need but thanks.'

She takes hold of them then puts them back on the chair. 'Ying again,' she begins.

'As bad as the previous game. Did Jennifer tell you about the cake throwing?'

'She did. Ying must have been furious. Have you spoken to her?'

'Not yet. I'm no good at stuff like this, I was waiting until we've talked it through.'

'I think she needs a final warning if she wants to continue playing in any of our teams.'

'Could we meet her together?'

'No. You asked me that last time: it needs to be you. It would be seen as ganging up unless it was a one-to-one chat.'

Laurie's phone is resting on the table. It vibrates and the pair of them watch it slide along the surface until Laurie reaches for it. He reads a message and starts to type a reply.

Helen would rather he was focused on their conversation.

'Sorry about that.'

'No problem,' Helen says although she doesn't mean it.

'I'm sure Ying wouldn't mind if both of us ...'

Laurie's phone is buzzing again. Surely he'll leave it be this time, but no. He reads then types, using a single index finger when everyone else she knows under the age of about ninety uses thumb-texting. She's angry.

'As I was saying, together we'd be perceived as the chair and deputy chair carrying out a club duty. That's hardly intimidating.'

'I've said no. I think ...'

There's another buzz and the reading and messaging is repeated.

'Is there anything else you want to cover tonight?' she asks snappily. 'I'm tired and I've got a busy day tomorrow.'

'Well, maybe the builders. I still haven't met the new site manager but today I got a request for a substantial additional advance to pay for materials.'

'Can they do that?'

'I'm not sure. I was thinking of asking Oliver.'

There's another buzz on the phone. This time Laurie looks across at Helen before lifting it up.

'Just deal with it,' she snaps.

Laurie reads the message but doesn't reply.

'Could we leave it at that this evening?' he asks.

Helen is already standing. 'You're the one who wanted to meet but it's been a complete waste of my time.'

Laurie watches her leave. She's forgotten the flowers. He'll bring them to the committee meeting tomorrow evening.

Helen is fighting anger as she walks home. He can shove his peace offering of flowers up his bum.

12

Seven turn up for the committee meeting – Laurie and Helen, the men's and women's team captains, the social events and the communication reps and the head coach.

Predictably, the level of interest is minimal.

The captains see their responsibilities confined to the summer leagues. As far as they are concerned, the winter matches are of no importance and they're happy to leave it to lesser tennis players to do the organising. They look thoroughly bored.

It is the head coach's final week in England before heading off to Courchevel in the French Alps for his annual stint as a ski instructor. He is passing the time at the meeting looking at his phone screen.

When Laurie asks the social events rep what she's planning, she reminds him that the Christmas event has already been organised but other than that there's nothing to do until she is given the date for the clubhouse reopening.

'I should have that soon and of course I'll let you know immediately. What about comms? Anything to report?' Laurie asks turning to Dee.

'I'm pushing for numbers for the Christmas social. Do you want me to send out a newsletter covering clubhouse progress?'

'Best not to for now. I need to let you know that the builders are behind schedule, but there's no need for concern. I'm chasing them up and expect to report on good progress at our next meeting.'

The head coach pauses his phone activity. 'We trust you will stay on top of that,' he states before resuming his scanning and texting.

'Definitely.'

There are nods and smiles all round with the exception of Helen who knows that Laurie has yet to meet the new site manager and that the builders have requested an early advance of the next instalment.

Everyone seems desperate to leave, surprisingly even Helen who hasn't provided a single contribution all evening.

Laurie wonders whether briefly to mention the Ying issue, but what is there to say ahead of meeting her? Nothing much. 'OK, I guess that's it and we can call it a day. Thanks everyone.'

'What about A.O.B?' the comms rep asks.

'Do you have something, Dee?'

'Yes, I do. I think what's going up on our WhatsApp group about Stephanie and Oliver is a disgrace.'

'I thought all that had died down.'

'Well it's back, as bad as it was after the AGM.'

The mix of self-righteous, vindictive and mocking posts directed at the Kilroys following the meeting had been shocking, with the nastiest attacks aimed at Oliver. Laurie never engaged in social media gossip and it was Helen who had alerted him.

Jordie's limerick, posted three days after the AGM, had taken the malice to a new level.

Jordie
There was an old man called Olé
Who was on the lookout for a lay
With just a stick of chalk
He was nothing but talk
Much to his women's dismay

Tony
Bloody brilliant mate!

Simon
It's the poet lawriate for you.

Ursula
It's Poet Laureate, Simon, and Jordie's vulgar rubbish isn't even worthy of toilet graffiti.

Simon
Soreeee

Tony
What's the matter with you, for f**ks sake Ursula, it's only a bit of fun.

Ros

It isn't fun for the subject of the post – it's nasty.

Jimmy
So wokism has reached our tennis club!

And on and on it went for several days until Laurie's hope that it would all die down without the need for intervention turned out to be correct.

Dee now announcing that nasty posts have resumed is news to Laurie. He looks across to Helen who remains disengaged. She's doodling on a pad.

'This rubbish when Stephanie and Oliver are trying to piece their lives back together is appalling. Her post was dignified; it didn't merit an attack, and it's up to you to stop it, Laurie.'

'I'll investigate.'

'You said that the last time and you didn't do anything.'

'I didn't have to because it stopped.'

'Well it won't stop this time because Oliver and Stephanie are back playing tennis,' Dee continues. 'Separately of course. It's reopened the online attacks and some members are refusing to play with them during social tennis, which is against club rules.'

'It is. We can't have who you play with during social tennis based on who you like or don't like.'

'Exactly, Laurie. As I've already said, Stephanie's post was perfectly reasonable, so why the hatred?'

'I haven't seen it so thanks for alerting me, Dee. And as *I've* already said, I'll look into it.' Laurie looks at Helen. She must know about this. Why hasn't she told him?

Helen continues to avoid eye contact. She does know, she's seen Stephanie's message and is keeping abreast with the responses. Not telling Laurie has been an act of kindness, an attempt not to burden him with another problem in the hope that, like the last time, the antagonism would die down without the need for action.

It's not looking promising though despite, as Dee has pointed out, Stephanie's post not meriting spite.

Stephanie
Hi everyone. Just to let you know that Ollie and I are in the process of an amicable divorce. I was harsh about him at the AGM and in my previous posts. I realise that marriage difficulties are the result of both party's actions. Could I request that you don't give Ollie such a hard time when he comes to the club to play? Come to that, me too. Thanks to those who have been happy to join in with us. I ask for forgiveness from those who to date have been unwilling to accept our friendship.

The replies came flooding in within minutes of Stephanie's post.

Frank
How much is the settlement bribe to get you to write this garbage, Stephanie?

Dee
Disagree. This is dignified. Well done, Steph.

Frank
Sorry but I'm suspicious. Something's not right to bring about the change in her attitude.

Jimmy
And I know what. I've seen her around The Broadway with a new bloke.

Gus
Me too. I didn't want to say, but now that someone else has ...

Jane
Simply malicious gossip, you've no right to put a wild insinuation like this in the public domain.

Gus
As much right as you have for saying it isn't true. I know what I saw.

Stephanie
What you saw is me with my brother if you must know, even if it's none of your business.

Jimmy
So you say!

Ursula

Honestly, what a disgrace not to believe Stephanie. This is most unpleasant. Have sympathy for the poor couple. Are you trying mediation, Stephanie? It worked for us.

Frank
As a reminder, Ursula, it is Stephanie who was the first to post.

Helen
Can everyone cool it please. This is a group to pass on information and make requests for players. It is not for juvenile gossiping.

Gus
This is a democratic social media group, not a propaganda outlet for the tennis club committee.

Abi
Agreed. It's for everybody to use and to write what they want.

Sam
Anything   Abi?   Racism?   Homophobia? Misogynism?

John
Excuse this interruption but I'm short of a player for next Saturday's men's first team match owing to several injuries. Don't feel intimidated if you don't

usually play at this level, being winter league it really isn't that high. DM me if you're available.

Abi

Yeah but I'm none of those things, am I? So fuck off accusing me.

Helen

This is really poor. I'm going to advise Laurie to shut down the group if participants can't stay civil.

Frank

Not surprising you're going to tell Laurie what to do because we all know about you two.

Jane

So what if they're in a relationship? What right do you have to suggest it's influencing decision-making. I'm sure Laurie can make up his own mind.

Dee

These posts are a disgrace. I'll be putting forward a motion that we form a disciplinary sub-committee with the power to ban rude members at our next committee meeting.

Rob

Fucking bullshit. Fucking bollocks. Has that got me expelled Ms Goodie-goodie?

Dee has her phone out at the committee meeting and is reading the posts to update Laurie. 'That message from Rob was sent last night at 3.00 am. I won't carry on reading but there has been more posting today. Now I'm under attack. As is Helen.'

'Is that right, Helen?' Laurie asks.

'I've tried to calm things down but haven't got anywhere.'

'But why didn't you tell me there was an issue.'

Because I know you're stressed and I didn't want to over-burden you. She can hardly say that in public. 'I was going to; it's only recently cropped up.'

'It doesn't matter whether Helen has told you or not, I'm telling you,' Dee continues. 'It has to stop and my idea of setting up a disciplinary sub-committee with the power to ban miscreants is the only way forward.'

'Honestly, what is the matter with people?' Laurie sighs.

'Does that mean yes to my disciplinary sub-committee?'

'I need to reflect on this, Dee. I'm minuting your concerns and suggestion and I'll get back to you soon. Can we now close the meeting?'

'There's one more thing?'

'Yes, Dee.'

'There are rumours going round that Ying has been antagonising players from other teams with her unsporting behaviour.'

The coach laughs. 'Her and her line calls!' He returns to scrutinising his phone.

'Perhaps we can keep this off the record for now. I am dealing with it and I'm sure there'll be an amicable resolution. I'll report back the next time we meet.'

'Let's go then.' The coach pushes his chair back noisily and stands up. 'See you all at the end of March.'

There is a rapid exodus with Helen set to join the rush until Laurie calls her back.

'Yes?'

'So you knew about the WhatsApp posts?'

'Yes.'

'But you didn't tell me.'

Helen stays silent.

'I suppose we have to consider Dee's suggestion.'

'Something for next Monday then, assuming we're still meeting,' Helen says. Assuming I haven't quit being deputy by then.

'Yes, we need to keep going with the meetings but I've arranged to see Ying quickly: tomorrow after work. Could we discuss what she says as soon as possible afterwards?'

'Like when?'

'Can you make an evening this week? Maybe Wednesday or Thursday? There's something else, something more important to think about. The builders want to up the cost of the renovation.'

'They can't do that.'

'They think they can.'

'Quite a lot to cover then.'

'Exactly.'

'OK, I can make Thursday. Latish,' Helen adds to avoid any suggestion of a meal together. 'At nine.'

13

Laurie isn't looking forward to meeting the hot-tempered Ying. When he'd called to arrange it, she was not happy.

'Why must we meet?'

'To chat about matches.'

'Andras has been telling you stories, hasn't he?'

'Not at all, but twice when I've joined you at the café after matches I've picked up an uncomfortable atmosphere.'

'What do you mean by uncomfortable?'

'The opponents seemed extremely unhappy.'

'I never saw that.'

Laurie decides not to mention the cream cake. 'That's why we need to talk it over.'

'I'm very busy.'

'This is a strong request, Ying.'

'OK, a short meeting. Say where and when?'

Laurie has considered location ahead of the conversation, ruling out Dream Café (too risky), his place (too personal) or a pub (too noisy). He suggests the Tesco café.

As he sits there waiting for Ying to arrive, he texts Helen.

Wish me luck! Hoping for a peaceful resolution.

Helen. *Fair enough but you do need to lay down the law. We can't have her antagonising every team in north London. We'll get a bad reputation.*

Ying bounds in, as ever a ball of energy, and accepts the offer of tea which Laurie orders at the counter.

Softly, softly, he's thinking as he brings the tray across to their table. He wishes Helen was with him. 'So, Ying, how are you?'

'How am I? Not good with this victimisation.'

'That's not the case. But we can't have the club getting a bad reputation,' he adds, borrowing the line from Helen's text.

'And you think that is because of me.'

'We have had matches ending unpleasantly because of disputes over your line calls.'

'It's not my fault if they have poor eyesight. The one doing all the complaining last weekend was wearing glasses.'

'But people wear glasses to correct vision so they can see clearly.'

'Obviously not in her case. I know my calls are good.'

'And there have also been questions about your scoring.'

'I don't make mistakes about scores, Laurie. You are creating a giant mountain out of a tiny molehill. There have been no complaints from opponents.'

'There have. I saw it myself at the café and your fellow team members agree.'

'Ha, my so-called friends.'

'Someone was angry enough to throw a cream cake at you on Sunday. We'll get kicked out of the café if things like that happen.'

'But it wasn't me who threw the cake.'

'Throwing a cake is not normal post-match tea behaviour. Something must have triggered it.'

'That woman was deranged.'

'I didn't see anyone in her team tell her off. All four of them left together.'

Laurie was getting an if-looks-could-kill glare. Reasoning hadn't worked. 'Ying, maybe it's a good idea not to play against other teams, at least for a while.'

'So you are calling me a cheat.'

'Not a cheat. Mistaken.'

'Whatever the word, you're agreeing with everyone else.'

'You've said it – everyone else. Your own colleagues as well as the opposition.'

'You want the best person in the team to stop playing?'

There is a pause. 'Yes, I do.'

'This would never have happened if Oliver was still in charge.'

'Well, I'm not Oliver and it's happening now.'

'Then it's goodbye to the club; I'll join somewhere else.'

Ying stands up.

'Don't be silly. Please sit down.'

'It's too late for apologies,' Ying says as she hovers by the table, perhaps with the expectation of Laurie caving in.

'There isn't going to be an apology,' he says. 'I'm not changing my mind about you representing our club.'

Laurie texts Helen as soon as Ying has stormed out.

Didn't go brilliantly, Ying leaving the club.

Helen. *I thought that might happen. Probably for the best.*

Laurie. *I do feel that I've failed though.*

Helen. *You haven't. We can talk it over on Thursday.*

Laurie. *Thanks. Sorting out the builders next!*

~

Lee Grimshaw is the new site manager. He has finally answered one of Laurie's calls and agreed to meet, insisting that it must be a daytime visit as he's off site at four o'clock.

'There's no point me hanging around when it's dark,' he explains when Laurie tells him that late afternoon would be more convenient.

'There is if it's to meet the person employing you for a big job.'

'Sorry mate, can't do. And anyway, surely you'll want to have a walk round to see progress. That won't work in the dark, will it?'

So Lee Grimshaw gets his way, meaning Laurie has to sacrifice an afternoon in the lab at a critical time when a series of tests are being carried out to a tight deadline.

He takes a deep breath as he gets off his bike and strides over to meet Grimshaw who is all smiles as they shake hands.

'Before we do any inspection you need to know that the insulation regulations have changed since we got the contract,' Laurie is told. 'That means more costs and to be honest it won't stop there. The price of everything has soared – cement, copper, wood, glass. You name it, it's more expensive. And then we're having to increase wages to attract good quality labourers. That's why we've had to up your bill.'

'I did read Mr Grayling's email and I must say it was a shock. Thirty-five percent, that's a massive increase so I want to see a copy of the contract before considering anything. I did ask your predecessor but I didn't get an answer.'

Could there be a contract that Oliver has refused to pass on? A spiteful act of revenge?

'There ain't a proper one. Not much was put in writing, it was all done through chats between my boss and your man. All I've got is the estimate of costs.'

'At least that's a start,' Laurie says, thinking of the expensive watch Oliver was wearing at the AGM. Oliver's negligence was criminal but contesting the point with a barrister wasn't something Laurie was prepared to take on. 'Have you got that with you?'

Grimshaw takes out and unfolds a water-stained sheet of paper. 'It's an in-house document really, so

I'm doing you a favour letting you see it. But this is the important bit.' He points to a handwritten sentence at the bottom of the page. *The builder has the right to raise the charge under exceptional circumstances.*

'Who wrote this?' Laurie asks, although he recognises Oliver's signature.

'Your man.'

'Is this common practice?'

'It's normally written into a contract, but since there isn't one ...'

'What counts as exceptional circumstances?'

'The things I've mentioned.'

'Which means anything you decide to be exceptional! I want to see an amended cost sheet with justifications for each item. And I want to see invoices for all goods supplied.'

Laurie rests the piece of paper on a stack of bricks, takes out his phone and photographs it.

'I'll let Mr Grayling know but I'm not sure what he'll say. Of course, you can always cancel the job and get someone else to finish it.'

This option has come to mind, but Laurie knows it's not viable. Finding another builder would be time consuming and reduce the likelihood of the clubhouse being ready for the summer season. And anyway, a new builder might be every bit as expensive as this one. Plus the fact that recently he'd authorised and handed over a sizeable advance.

He gives the sheet back to Grimshaw. 'You need to speed things up. I want regular weekly meetings with you to assess progress.'

'I'll see what I can do.'

'You do that.'

'All good then, so I'll head off now then,' Grimshaw announces, the site inspection seemingly no longer on offer.

Just as well because I've had more than enough for today Laurie is thinking as he texts Helen.

We haven't got a leg to stand on regarding the builders increasing the cost.

Helen. *What's in the documentation?*

Laurie. *There isn't anything. Only a scrap of paper with handwritten permission to up the charge under exceptional circumstances.*

Helen. *Meaning?*

Laurie. *Exactly.*

Helen. *Great! Another thing to talk through on Thursday. And there's something else to worry about.*

Laurie: *What?*

Helen. *Ying has just posted on the WhatsApp group. Take a look. Must go.*

Laurie reads the spiteful post attacking him for kicking her out of the club without justification.

He calls Dee.

'Have you seen Ying's post.'

'I have. Is it true you've kicked her out?'

'No it isn't. I suggested she step down from playing in the Mixed C Team because of accusations of cheating with line calls –'

'Which we all know is the case.'

'I was as diplomatic as possible but she decided to resign.'

'At least there are no comments on the thread sympathising with her. Well, not yet anyway,' Dee adds.

'Why would anyone want to do that?'

'You know what people are like on social media. What do you want to do about Ying?'

'You're the group administrator, right?'

'Correct.'

'Well, since she's no longer a club member we should remove her from the group. I think you have the means to do that.'

'Yes I do, but what about those vicious posters I mentioned at our meeting? Can I remove them too?'

'It's hardly the same. They're still members.'

'I'll only remove Ying if you agree to my idea.'

'Which is?'

'The disciplinary sub-committee. However, I've been reflecting on that and I think it's a cumbersome solution. Instead, what about running all posts past me before they go live?'

'I'm not sure. For a start, have you got the time to do it quickly enough, for instance when a team captain needs a player at very short notice?'

'I am retired so yes, I do have the time on my hands. I could set it up so that captains' posts go straight on without me having to check them.'

'And the coaches?'

'Them too.'

'But who decides which posts are banned? It can't only be you.'

'Why not?'

'It's undemocratic, it's open to bias.'

'Is that an accusation, Laurie.'

'Of course not. Look, I'm meeting Helen tomorrow. We'll talk it through and then I'll let you know.'

'Fine, but Ying stays in the group until I have an answer.'

'That's blackmail.'

'Call it what you want, but I'm not shifting,' Dee says.

'And I'm not making the decision on my own.'

'You know, one good thing about Oliver was that he got things sorted quickly.'

'Thanks for that. I'll get back to you. Enjoy your evening.'

Is Dee right? Should he be making decisions without consulting anyone else? Without consulting Helen?

He sends her a text.

I wanted Ying off the WhatsApp group but Dee has imposed conditions. I don't agree – so that's another thing to cover with you.

Helen. *The plot thickens!*

Laurie. *I'm afraid so.*

Helen. *OK, we'll sort it all out on Thursday.*

Laurie drops his phone onto the sofa, goes to the fridge and grabs a beer. Once again he's wondering why he accepted the post of chair: there are too many problems to deal with. He has a sense of duty but nothing is working out and he's doubting whether he has the competence to succeed. Perhaps the sensible thing is to resign.

Helen flicks through the texts Laurie has sent over recent days and wonders what she's let herself in for. She's discovered that Laurie is indecisive which is putting pressure on her to make the decisions. With rehearsal time at a premium she hasn't got the space to problem solve for the tennis club. Both of them were the wrong appointments, spontaneous and euphoric on the evening of the Kilroys' demise, but poorly thought through. What was needed were people with more time on their hands, possibly retirees and definitely those with the wisdom that comes with age.

He's not going to like it, but when they meet on Thursday she's going to tell Laurie that she's resigning.

14

They meet at Dream Café, Laurie's choice of venue. His text to Helen had ended with, *The café has a much needed calming atmosphere.*

Helen. *Yeah, right! As in hooligan chanting, fights and cake-throwing.*

Laurie. *Exactly! Is 9 still OK?*

Helen. *Sure. See you then.*

Laurie is the first to arrive and sits at the table furthest from the watchful eye of Bridget who is chatting with Jennifer and Gareth. They're in fits of laughter about something or other.

He waves as Helen enters the café and she strolls over to join him. There's no smile though, just a nod as she sits down. What's going on? It was the same at the committee meeting when she was totally disengaged.

'Hi Helen. What do you want to drink?' he asks.

'A beer's fine.'

'Right, here's the list of problems we need to tackle,' he says as soon as he's back with the drinks. 'Number One: the builders want more money. Thirty-five percent more. Number Two: they are way behind schedule. Number Three: Dee's WhatsApp blackmail demand. Number Four: the possible fall out after my meeting with Ying. And should we let Andras partner Zadie?'

'Do you want to go through them in that order?' Helen had intended to resign immediately on arrival, but since she's there she might as well work through the issues with Laurie. One final attempt to help.

'I think so,' Laurie says. 'They're probably ranked according to urgency.'

'Right. The builders want thirty-five percent more. The first question is, can we even afford that?'

'We do have sufficient funds in reserve but that's not the point. It isn't there to pass on to the builders without an assessment of value for money.'

'No, I understand that. So –'

'Hang on a sec.' Laurie takes his phone out of his pocket and reads a message. 'Sorry about this,' he says as he starts tapping out a reply, a long reply.

Not again! Helen looks away, dismayed. Laurie was the one desperate to meet to cover tennis club problems, but once again she's been relegated to second class citizen. She envies Jennifer who is laughing away with five others at a table on the other side of the café. She wishes she was with them.

'All done,' Laurie is saying matter-of-factly, his tone assuming she is prepared to give him her full attention the instant he stops texting. 'Where were we up to?'

His phone remains on the table.

'Nothing as important as what you're doing,' she mutters. Could all this texting be related to his issue whatever that might be. She goes through options. A partner? An ex-partner? Or something left field like an addiction to gambling? Next time he's texting she might try to see what he's writing and to who. Except that she doesn't care anymore.

'Oh yes, the builders. What were you saying?' Laurie is asking.

'Do we have to do this tonight; I'm not feeling great? Unless there's something absolutely urgent, I think I'll go.'

'I thought that was why we were here – to sort things out. I'd like –' Laurie's phone vibrates and slides towards Helen's side of the table.

Laurie takes hold of it and presses a button. 'It's OK, I'll leave it.'

'Maybe you could actually put your phone away.'

'Yes. I'll –'

Another vibration, the soft buzz quite possibly the most infuriating noise Helen has ever heard.

'For fuck's sake, Laurie!' she shouts. 'This is ridiculous. Whenever I'm with you you're on the phone. I'm surprised you don't keep it in one hand when you're playing tennis.'

'Sshh Helen. Bridget's listening.'

'Well, fuck Bridget. I'm off.'

Helen pulls the chair back with force and it topples over.

'Wait!' Laurie is standing and he grabs hold of her arm. 'Please wait,' he says softly.

She relents, unsure why, lifting up the chair and sitting back down. 'Who *is* this person you seem to be non-stop messaging with? Work? A girlfriend?'

'Neither.'

All dreams of a relationship with this man have gone out the window. 'It doesn't matter who it is other than the fact that you are astonishingly rude.' She is fighting off tears of anger and disappointment. 'Fucking Phubber,' she hisses.

'What?'

'Phubber. A person who ignores who they're meant to be with because of their obsession with their phone.'

'But why Phubber?'

'Does it matter?'

'I was just interested.'

'Snubbing. Phone snubbing. Phubbing.'

'That's clever.' Laurie gives a little snort-like laugh which makes Helen consider killing him.

'It's not meant to be funny. The issue is the rudeness not the bloody word to describe it! Anyway, I am going now and you can take this as my resignation as deputy.'

'It's my stepfather.'

'What is?'

'You asked who I was texting. It's my stepfather. Will you let me explain?'

~

Laurie's memories are of doting parents and a happy childhood, but at some point during his mid-teens there was a huge change. Long periods of silence from his father were followed by yelling and the slamming of doors. Although recognising that these actions were out of character, Laurie was too immersed in his own adolescent anxieties to take enough notice to investigate the reason. He wasn't told about the tests being undertaken until a brain tumour was identified and a prognosis of months to live was given. How self-absorbed teenagers can be. Of course he was upset, for both his father and his mother, and of course he did help with whatever he could, but how he now wishes he'd spent more time at his father's bedside during those final days.

His father died at the start of Laurie's final year at school. There was discussion about whether to take up his university place or have a year out to support his mother Jean, but she insisted that he go, so he did. When he came home during holidays he was glad to see that she was coping remarkably well, a surprise because he'd always regarded his father as the strong one in the household. She'd admit that it felt strange to be in an empty house, but beyond that she chatted about friends old and new, a job she enjoyed and a range of outside interests.

It never entered Laurie's head that his mother might be in search of a new partner, so it was a shock during a visit home ahead of finals when he introduced to the man she planned to marry.

It was a double surprise because Keith was twenty years older than his mother.

The ever-diplomatic Keith didn't stick around much while Laurie was at home that holiday which enabled heart-to-heart chats between mother and son.

'I like him, Mum. He's friendly, he's kind, and I'm pleased that he's not over-pushy with me. But you do realise that you could end up as a carer in the not too distant future.'

'I appreciate you thinking of my welfare, and yes, there is an age difference. The thing is, Keith is super fit. He jogs, he does yoga, he's constantly dragging an exhausted me to the cinema, a play or a concert. He's an absolute bundle of energy and I can hardly keep up with him. I think we'll have a good few years together to enjoy ourselves.'

'In that case I'm very happy for you. For both of you.'

At first it was as his mother had predicted, she was kept entertained by Keith with his boundless energy, and Laurie had never seen her so happy.

Then she was diagnosed with cancer. She deflected his questions about the severity and time frame for recovery.

'You're treating me like a kid,' he complained.

'It's not that. I really don't know the answers.'

That was a lie. She did know and it was left to Keith to tell him.

'We aren't far from the end, Laurie, I'm afraid it's at Stage Four. Terminal. Jean mustn't know that I've told you; she's intent on protecting you. But I think it's only fair that you're aware.'

~

'So it was the exact opposite of what I'd expected. Instead of my mother caring for my stepdad and being left a widow, it was Keith who did the caring and is now left as the grieving widower.'

'That's so sad,' Helen says. She has taken hold of Laurie's hand.

'And he's fallen to pieces, he's an utter wreck. It's been over a year since Mum died – I know that isn't a huge amount of time for grieving – but he's not coming to terms with what's happened at all. If anything, he's getting worse.'

'I don't think you can set a time limit on how long it takes to heal.'

'I know, but Keith's at crisis point. Everything I've googled – panic attacks, lack of sleep, depression – you name it, he's got it. He's mentioned suicide and he's not one for giving false alarms or seeking attention.'

'He obviously trusts you; take it as a compliment. But doesn't he have any family who can help?'

'That's the problem, I'm the only one around. There's a son living in the Middle East who offers to pay for things but apart from that has little interest in getting involved. Then there's a sister. She lives in a warden controlled flat down in Worthing and is more or less housebound.'

'And his doctor?'

'Definitely concerned and she prescribes medication, but she tells me I'm the one best placed to help him and that I'm doing a great job. I'm not though, Helen, I'm struggling. I try to cheer him up and when that doesn't work, which it never does, I step back which upsets him. So I feel guilty and attempt to cheer him up again. It's a vicious circle.'

'It's tough, I can see that. It's not a parallel but I've been around musician friends who are in a state of permanent despair – "I'll never be good enough", "I can't get any work", "I'm too busy to make a success of a relationship" – and I run out of things to say to them. "Poor you" never works. "Snap out of it" doesn't either, of course. So, what's left to try?'

'Exactly. But that's what all my texting and calling is about – not work, not a girlfriend – just trying to help Keith survive. I'm his personal Samaritan, responding to his frequent cries for help, trying to calm him down, consoling him, arranging another appointment to see the doctor.'

'Why haven't you told me what was going on before now? Of course I wouldn't mind the texts and calls.'

'Because I fancy you like mad. I want to impress you and the last thing you'd be interested in is how I'm failing to deal with my stepfather's distress.'

Laurie reddens. Coming out with fancying Helen was not planned.

'You're wrong, it does impress me. Massively. He's your stepfather, he's not even a blood relative, and yet you're prepared to be there for him.'

'He is a really good bloke – or was before Mum died. And besides, I can't leave him to suffer.'

Helen gets back to what Laurie has blurted out. 'Oh, and by the way, I fancy you too.'

Laurie's look oozes despondency. 'But you can see why I can't be in a relationship with all this going on.'

'That's not true if the person you start it with is understanding and willing to help.'

Helen wonders whether it was OK to say that. She breaks the awkward pause, her tone light. 'We fancy each other – that's promising! Why don't we put that on hold for now and race through these tennis club issues.'

Laurie nods, leaving Helen to reflect on her abrupt change of subject and Laurie's compliance. Crazy really. They're in their late-twenties and both have admitted to fancying the other. Shouldn't they be racing to the nearest inappropriate place to strip off and have wild sex, just like you see in the movies?

Well, that scenario has passed them by – at least for now.

'What was your Number One problem at the club?' she asks as she struggles to dismiss the thought of a naked Laurie.

15

Laurie switches off his phone and drops it into his jacket pocket. He has zero interest in tennis club problems because his thoughts are about removing clothes, caressing Helen's gorgeous body, making love, and waking in the morning with her tight up against him.

Focus, he tells himself. Focus. 'The increase in the cost of building is the first item.'

'What have you told them?'

'I've only spoken to the site manager. I've said I want his boss to pass on details of their amended costs and from now on I want to see copies of all invoices.'

'That's a good start, but I do think you need to speak directly with the company owner. We should hold back payments for materials until we see the delivery notes. They won't be out of pocket if we do that because suppliers always give a month or more to settle accounts.'

'Agreed, I'll tell him that. The second clubhouse issue is them falling behind with the work. I've asked for weekly meetings to inspect progress.'

'Yes, insist on that. And during those meetings ask for details – in writing – of what they intend to complete the following week.'

'I agree with that, too, though it still doesn't solve the problem if the delays continue.'

'If we insist on an updated contract to reflect the increase in costs, we can include a penalty clause for late completion.'

'And that will be a first contract as far as I can see.'

'Good. Number Three?'

'Dee wanting to mediate WhatsApp posts.'

'No, she can't.'

'She's threatened to step down from comms.'

'Call her bluff and if necessary let her go. It'd be easy to find a replacement. Number Four?'

'Ying.'

'I've looked and there haven't been any follow-up comments on her WhatsApp post. She's decided to leave. End of. And that makes Dee's blackmail threat worthless. She won't be happy so we should get the ball rolling to find a new comms person.'

'Great, Helen. I'll start working on all of this tomorrow and report back when we meet on Monday.'

'I can't do next week.'

'You're not going to resign, are you?' Laurie asks with a cross between an anxious frown and a smile.

'Actually I was going to this evening. But no, I'm staying. It's just that one of my string quartet sponsors is a travel company and they've offered us a week away to rehearse in peace and quiet at one of their hotels.'

'String quartet?'

'My group. Me on cello, two violins and a viola. I have mentioned it before.'

'Have you? Maybe I'll see you play one day.'

'That would be nice. We'll be performing in London in spring. We haven't been going for long so we need all the practice we can get before making our first recording in January. That's why our sponsor's offer is brilliant.'

'Where are you going?'

'Some spa hotel in mid-France. We leave tomorrow.'

'I must be in the wrong job. When I'm not stuck in a basement lab in London I'm at a conference in some lookalike hotel in a big city.'

They are on their way out. Stepping onto the pavement, they face each other.

'You know that other stuff we mentioned...' Helen says. They kiss, a soft and gentle kiss, not the frenetic one in that inappropriate place while tearing off clothes in the make-believe blockbuster movie. Better than that, much better.

'Mmmm. Nice.'

'Do you want to ...'

'No. Laurie. Well, yes I do, but let's wait until I'm back. I want it to be special and I'm not sure tonight would be. It's been such a rollercoaster evening – at one point I was hating you. And I have loads to sort out for the trip.'

'Maybe it is best not to rush things.'

'You do a lot of agreeing, don't you? Good, that sets the tone for our relationship! I'm assuming you'll agree to another kiss now.'

This one is different. Passionate. Long-lasting.

There are footsteps to their side.

'Oh to be young again,' Jennifer teases as she and Gareth pass them by.

~

Laurie takes the next afternoon off work to get to grips with tennis club matters. The starting point is to sort out the builders, as forcefully as necessary because he is tired of being messed around. He calls Mr Grayling and leaves a message, Then another and another. He makes no progress and is wasting the afternoon.

If it means flooding Grayling's voicemail box until it's full then that's what he'll do.

'Mr Grayling, I voicemailed and sent you several emails today but still haven't heard back from you. Could you please call me as soon as you pick this up?'

The voicemailing continues over the weekend.

'Mr Grayling, I won't begin to consider your request to increase the cost of the tennis club refurbishment ahead of a discussion.'

Laurie is still trying to make contact at the start of the next week.

'Mr Grayling, having wasted my weekend trying to make contact with you, I took time off work this morning in the expectation of meeting Mr Grimshaw at the club. The project is behind schedule so why, on

a perfectly reasonable day for working outdoors, was no one there?'

'Mr Grayling, this is the second weekday with no one working at the club. It's simply not on. Please make contact.'

Laurie has yet to hear from Grayling but does from Dee who has sent him a rather offensive email to announce her resignation as the committee comms person. Her message ends with notification that Ying is reaching out to members to back her reinstatement in the Mixed C Team. When he accesses the thread on WhatsApp he notes, judging by the comments, that she has few supporters, definitely not enough to justify immediate action. The builders are more important.

Laurie hates conflict but enough is enough. It's time to get tough.

'Mr Grayling, in the light of the bribery that resulted in your company gaining this contract, I am set to report this to the police. You might want a conversation ahead of me doing so.'

It's worked. The word *Builder* is up on his screen seconds after leaving the voicemail. He answers the call.

'At last, Mr Grayling.'

'Don't you at last me. I don't appreciate threats.'

'I'm merely –'

'Oh, you're merely, are you? You posh twat.'

'Excuse me, but –'

'Oh, *do* excuse me, I pray!'

'There's no need for that.'

133

'Then don't you dare accuse me of bollocking fraud.'

On the verge of apologising for leaving an over harsh message, Laurie becomes the new Laurie: he'll take Grayling on. The man is getting good money and failing to do a job properly.

'I am NOT lying about you offering a backhander of an expensive watch to get Oliver Kilroy to give you the tennis club contract.'

'I did no such thing.'

'Yes you did.'

'I know Ollie, he's a mate of mine. What's wrong with me giving him a gift?'

The thought of Oliver Kilroy, a prominent barrister, being a mate of a small scale builder strikes Laurie as somewhat unlikely. 'A gift at exactly the time when the project had gone out to tender.'

'You need to be careful what you're accusing me of, matey.'

Laurie presses record on his phone. Just in case.

'How are you going to prove it, clever boy?' Grayling continues, his tone menacing.

'Oliver's wife Stephanie has admitted it.'

'They're fighting each other over a divorce, ain't they, so she's hardly an independent witness. And anyway, you'd need to prove that she told you, which you won't be able to do because she'll deny it. She don't want her name dragged through the mud, does she?'

'I wasn't the only person she told. She announced it during a packed public meeting.'

134

'Silly cow, that is if what you're saying is true.'

''It is true. There are almost a hundred witnesses.'

'Look mate, let's not fight,' Grayling says, his voice now conciliatory. 'If it's a watch you're after, that ain't no problem.'

'So it *was* a bribe. And now you're trying to bribe me?'

'A gift. Keep schtum and I can get you one just like his.'

'No thank you. I'm not interested.' Laurie looks at his Fitbit, considered an extravagance at time of purchase but costing a small amount compared to the watch Oliver had been wearing.

'And I'll let you into a secret, matey. If it came to it, Stephanie would say she lied at this meeting of yours. She'd say it was only to get at Oliver.'

'Why would she change her story?'

'Because, my son, she got a watch too. So, when she admits to lying there goes your proof.'

'Actually I still have proof because I'm recording this call.'

'That don't hold up in court, recording a conversation without permission. You know that.'

'Since I've never been to court I don't. I'd have to check it with the police.'

'You fucker.'

Laurie pauses. Where is this going? He has no intention of reporting the watch bribe, two watches it seems, to the police. He made the accusation to force the builder to cooperate and it's backfiring. Severing ties with the Grayling firm would end all chance of finishing the clubhouse on time which would be a disaster.

Morality or pragmatism, this is the decision he needs to make.

'I'm not happy with the situation but I am prepared to let you continue with the project subject to certain conditions.'

'Before any of that I have a condition meself, son. No criminal charges.'

'Agreed.'

Grayling moves on to accept all that Laurie and Helen have discussed – for the club to reduce the size of the monthly advances and to pay for supplies only on receipt of delivery notes, and to have a cast iron guarantee for completion before the start of the summer season, with a penalty if they fail to deliver.

'I'll have people working there tomorrow, matey,' Grayling tells him before cutting the call.

Laurie realises that this is nothing more than another verbal agreement, but it's better than nothing. He's hardly optimistic when he cycles to the club the next morning, but sure enough four builders are busy working, supervised by Grimshaw who is perched on a breeze block eating a pastie. Laurie cycles off without speaking.

He has another tennis club issue to sort out having decided not to respond to Dee's email directly. Instead, taking pleasure in the likelihood that it will infuriate her, he posts on the WhatsApp group.

Dee is stepping down as comms rep on the committee after five years of sterling work. Our huge gratitude for all she has achieved. We now need a replacement. Please DM me if tentatively interested.

He smiles as he checks the message before posting it. He is happy with his wording, replicating the style used by a football club when they sack their manager or a prime minister dismissing a member of the government.

Do people keep their social media open permanently because within an hour he has seven members interested in the comms role?

Builder sorted. Dee sorted. Replacement strategy in place. That leaves Ying.

Ying will not be playing the next match whether she's left the club or not. What about another partner for Andras though? Can it be Zadie? There's no Mixed C match for a few weeks so he'll leave that one until Helen is back.

At last he's getting a buzz from sorting out tennis club affairs, the negativity replaced for the first time by an enjoyment of the responsibility. While setting up a spreadsheet to process comms applications an email from Grayling arrives. Much to his surprise, the builder has attached a document listing the terms agreed. It isn't a contract so nothing is legally binding, but at least he now has something in writing.

Brilliant, brilliant, brilliant! And that has nothing to do with the tennis club – it's about Helen. He had been fretting over what to tell her about his stepfather and the answer turned out simply to be the truth. He'd been sure a relationship was impossible until her reaction changed everything. He can't wait to be with her again.

Did she say she would be back on Saturday or was it Sunday? Hopefully they'd be together at some stage that weekend; if not, he'd have to wait until their Monday evening meeting.

Three, four, five days, it hardly matters, but as he awaits her return there is a fair amount of nighttime fantasising going on.

16

There's no let up during the rest of the week because Laurie is working flat out at the lab to finalise test results essential for a grant application. After work he's scrutinising the emails sent by members interested in taking on the role of comms rep. Although they haven't been asked, they are attaching CVs which are amazing. How can so many high-level media, marketing and IT specialists who enjoy tennis and want to serve the club live in one small part of the city? To be fair interviews will be needed and he'll ask Helen to join him on the panel.

He's got a couple of texts from her but has kept his replies brief. It's a trip for the quartet to immerse themselves in rehearsals and he doesn't want to distract her. Since she hasn't indicated a return date he's assuming that he won't be seeing her until their Monday evening tennis club meeting. That will be weird. Will they actually deal with anything to do with tennis? Will they sleep together that night?

A Friday evening email from Stephanie Kilroy pops up. As he clicks into it he wonders whether she is applying for the comms post. Absolutely no way would she get the job.

Dear {name$}

Time has passed and water has flown under the bridge since the Annual General Meeting. Both Oliver and I are deeply embarrassed, nay, humiliated, by our poor conduct, even though the behaviour of some club members was far worse than our own and totally unwarranted. Nevertheless, we do offer our sincere apologies and would like to make amends in some small way by inviting you to dinner at Granville Villa on Thursday 11th December. We hope you are free to attend. Please RSVP.

With fondest affection
Stephanie

Stephanie's message irritates Laurie. Her attempt at an apology is hardly that if she's implying that club members are more to blame. Her salutation error is annoying, too, the failed name merge indicating that she can't be bothered to send tailored messages to those invited. Being a post to a group suggests that it will be a big event. Laurie doesn't enjoy dinner parties, definitely not large scale ones and definitely not one hosted by the Kilroys.

He won't be going, of course.

As he closes his laptop for the night there's a ping on his phone. He's set up a personalised alert for messages from Helen.

Hi Gorgeous. Just to let you know I won't be back tomorrow. We're staying on until Wednesday because our sponsors have given us some all-expenses paid relax time! Poor me because that means galleries, a vineyard tour, shopping of course, and lots of delicious food. Yes, I do miss you but this is rather great! XXX

Laurie. *Lucky you – hope you have a good time. A quick question before you disappear. Have you been invited to the Kilroys next Thursday?*

Helen. *Yes. What about you?*

Laurie. *Me too. I'm assuming you won't be going.*

Helen. *If there are no travel delays I was thinking yes.*

Laurie. *Why?*

Helen. *Curiosity. What are the Kilroys plotting? It's probably a good idea to have a club rep there.*

Laurie. *I was about to reply with a no, but if you go I will.*

Helen. *Great – our first date! Will you RSVP for both of us? Must go, will catch you as soon as I'm back XXX + XXX = 2(XXX). See, I can do science too!*

Everything is encouraging, the kisses, the Maths joke, calling him gorgeous, saying she's missing him, labelling the Kilroys dinner as a date.

He replies to Stephanie, accepting her invitation. Adding *We'd be delighted* in his brief message grates.

~

'What do you make of this?'

David and Bridget are in the back office at the café finalising the second quarter accounts. She hands him her phone.

David chuckles. '{name$}, that's interesting!'

She takes back the phone. 'I didn't notice, it's the dollar sign in the wrong place, isn't it? If she's attempted a name merge it must mean she's inviting loads of people.'

'I suppose so. I'm assuming we aren't going so it doesn't matter.'

'It is the grandest house in the area. I've always wanted to see what the inside is like.'

'I'm still not tempted.'

'We are free next Thursday.'

'Exactly. Free to have a quiet evening in for a change.'

'I think we should go,' Bridget persists. 'Perhaps they're planning to do the decent thing, apologise, even if it has taken a while.'

'It's hardly an apology in the email. She's blaming everyone but themselves.'

'I don't see it like that. Let's accept. It'll be fascinating to see who else they've invited and whether anyone from the tennis club will be there after what happened.'

'I want to find out who else is going before deciding.'

'I can't see what difference that makes, but if you want to then fine.'

The next morning David is at the hotel and he asks Jennifer whether she knows anything about the Kilroy dinner party. She says she'll ask around and calls Helen. The phone service is unavailable so she texts Laurie to enquire.

Laurie. *Both of us invited and we're going though not sure why.*

Jennifer. *I tried calling Helen but couldn't get through.*

Laurie. *She's switched her phone off. She's in France.*

Jennifer. *How come?*

Laurie. *A mix of work and holiday. Are you invited to the Kilroys?*

Jennifer. *No, obviously I'm not important enough.*

Laurie.. *Any idea who else is going?*

Jennifer. *Yes, Bridget and David.*

Jennifer lets David know that Laurie and Helen have been invited, "normal people" he defines them when informing Bridget, so he's happy for her to send an acceptance email.

~

The four guests are standing in the hallway, a space as large as Laurie's entire living room and kitchen area. Bridget is inspecting the Escher-like marble floor, weighing up whether it's an Art Nouveau original or an impressive replica. She intends to ask Stephanie as soon as the two of them are alone together. Laurie is wondering whether the woman who had opened the door and is now collecting their coats is called a maid, housekeeper or servant. What do posh people say these days?

143

Stephanie descends the sweeping staircase to greet them and the group are escorted to the library.

Oliver eases out of a voluminous maroon leather armchair which emits a soft farting noise as he stands. He strides across to shake hands, first with David who is unimpressed with the host's competitively tight grip. When Oliver shakes Laurie's hand firmly, he responds with a squeeze that makes Oliver wince as he pulls his hand free.

'It is so kind of you to join us,' Oliver says as he turns to face the women. In turn they are gripped and kissed, one on each cheek.

'Sherry everyone?' he asks as he wheels a fussy gilded trolley to the centre of the room. On it are three cut glass decanters, the liquids inside rich, warm colours. He holds up one of the small crystal glasses. 'Dry, medium or cream,' the question firstly directed at Bridget.

Laurie hates everything about the man and his wife. Oliver's cravat. Stephanie's pearls. The smell of the faded leather. Two oil portraits side by side above the fireplace – one of him, one of her. When offered a sherry he fights off the mild anarchy of asking for a beer, refusing a glass and drinking from the bottle. Having weighed up rebellion against immaturity, he settles for a dry sherry.

Catching David's eye, Laurie senses that the other man shares his loathing as they smile conspiratorially. He's unsure what Helen is thinking though. Looking across at her, she doesn't seem out of place in this setting, sipping from her little glass of honey-coloured alcohol. She's wearing what he remembers his mother used to call a cocktail dress, a knee length, emerald green off the shoulder garment. She looks gorgeous.

They'd only snatched a brief conversation following her delayed return from France due to a strike by French air traffic controllers. It meant he'd be meeting her at the Kilroys, not beforehand. He's desperate to be alone with her.

David watches Stephanie escorting Bridget across the room from wall to wall to view the portraits and other paintings. With her arms gesticulating wildly as she points, he hears Bridget outlining features of the artwork – the popularity of a particular colour, a rule adopted by landscape painters during the early nineteenth century, and so on. He's hit by a wave of admiration and affection.

Laurie watches as Helen edges away from Oliver to join the other two women. They are looking at portraits of the Kilroys above the fireplace, paintings way more complimentary than the actuality. He would expect Bridget, an artist, to have lots to say about them, but Helen seems equally engaged. His own ignorance about the arts, theatre and classical music is an embarrassment: beyond science his cultural interests are confined to action films, rock music and the occasional fantasy novel.

He finds himself questioning whether he might be out of his depth with Helen. Is a relationship workable? Helen's sexy off the shoulder green dress is telling him yes, a relationship is a good idea.

David is by his side. 'Look how comfortable the women are chatting away together.'

Laurie has only been looking at one of the women.

'You know what I think?' David continues. 'Women find it easier to slot into any social situation than men do.'

'Maybe, but is it easy for them this evening or are they just being polite?'

'I think easy. Bridget is as engaged chatting to a lorry driver delivering supplies to the café as she is here. She seems able to morph into everybody's best friend.'

'She's certainly welcoming at the café whenever I'm around.'

'Exactly. The customers love her, even if she's reprimanding them for poor behaviour.'

Is there a hidden agenda Laurie wonders? Is David going to bring up tennis club events?

'Her friendliness is great for business,' David continues. 'Whereas me, I see everything as a job to get done.'

'You don't come across like that when you're hosting café events. And anyway, sorting things out when you're running a place is important.'

'But Bridget does that and is also sociable.'

They watch Oliver approach the women and say something that makes them laugh.

'I'd struggle to laugh at anything he does. The man is obnoxious,' Laurie says.

'Which backs up what I've said. Bridget dislikes him intensely, I wouldn't have thought that Helen thinks much of him either, and Stephanie is filing for divorce. But there the women are, all smiles and laughter.'

The maid-housekeeper-servant has entered the room. She strides across to speak to Oliver.

He claps his hands loudly which, Laurie notes, has made Helen jolt with surprise.

'Excuse me,' he booms unnecessarily given the close proximity of his audience. 'Cook wants to know if there are any allergies or suchlike.'

'I'm a vegetarian,' Helen tells him.

'That's not a problem,' Stephanie says. 'It's a buffet. The cook has made plenty of veggie options.'

'Anyone else?' Oliver booms again.

There is silence and the woman leaves.

'So there's a cook as well as that woman,' Laurie remarks. 'Stephanie hasn't bothered to sort out the food herself on her apology evening.'

'Are you expecting an apology?' David asks.

'You certainly deserve one after what happened at the AGM. I thought you'd be cancelling the arrangement.'

'I'll let you into a secret. We were in hysterics seeing what was happening in our peaceful little café and were still laughing at home. Our kids thought we were drunk.'

'Who's drunk?' Helen asks as she places an arm around Laurie's shoulder and draws him towards her for a brief lip to lip kiss. 'Hello,' she whispers.

'We were reminiscing about the AGM night,' David says.

'I'm assuming that's why we're here because we're hardly typical Kilroy guests,' Helen says.

'You look like a perfect fit,' Laurie tells Helen. 'You look fantastic.'

'Flattery will get you everywhere,' she says, 'and I do mean everywhere.'

Laurie wants to skip dinner and take Helen home that minute.

The maid is back to announce that dinner is served and she's asking the guests to follow her to the dining room.

17

They enter the dining room, its focal point being a large oval table with a crisp white cloth and two multi-arm candelabras.

'Look at that, it's wonderful,' Helen says, pointing up at the ultra-modern light fitting, eight metal cylinders of different colour and length that are projecting pinpoints of light onto the table. 'Much better than the crystal chandelier I expected to see.'

Laurie nods, unsure why she's getting so excited about a light.

A low cabinet runs the full length of one of the walls. Two women, the one they've already seen and presumably the cook, are in front of it ready to hand out plates.

'There are labels by each dish but you can always ask,' Stephanie announces.

Helen comes from a foodie household and this display is taking her back to a childhood when her parents frequently had friends and family over to dinner. Since leaving home her interest in food has suffered because she has neither the time to cook nor the income to pay London restaurant prices.

She's the first in the queue and takes her time reading labels before selecting a little of everything marked with a green V on the right hand corner of the tags.

With her plate full and set to return to the table, she notes Laurie peering down at the labels with what looks like either perplexity or suspicion. She can understand why, some of the concoctions are pretty left field, like cheese quesadilla with papaya, and coffee grinds with bacon.

Oliver, in charge of the wine, is circling the table with a red and a white on offer, a bottle in each hand.

'Your preference, dear?' he asks Helen.

'Red please.'

'It's a Mâcon 2013, an absolutely super year,' he explains as he leans over her – uncomfortably close – and pours a small volume into the larger of the two glasses.

Laurie opts for the red, too. He's never understood the convention of serving a glass only a quarter full during an evening when a fair amount of alcohol is sure to be consumed. It's the same at work receptions and before that, at formal meals in college. Outside of those occasions he and his mates fill their glasses to the brim or drink directly from the bottle, this probably not brilliant for hygiene.

A quietness descends as they eat, broken by the clinking of cutlery. The food is delicious and Laurie resolves to learn how to cook beyond the basics. Perhaps he could take lessons. Yeah, right, there's no time and he's not that interested.

If he and Helen ever get to live together will they share the cooking?

What's going to happen this evening after this meal?

Will they spend the night together? He feels a pang of nervousness at the thought: he hasn't had a girlfriend for ages.

Oliver is tapping his fork against his glass.

'Apologies for interrupting your meal, dear souls, but some words must be said. I would like to take this opportunity to offer a formal apology to all four of you. At the time of the tennis club annual meeting we were in a difficult place as far as our marriage goes. All is now resolved and we are getting divorced.'

That's hardly resolved then, Helen is thinking as she sees Stephanie wince and David shake his head in puzzlement.

'We do have a little something for each of you as a thank you for your understanding,' Oliver continues. On cue, the two women who have been supervising dinner reappear, one carrying two bouquets of flowers, the other two bottles of whisky. Stephanie takes the flowers and passes them to Bridget and Helen. Oliver hands the drinks to David and Laurie.

'We recognise that the whole affair was an embarrassing inconvenience and we hope that all can be forgiven and forgotten.'

'Hardly forgotten,' Helen says. 'I hope I never see anything like that again.'

This stops Oliver in his tracks. 'Well,' he says cuttingly, 'my apology was more directed at Bridget and David.'

'Oh, it was highly amusing to see such prestigious citizens behave like that,' Bridget jokes.

Oliver ignores the remark, his gaze fixed on Helen.

'Let's be truthful, Helen, the kerfuffle didn't inconvenience you at all, did it? In fact, quite the opposite. A position as deputy chairman, or should I be saying chair? And a relationship with young Laurie here.'

Laurie is sitting by Helen's side and she can feel him bristling, his fists clenched. She places a hand on his thigh and squeezes. 'Let it go,' she whispers.

'On the subject of tennis club posts, that is one reason for this evening's gathering. Now that an apology has been made and our good behaviour is restored, I suggest Laurie steps down and I am reinstated as chairman. There are busy months ahead and I am the best placed to steer the refurbishment of the clubhouse.'

Laurie receives another squeeze on his thigh, this one firmer, but it doesn't stop him speaking. 'You're joking.'

'Not at all, dear fellow. From what I understand you haven't been making much headway. The builder is extremely unhappy, our communications manager has stepped down, and one of our prominent members has been expelled. Whatever next?'

'You're twisting things.'

'Am I? Well anyway, I'm not intent on criticising you. To put it simply, chairmanship is a difficult job. It needs a man with greater experience than you have to manage the unavoidable ups and downs. When you were my deputy you told me how busy you were with your job. I'm offering you an exit from this added responsibility.'

'And since Ollie and I are back on good terms, we think it might be sensible for me to take on the deputy role.' Stephanie looks across at Helen. 'What do you think?'

'Interesting,' Helen gets in before Laurie has time to react. 'Thank you for the offer,' she continues, all sweetness and light. 'I'll certainly consider it and I'm sure Laurie will, too.'

'Excellent. On with our feast then,' Oliver says before taking hold of the two bottles of wine to top up Bridget and David's glasses.

'Last chance for main course before the counter is cleared to make way for afters,' Stephanie says as she heads for the buffet with her empty plate.

'Like fuck they'll get our posts,' Laurie whispers.

'Agreed, like fuck they will,' Helen responds. 'Well put.'

'But you told Stephanie ...'

'Tactics.'

Oliver is behind them. 'More wine?' he asks.

Helen holds up her glass. 'I'd love some, thank you so much. And the food is delicious. Do please thank your cook if I don't get the opportunity.'

'I will, dear, I will. I hope you weren't offended by our suggestion.'

'No, not at all. It's brave of you to want the post back bearing in mind what most club members think of the pair of you. Not to mention the risk of an investigation into financial irregularities.'

Oliver is good at handling such situations; he doesn't flinch.

'More wine, Laurie.'

'Certainly. Thank you, Oliver.'

He's learning something from Helen. He'll need to reflect on exactly what that is, but her tactic is a cut above his customary reaction of losing his temper.

Helen is smiling at him. 'Well done. I've got a funny feeling there's more drama to come this evening. Watch this space!' she adds as she sees Oliver bring two more bottles to the table. 'To fully appreciate the entertainment I'm stopping drinking,' she adds.

Helen isn't the only one; all four guests are putting hands over wine glasses to prevent Oliver from topping them up. Stephanie though is pointing her glass towards Ollie for a refill, and soon afterwards, for another.

Laurie and Helen leave it to Bridget to engage with the hosts. Bridget is questioning Stephanie about her refurbishment of the house. She seems genuinely impressed with how meticulous Stephanie has been in restoring original features.

David is beaming, struck with admiration for his partner's knowledge and how well she conveys it.

There's a feeling of guilt, too, that business pressure is preventing her from involvement in the arts as much as she would like. Perhaps taking on the hotel in addition to the café was a step too far? Both are highly profitable so they could easily find a buyer if they decided to offload one of them. But which one? The café, his dream, or the more lucrative hotel?

The chat about the refurbishment of Granville Villa has dried up. Dessert plates have been cleared from the table and Oliver is offering port or brandy, declined by the guests. Oliver opts for port, Stephanie a brandy.

David asks Oliver to identify his most difficult court cases and there's no holding back as Oliver promotes his brilliance, frequently interrupted by Stephanie ridiculing her husband's claims of success and elevating her own achievements.

The allegedly restored harmonious relationship between husband and wife is collapsing. Stephanie suggests that the majority of her husband's courtroom victories are the result of prosecution incompetence or malpractice rather than his own skill.

'You only take on cases that you're sure to win, don't you darling?' she taunts.

'Every single one I've accepted is on a grander scale than anything you've dared to tackle.'

'Mine are about people's wellbeing, protecting women against domestic violence or fighting racial abuse. Yours are about getting criminals off scot-free.'

'Mine fund the absurd amounts of money spent on refurbishment that you've been boasting about all evening. And you have failed to mention that an interior designer has done all the donkey work, leaving you with the grand task of selecting the fucking Farrow & Ball colours!'

'That's not true.'

'What else have you done then?'

'This light,' Stephanie says, looking upwards.

'Which looks like Pick Up Sticks thrown together by an infant.'

'I rather like it,' Helen says.

'Me too,' adds Bridget.

'Yes, it's nice,' David says.

'And very different,' is Laurie's contribution.

'Go on all of you, take her side. As expected,' Oliver slurs.

Something resembling telepathy strikes as Laurie and David declare in harmony, 'It's probably time to head off.'

'Yes, a busy day at work tomorrow.'

'It's been a lovely evening.'

'Don't forget to thank your cook.'

They race to the hall where the maid-housekeeper-servant is already standing, holding their coats.

'Thank you so much for coming,' Stephanie says. 'And here are your flowers, ladies,' she adds, gesturing towards the bouquets which have been placed on the hall table.

Oliver has joined his wife and he puts an arm around her waist. 'Yes, much appreciated. Don't be concerned about our little tiff just now, it's part and parcel of the joy of marriage.' He's looking at Laurie.

'You will consider what I suggested, about chairmanship?' he says as he holds up one of the bottles of whisky which Laurie had deliberately left in the dining room. 'Don't forget this.'

Laurie takes hold of the proffered bribe but can't bring himself to say a thank you.

With the false thanks for a lovely evening over, the guests are ushered out and the front door is closed. They can hear arguing as they make their way down the driveway.

'What fun!' Bridget says ahead of farewell hugs.

'You will stay in charge of the tennis club, won't you?' David asks Laurie. 'If not, us hosting your events would have to end.'

There's no reply because Helen and Laurie are kissing.

David observes them for a split second before taking hold of Bridget and kissing her.

'That was a nice surprise,' Bridget says as they separate. 'Right then, we'll see you two around.'

'Yep. See you.'

Laurie and Helen stay put outside the Kilroys' house.

Helen answers Laurie's unspoken question. 'This is hard to say, but I'm thinking not tonight. I was stuck at the airport all night yesterday and didn't sleep a wink and when we finally got to London I had about half an hour to get ready for this. I want our first night together to be a special one but I'm a mess now. Can you wait one more day?'

This is her second postponement: has Helen gone off the idea? 'I suppose so,' is all Laurie can say.

'Definitely, definitely tomorrow night, and the next and the next and then more. Come to mine and I'll cook.'

Laurie nods. 'I'll walk you home.'

They stop outside her house and there's more kissing and Laurie doesn't want to leave.

Helen edges away. 'I'm going to drop with exhaustion if I'm not careful. Tomorrow Laurie, and I'm so excited about us.'

After all that's happened, all that's been promised, it feels odd for Laurie to be walking away. One more day though; that's not the end of the world.

18

As Helen watches Laurie walk away she's regretting her decision and considers calling him back. His disappointment at not being able to spend the night together was obvious and it matches her own. So what if she's already exhausted and will be even more so the next morning after a night with little sleep?

She doesn't call after him though.

She hasn't given him the principal reason for her decision. There's a breakfast review meeting in central London with the sponsors and it's hugely important. This is such a critical time for the quartet; they're balanced on the boundary between success and failure. Out of the four of them she's the one the others rely on to ignite the enthusiasm that leads to further funding. Her social life is important but she can't ignore her career.

Helen hopes Laurie isn't thinking that she's having doubts or isn't interested in him. She sends him a text. *Night-night. Can't wait for tomorrow XXX + XXX = 2(XXX)*

Immediately she receives a smiley.

She considers replying with "Love you!"

Will she never learn? She's been too quick in the past to throw in the word love, expecting a relationship to progress on her terms. She then discovers that the man in question is merely looking for a short-term fling or has turned out to be someone who she doesn't love at all.

But it's different with Laurie, the mention of love in a message wouldn't be a throwaway gesture. As soon as he'd told her what was preoccupying him everything fell into place. His concern for his stepfather has made her love him all the more. Kind and sexy, that's a pretty good combo.

Love? She's doing it again, behaving like an infatuated teenager. They haven't even started a relationship; their first night together could be a disaster.

She doesn't chase his smiley with those two words.

~

Helen's morning meeting is over and it's been a success with the promise of a further year's sponsorship. The others are full of praise and suggest a couple of hours of rehearsal but she turns them down. With Laurie not scheduled to arrive until seven-thirty she would have plenty of time to practise, but she'd never be able to concentrate. And a wandering mind for even a second can mess up a whole piece.

While on the bus home she receives a text from Iris, her first team tennis partner, asking if she fancies a hit ahead of their next mid-week match.

Helen types *No* then deletes it. She's anxious about her first night with Laurie and playing a bit of tennis might help her chill.

Sure. I've got something on this evening but I can fit in an hour or so. Maybe at two?

Back at home she grabs a sandwich, gets changed and heads off to the club on her bike.

A single builder is there on this bitterly cold day, sitting on a stool in a sheltered corner drinking from a thermos flask.

'Just you today?' she asks him.

'Yeah, the others are on another job. There ain't much I can do on me tod.'

'So what exactly are you here for?'

Helen gets a look which she interprets as "What's that got to do with you?"

'I'm the deputy chair,' she tells him.

He looks confused.

'Deputy Chairperson,' she says, hardly a term that rolls off the tongue. 'I'm on the committee that runs the club.'

'Oh, right. I'm doing some tidying up.'

Helen surveys the piles of bricks, breeze blocks and timber, all neatly stacked. 'Tidying what?'

'Good question, darlin'.'

She considers telling the workman off for calling her darlin', but with Iris already on court shouting for her to get a move on, she lets it pass.

'On my way!' she yells as she considers what to tell Laurie about the lack of builder activity. Definitely nothing tonight though.

She's wrapped in her thickest tracksuit and it stays on as they start rallying. But even during a friendly hit she's competitive and before long is racing round the court with layers of clothes discarded.

There's a small patch on the artificial grass court close to the base line that doesn't see the sun for a few weeks during the darkest days of winter. At best it is soggy, at worst, icy. Wet or icy, the outcome is the same, it's as slippery as hell. Everyone knows that.

Helen is one point away from losing her service game when Iris whips a ball deep into the backhand corner. She chases it down at full stretch and manages to return it but goes flying, turning her ankle and ending up sprawled on the court. She leaps up without further thought, claiming that it's only a tumble and she's OK. She isn't. Crying out in pain, Helen hobbles to the side of the court.

'You alright, luv?' the builder shouts.

'It's fine thanks, I'll sort her,' Iris tells the man who has remained seated.

The things on Helen's mind in order of emergence are will she be fit to play the next match, will this injury affect rehearsals, and will it mess up the night with Laurie. This, she realises, is the opposite of the order of importance.

She opts for denial: this is a minor inconvenience that will soon disappear. 'Just give me a minute, I'm sure I'll be OK,' she tells Iris. 'Perhaps I shouldn't cycle home though. Would you give me a lift?'

Iris looks at Helen's ankle which has swollen to double its normal size. 'I can give you a lift, but it'll be to A&E, not home.'

'Don't be silly,' Helen says despite noting her swollen ankle.

'Come on,' Iris says, supporting Helen as she hops to the car.

'Need any help, luv?' The builder has stood up, his first physical activity for the forty minutes they've been at the club.

'No, I can manage thanks,' Iris tells him and he sits back down.

'A pity there's no clubhouse yet; I would have put on some ice to stop the swelling,' Iris says as they drive to the hospital. 'They're slow with the rebuild, don't you think?'

'They have a schedule. Laurie has it all under control.'

While Helen is waiting to be seen in A&E she texts him. *I got injured playing this afternoon. Still OK for tonight though!*

Laurie. *Where are you?*

Helen. *At A&E.*

There is a pause. The three dots are indicating that Laurie is typing but nothing is arriving. It must be a long message.

Laurie. *Oh!*

Helen. *Yes, oh.*

Laurie. *It could be ages before you're seen.*

Helen. *No prob. Got hours before we meet.*

Laurie; *Want me to join you there?*

Helen. *No need tho thanks for offer. Iris is with me. I'll keep in touch.*

Laurie. *Hope it's not serious. Poor you.*

She's about to send XXX + XXX = 2(XXX) when her name is called out.

All the hanging around is frustrating. Firstly, waiting for the doctor, then the X-ray department, then another doctor, then a nurse to strap the bandage – yes, a bandage, not plaster, because thankfully it's a sprain and not a break – and finally a third doctor to prescribe painkillers, provide a list of things she should and shouldn't do over the next few days, and at last give the all clear for her to leave.

While being seen she has missed three texts from Laurie, each one simply *And?*

Finally she can reply with the relatively good news. *And ... I'm finished here so on my way home. It's a sprain, not a break, so definitely OK for this evening.*

She's texting this while being driven home by Iris, aware that time has leapt ahead at an impossible rate since she last checked at the hospital. It's half-past six. Caught in Friday rush hour traffic, they're still a couple of miles from home. She tots up the negatives. Top of the list, the painkillers are wearing off and her ankle is hurting. Secondary issues, she has no idea what to do about food and she might well stink to high heaven. And she isn't even allowed to shower for a couple of days. Despite all this, she's desperate to see Laurie.

As soon as Iris has dropped her off she heads to the bathroom to tidy herself as best as possible. A touch of mascara, lip gloss, a brush through her hair, teeth cleaning, a spray of perfume.

The doorbell chimes while she is still in the bathroom.

'I'm coming,' she shouts as she makes her way to greet Laurie. Using the crutches provided by the hospital is harder than she expected.

Laurie is holding flowers and a bottle of wine. He's frowning when there is really no need; Helen would rather see him smiling. She drops her crutches and flings her arms around his shoulders, gripping tightly for support as they kiss. He can't take hold of her properly because he's still clutching the gifts, but he is doing well with the kissing.

There is a problem because her crutches are now out of reach. She can't let go of Laurie since he has no hands free to support her. She shuffles him towards the wall which she leans against while balancing on one leg.

'Could you hand me those, please?'

Laurie puts his gifts on the floor and retrieves her crutches.

'Flowers and wine, thank you,' she says.

'No wine tonight though, not if you're on painkillers.'

'I'm sure one glass can't harm.'

'Another thing on my mind is that you wouldn't have had time to organise food. So I was thinking maybe a takeaway.'

'Yeah, good idea.'

'What do you fancy?'

'We can sort that out later.' Come on, Laurie, priorities. This is our first night together.

There's a shooting pain in her ankle. She winces and he notices.

'Are you sure it's OK me being here?'

'Of course.'

'At least it's a sprain and not a break. Remember Glen, he was out for months with a broken ankle.'

Helen *does* remember Glen's broken ankle. She *is* glad her injury is only a sprain. She *agrees* that a takeaway is a good idea. She *knows* that drinking alcohol is probably unwise.

And then it strikes her that Laurie's rambling conversation is because he's nervous. As nervous as she is.

Helen leans across and takes his hand; a crutch drops to the floor and they laugh at the clattering. As they kiss again, a soft and tender kiss, Helen can sense that Laurie is less tense. She unbuttons Laurie's shirt and runs her hand over the little wisps of hair on his chest. Her heart is racing as she stretches down to unfasten his belt, pull the zip and yank down his trousers. It's not easy using one hand. She is all set to take off his boxers.

'Wait! Shouldn't we discuss Oliver and Stephanie's proposal to take on the chair and deputy chair posts first?' Laurie says. Helen looks up from boxers to face in disbelief then catches his broad grin.

Laurie removes Helen's top as she balances on one leg. She sways and they giggle. After unhooking her sports bra the laughter ceases. He grips the waistband of her tracksuit bottoms and edges them down. 'This isn't going to work with you on one leg,' he says, pausing between kisses.

'Pull them back up then, I'll hop to the bedroom,' Helen suggests.

A topless man and woman, one edging along with his trousers round his ankles, trapped by his shoes, the other shuffling along with one functioning leg and one crutch, make their way to her bedroom.

Helen drops down onto the bed.

Laurie pauses to assess the situation.

'It's OK, just pull them off,' Helen says.

'They're tapered. I won't be able to get them over the bandage.'

'They're an old pair, you can cut them.' Actually they are fairly new and quite expensive but Helen has a higher priority. 'There are scissors in a kitchen drawer,' she continues.

Helen watches Laurie hobble away, wondering why he hasn't taken his trousers off first or at least pulled them up. It obviously crosses his mind while in the kitchen because he returns naked, trousers, boxers, shoes and socks removed, holding up a pair of scissors.

He cuts and pulls and they're giggling again. 'My ankle might be messed up but the rest of me is working fine,' she jokes.

'Good,' is the last word spoken for a while.

~

When Helen wakes and turns to face her man, he's missing. She's all set to spring up to find him, then realises that any leaping out of bed is impossible. Was having Laurie with her an injury-induced hallucination? When she touches the empty side of the bed it's warm. No dream then.

She's satiated and content as she reflects on their night together. The laughter as they struggled to undress. Her dozing then waking to see Laurie sitting up in bed, phone in hand.

'Your stepfather?' she'd asked.

'No, I'm checking out takeaways.'

'But it's the morning.'

'It's not. You've only slept for a few minutes.'

Opting for Thai food and eating in bed.

More laughter.

More lovemaking, so comfortable and natural, without the inhibitions she'd felt during the first time with a boyfriend in the past.

Now, with the light from the low winter sun streaming in through a chink in the curtains, she can hear clattering in the kitchen.

'Laurie?'

'Coming.'

He's back carrying a tray with a pot of coffee, two mugs, a jug of milk and two bowls of fruit and yogurt. He's wearing boxers, nothing more, and she admires his well-toned body.

'How's the leg?' he asks.

'Not bad at all.' She sits up, initially self-conscious of her own nudity. 'Take a look at it if you want.'

She sweeps the duvet to the side so they can inspect the extent of the swelling and she notices Laurie's attention straying from the injured ankle to other parts of her anatomy. She's usually modest but is happy to be observed in this way with him.

'The swelling's definitely gone down,' he says.

Perhaps it has, just a little, but it's aching and Helen is desperate for one of the painkillers prescribed at the hospital. 'It's still a bit sore though so could you get me one of the pills from my bag? I think I left it by the front door.'

'We didn't get much sorted last night, did we?'

'I think we got loads sorted!'

19

Laurie has been reflecting on his night with Helen. On how, a short while ago, he was certain this couldn't happen while he was responsible for his stepfather's welfare. The burden was too much – time consuming, upsetting and stressful. And then he'd told her how his situation made a relationship impossible even though he fancied her. There hadn't been any ulterior motive, he wasn't looking for sympathy or trying to impress her with an account of his kindheartedness. Quite the opposite, he'd gabbled on incoherently, increasingly embarrassed as he spoke. Her response had been simple, that they could get round any difficulties within a relationship.

They are sitting on top of the covers in bed, drinking coffee and eating fruit and yoghurt.

'Why are you grinning?' she asks.

'Because I'm happy,' he says reddening, sure that Helen has noticed his attention on her nakedness way above the injured ankle.

'Me too.'

Laurie shifts his gaze back to her ankle, the skin tight and red against the top of the bandage.

'It's bloody killing me,' she says, 'but there was no way I was going to cancel last night.'

'I was playing the super cool guy but then I realised what an idiot I must look shuffling around with my trousers around my ankles.'

'I did wonder.'

'It could have been the most embarrassing moment ever but I didn't feel that with you: we just laughed.'

There's a moment of quiet reflection. Laurie is thinking that last night was more exciting and natural than anything he has ever experienced. He wants to tell Helen that's the case, but of course he won't. You can't tell someone she's *the* one after a single night together like in some tacky romance film.

Helen's thoughts have shifted from last night's bliss to a consideration of her injury. At hospital she was advised to have complete rest for a few days, whenever possible keeping her leg raised to reduce the swelling. "Use a footstool during the day and put a pillow under your leg in bed at night," the nurse had told her. Well so much for that because her injured ankle had twisted and turned during their lovemaking, far removed from the recommendation.

The nurse's final words now seem threatening. "As long as you're sensible and stick to the guidelines during the critical first week, you'll be fine. Do stick with it though or else recovery could take a lot longer." On Day One, make that Night One, she has ignored the advice. Recommendation or not, she is anticipating similar ill-advised activity with Laurie through these critical first few days.

Laurie is worrying about time pressure. Of course he wants to spend as much time as possible with Helen and he'll offer all the support she needs while she's injured. That's fine but it's on top of caring for his stepfather, a hectic work schedule and running the tennis club.

His stepfather has been urging him to find a girlfriend for ages. Mission accomplished and Laurie is sure that Keith will be charmed by Helen, but he'll need to take on board that this means less time for Laurie to spend with him.

The demanding timetable at work is for a good reason. Recent lab test results have been encouraging and one of the pharmaceutical giants is interested in providing a substantial grant for further synthesis experiments. The deadline for submitting the bid is tight and Laurie is a key member of the team writing it.

And then there's the tennis club. The building. The committee. The teams. Social media. The Kilroys. He wishes he could return to the original reason for joining the club – to play tennis.

Laurie starts filling the tray with cutlery and crockery. Helen smiles as she watches him carefully placing things in neat stacks, removing and resorting items to fit some system he has in his mind. Finally filled, he carries the tray out of the bedroom and Helen is back to thinking about how long it will be before she recovers. An extended period of injury will have consequences for the quartet. Their recording session is in less than four weeks' time with the

Christmas to New Year break in the middle. Rehearsals have been going well, but all the same, fine-tuning is still needed. And then there is the tour to prepare for, their first beyond performing at small London venues.

One problem that comes to mind is travel. She uses a mix of buses and the Underground to reach the rehearsal room. She won't be able to do that for a while, not when carrying a cello. She'll have to use taxis. The quartet's budget won't stretch to cover the fares so maybe an S.O.S. to her parents for funds might be needed.

But travel is the least of her worries. She's a physical musician, swaying her legs, pressing her feet down, her whole body immersed as she plays. Will she be able to perform properly with a damaged ankle?

It isn't looking likely. 'Fuck!'

'What?'

'Did I say it aloud? Sorry, I was just thinking about work. I hope my ankle doesn't affect my playing.'

'Tennis?'

'No, cello. There's something I need to do; I won't be long. You can take a shower while I'm busy if you'd like.'

'OK.'

She can't take her eyes off his back, bum and thighs as he walks away. She's all set to follow him to the bathroom before realising that her ankle injury makes that impossible. Or should she break another of the nurse's recommendations? No, that would be beyond reckless, and anyway, what she has to do is urgent.

Slowly she gets up, stoops down to pick up her crutches, slips on a dressing gown and makes her way to the living room.

The jet of shower water is distorting sounds that are unlike anything Laurie has heard before. He quickly finishes washing, wraps a towel round his waist and heads into the living room. He is greeted by a rush of notes, from high to low and back to high again, like in a heated conversation. Confrontational. Enticing. Emotional.

Helen stops playing and looks across at him. 'Say hello to my cello.'

'Hello, cello. That was amazing.'

'Thank you. It's definitely acceptable so the good news is that I can play without my ankle being a handicap.'

'Music is your full time job, right?'

'Sure is. For as long as I can remember, even when I was tiny, I knew it was the cello for me.'

'It's big for a tiny tot.'

'There are half-size instruments but yes, it isn't one of the usual choices. At least I didn't go for a double bass.'

Helen started playing the cello at a prep school where learning a musical instrument was the norm. When her parents took her to a magical BBC Proms performance at the Royal Albert Hall she fell in love with the deep, mellow tones of the cello and knew she was going to be a musician. She did well, joining the

National Youth Orchestra in her early teens, and several years later she gained a place at the highly competitive Royal College of Music.

'But you don't play in an orchestra. Why not?' Laurie asks.

'Because the competition is severe and once you're in the rivalry can be ruthless,' she explains.

There followed a few years of ad hoc pop, jazz and classical recordings and performances until she joined three equally frustrated and impatient ex-college friends to form the string quartet. It was a brave step because even this market was highly competitive, but they knew they had appeal in addition to being outstanding musicians. They were fresh and were soon to discover organisations keen to sponsor young musicians.

'And one of them has paid allegedly for your rehearsal but more likely for a holiday in France.'

'Exactly. If I'm honest, being OK looking and a bit cool in how we dress and behave has helped. It also helps that we're savvy with social media which has raised our profile. Some classical musicians are snooty about that, they think it's below them, which is fine because it gives us more space to promote ourselves.'

'Snooty? I'm not a social media fan but that isn't the reason.'

'I know you hate it. Anyway, the good news is that the ankle isn't affecting my playing. The other good news is that we're together.'

Laurie stays in the living room, his towel round his waist, listening to her practise for a while. 'I'm so relieved I can play as well as ever,' she says as she carefully rests her cello on the floor. 'We've got tight deadlines. Our first recording is in January then in March we start our tour at Wigmore Hall.'

He'd like to talk to her about her music but knows nothing about it. What's so important about Wigmore Hall? He's never heard of the place.

'Do you play that as well?' he asks, gesturing towards the piano.

'It's a distant second instrument though I do teach it. There are a lot more takers than for cello.'

'I wish I'd learnt to play an instrument when I was a kid. I begged my parents for a keyboard, one of those cheap electric ones. I remember being furious when they said no even though I knew we were strapped for cash.'

'In my family I would have been regarded as an outcast if I hadn't played an instrument. I was four when I started piano lessons. Come to think of it, I was about that age when I had my first tennis coaching.'

'I didn't realise you were that posh.'

'Oh, I was. Am. Independent schools, flash cars, holidays abroad, you name it, we had the lot.'

'My dad, not Keith, my real dad, would have hated your family – he was an ardent socialist.'

'My lot are rich but they do care about the community. They're always giving to charity. Listen, it's never too late to learn an instrument. I can get you started on piano.'

'You haven't got the time,' Laurie says while thinking that he's the one who hasn't got the time.

'On the assumption that this hasn't been a one-night stand, there's no rush to get started. Whenever we have a spare half hour we can give it a go.'

'I accept.'

'I will charge of course and I'm not cheap!'

'In that case, I'll be charging you for sorting out last night's takeaway, for making breakfast and clearing up in the kitchen this morning, and I assume for helping you to get dressed now.'

'But I've done that myself.'

'A dressing gown doesn't count.'

'No, you're probably right,' Helen says as she unties her robe cord. He's by her side and she is tugging at his towel. 'Oh, and I will be charging for sex,' she adds.

'Fine, I'll pay.'

~

An hour or so later, Laurie is looking at his phone. Several messages have come across and he is mindful of the promise made to visit his stepfather. Keith's texts indicate that he's having a difficult day and Laurie's encouraging words in an attempt to ease his depression have, as ever, failed.

'I'd better go soon,' he tells Helen.

'Your stepfather?'

'Yeah.'

She doesn't mind Laurie leaving because there is something she must do even though she isn't looking forward to it.

He is already out of the bed and dressing. 'Do we need to cover anything to do with the tennis club?' he asks as he is buttoning his shirt. 'Or can it all wait?'

'What's on your list?'

'Oliver and Stephanie's suggestion for a start. Whatever we think of it we will have to reply.'

'Will we? We were fairly elected and the members would go bananas if Oliver was back in charge. We saw what he was like at the dinner party, worse than ever. Stephanie, too. I wouldn't be surprised if one day there's a Granville Villa murder. I suggest we ignore them; they don't deserve a response.'

'OK, that was easy. There's the clubhouse though; it's a worry that won't go away.'

'It wasn't encouraging yesterday. I saw a single builder who had no idea what he was meant to be doing.'

'I'll chase Grayling on Monday.'

'We want the builders there at the start of next week so don't leave it until then. Text and email a complaint today and say you'll be checking that people are there on Monday.'

'I'm not optimistic about hearing anything over the weekend. I'm beginning to think he doesn't care.'

'Surely he wants to get it finished so he can get paid.'

'I've just got a bad feeling about it.'

'Let's hope you're wrong,' Helen says as she slides out of bed, stoops to pick up a crutch and hops towards the bathroom. She turns. 'Can you spare a couple of minutes to round up some clothes for me before you go? Anything will do.'

20

It's already midday and Laurie is worried about keeping his stepfather waiting much longer; the man's texts have been disturbing. He has no idea where to start rounding up clothes for Helen as requested, so waits until she's out the bathroom. She returns naked which doesn't encourage Laurie to rush things despite guilty feelings about being late for Keith.

She sits on the bed, resting the crutch on the floor by her side. 'Underwear from there,' she says pointing.

'These?' he asks, pulling a pair of red skimpy knickers out of the drawer and holding them up.

'Maybe something a bit more comfortable for today. One of the black ones.'

He puts the red pair away, lobs her choice onto the bed by her side, and pauses to watch her slide on the knickers. Is she toying with him?

'Matching bra, please, from the next drawer down.'

Rummaging through women's underwear is a new experience for Laurie and combining this with watching Helen dress is turning him on.

'You're enjoying this aren't you,' she says teasingly.

'I am.'

'Me too. We know trousers won't work over the bandage so it'll have to be a dress today. They're in that cupboard,' she says, again pointing. 'No, I don't think that one, I'm not off to a party today. The blue one next to it is fine though.'

He comes over and hands her the bra and dress. 'Need help putting them on?' Laurie asks.

'Weirdo! Now find me a cardigan from the shelves on the other side of the cupboard. What fun, this is like having my very own manservant. Dishy manservant.'

He watches her put her bra on; she isn't rushing.

He brings over a plain navy cardigan as Helen is slipping the dress over her head. 'Could you zip me up please?' she asks as she wiggles to pull the dress down over her bum. Helen rests her hands on his thighs as he stretches behind her to pull up the zip. He'd happily take everything off and start all over again but there is Keith to consider.

Helen is dressed. She stands up and pecks Laurie on the cheek. 'I might let you help me to dress even when my leg is better. As long as you're up for it,' she adds, grinning as she looks down at his erection.

'I don't want to go but I think I'd better.'

'That's OK because I need to let some others know what's happened sooner rather than later,' Helen says. She picks up her phone from the bedside table.

'Others?'

'The musicians and my family.'

There's a ping on Laurie's phone. The text is from Keith. *I hope you won't leave it too late. I'd welcome a chat.*

Laurie. *I'm leaving soon. I'll be with you as quickly as I can.*

'Done it, I've messaged the other musicians,' Helen says. 'So they know about the accident.'

She is reading replies.

'I said it wasn't affecting my playing but the three of them are doubters. Bradley's arranging for them to come over this afternoon – which I can do without.'

'Maybe they want to see you to offer support.'

'Maybe, but that didn't come across in Bradley's message.'

'I bet it'll be fine once they're with you. Can I do anything before I go?'

'No, I'm good, thanks.'

'I'll head off then. I can't stay with Keith for long because I've got work stuff to do.'

'On a weekend.'

'We have a tight deadline for something.'

'I'm creating extra work for you with this,' Helen says, touching her leg. 'I'm sorry.'

'No problem, especially when it's things like helping you to get dressed.'

Helen smiles that lovely smile of hers, chased by a serious expression. 'I've really enjoyed everything, Laurie. Will I see you tomorrow?'

'You bet! I'm playing tennis in the morning then I'll be with Keith for a bit and I'll be checking on the tennis team at the café in the afternoon. I'll come over straight after that.'

'Great. I can cook that meal you missed out on yesterday. I might text you with a list of things to pick up from the shop if that's OK.'

'No problem but will you be able to cook?'

'Of course. I can do it standing on one leg. Look.'

She balances for a few seconds then grabs hold of her bedside cabinet.

'You're crazy,' he says.

'Crazy for you, honey,' Helen says with an attempt at an American drawl.

~

By the time Laurie reaches his stepfather it's apparent that it's another difficult day for the man. Keith is still in his pyjamas and it looks like he hasn't shaved for the three days since Laurie's last visit. Until the death of his mother he'd taken such pride in his appearance, but that's no longer the case.

Laurie has learnt from experience that the best tactic on days like this is to talk about himself rather than dwelling on Keith's plight.

'I followed your orders and I've got a girlfriend.'

Keith smiles. 'It's that woman from the tennis club, isn't it? Helen.'

'Yep, that's the one.'

'I could tell you were keen whenever her name came up. I'd like to meet this Helen.'

'And she wants to meet you. I think you'll like her.'

'I already do because I can see she's made you happy.'

Laurie smiles. Keith has such a warm-hearted personality.

They sit in the living room drinking tea as Keith tells stories about Laurie's mother that he has heard many times before, how the couple met, their first holiday together, Keith helping his mother to overcome her fear of flying. Then comes the darker stuff about the short period of illness.

At this point during a visit, and they always reach this point, Laurie feels under pressure to stay on to support Keith but wants to leave so as not to get dragged down by the sadness.

He springs up. 'I've got loads of work to do; I must go.'

'Work? But it's the weekend.'

'We're nearing the deadline for a big project.'

'Oh yes, I remember you saying that. Off you go then.'

As they hug Laurie has the usual unease about parting.

'Don't forget the first episode of the new *Shetland* series is on tonight,' he says as he stands by the door, this to give his stepfather something to look forward to.

'It's already on BBC iPlayer. I can watch the whole lot together,' Keith says as if it were a punishment rather than of benefit.

'I'll come over for lunch as usual tomorrow.'

'You're not going to be with Helen then?'

'No, not until the afternoon.'

As he cycles home, Laurie is working out how the relationship with Helen and support for his stepfather will fit together. There has to be a creative way forward but nothing obvious comes to mind during the short journey.

He takes Helen's advice, emailing and texting Grayling to request a Monday morning meeting to set the weekly work schedule that the builder has agreed to. He's not optimistic.

Laurie is usually bursting with energy and full of good ideas when tackling anything to do with his job, but today it's a chore.

~

The three other members of the quartet turn up soon after Laurie has left. They arrive together. Strange Helen is thinking as she opens the door because they live well away from each other.

There are flowers, hugs and "poor you" comments but it's soon apparent that offering sympathy and support is not top of their agenda. This is an interrogation, the questions carefully scripted and distributed between the three of them, making Helen realise that they've met beforehand to plan this visit. That would explain them arriving together.

Yvette starts the inquisition, a good choice, she being the closest to Helen with oodles of female warmth to conceal a ruthless, no-nonsense edge.

'Naturally, we're all wondering how the injury will affect your playing.'

'It won't, it doesn't. I told you when I texted that I'm able to play as usual. I've tried it out.'

'But you're such an energetic player, the way you use your body, stamp your feet …' Yvette pauses as she looks down at Helen's bandaged ankle. 'But now this.'

'I've said, no worries. Honestly, it's fine.'

'Perhaps we could hear you play.'

'You mean you want me to show you that I'm OK. That means you don't trust me.'

'No, don't be silly, not at all. It would just be comforting to be reassured.'

'Comforting! Honestly! Hand the bloody thing over then.'

While Yvette is collecting the cello Bradley fires the next question. 'How are you going to be able to transport you and the cello everywhere?'

'Everywhere only means to the rehearsal room and back for a couple of weeks until my ankle is healed. I'll use ubers and don't worry, I'll pay the fares.'

Yvette hands her the cello and bow and the three of them sit in silence as she prepares to play.

The silence is deafening and Helen breaks it. 'There's nothing to worry about. The doctor said my ankle will be fine by the time we're booked into the recording studio.' He didn't but Helen reckons it's probably the case.

She plays the first movement of Schubert's *Death and the Maiden*, her rendition as rich as ever. She doesn't tell them that her ankle is throbbing as she presses down onto the carpet. She's knackered, too, after the almost sleepless night.

'Great apart from that arpeggio run near the end,' Yvette tells her.

'Sorry, I lost concentration, I was thinking of something else.' She was thinking of *someone* else.

'OK, that was really good,' Sardine says. That's his preferred name. No one knows the origin and he keeps it a mystery. Helen thinks it's pretentious. He's hardly a Stormzy, Eminem or Bono.

Having passed her music audition Sardine moves on, questioning her about whether a cellist playing tennis is a good idea.

'Well, for the foreseeable future I won't be playing, will I? Not with this.' She taps her leg. 'Possibly not until after we've made the recording.'

'But then we have the tour,' Sardine persists. 'It would be a disaster if you got injured again.'

'Look, I've been playing tennis and the cello for over twenty years. This accident is a one-off, for God's sake.'

'Shall I make us tea?' Yvette asks with false camaraderie.

'I can do it,' Helen says, laying her cello down, grabbing a crutch and hopping towards the kitchen.

'Don't be silly, Helen, sit down. Let me do it.'

Helen emits a silent scream of annoyance but allows Yvette to get on with it while she puts away her cello.

There is small talk, including the smallest of small talk about the weather, until Yvette returns with the tea things on a tray. She's used the wrong teapot, the one Helen keeps for peppermint tea. She's brought in mugs instead of cups and saucers, a pet dislike. The milk is still in the plastic bottle rather than in a jug, another pet hate. She's opened the packet of luxury Florentines that Helen had bought to take to her parents at Christmas.

Helen is not happy. She wants them out so she can unwind. She's fighting off anger. On the rare occasion when she reaches boiling point it's not a pleasant sight and currently there is a risk.

She watches Bradley nibbling the side of a biscuit, hesitating when he meets her eye. Helen knows Bradley has a crush on her, she's been told so by Sardine and Yvette, but even without anything said, it's pretty damn obvious. The feeling is not reciprocated.

'I hear you're dating,' he declares.

'Yeah.'

'Not affecting your beauty sleep, I hope.'

'WHAT!'

'I only mean that we need you alert and sharp every morning for rehearsals.'

'Are you suggesting that's not the case, Bradley?'

'Can't say yet because from what I've heard, the relationship has just started.'

How on earth could Bradley know that, unless he was spying outside her flat last night? Then it twigs. His parents are members of the tennis club and there has been gossip about how close she and Laurie seem

188

to be. And that was before they'd even started their relationship, their one day old relationship.

'I suggest you stop this right now, Bradley. It's none of your business.'

'Shall I pour the tea?' Yvette suggests.

'No, I'll do it. But you can go back to the kitchen to get cups and saucers. Please,' she adds forcefully.

Yvette does so and the interview appears to be over. Conversation turns to Christmas plans. Helen keeps quiet as she thinks about how the annual stay with her family will fit in with what Laurie wants to do. He might be occupied with his stepfather. With less than two weeks to go they'll need to get it sorted.

'Agreed?' Sardine asks.

'Agreed what?'

'It would be complicated to fit in any rehearsals between Christmas and the New Year, but with everything going so well we can afford to have a break. That will still give us a couple of weeks afterwards before we go into the studio.'

'That's fine by me,' Helen says, recognising that it provides enough time to see her family and be with Laurie. Maybe that can include meeting his stepfather. 'Thanks for coming over to see me,' she says, her tone making it clear that she wants them to leave. 'It's been one hell of a couple of days and I haven't got much sleep so if you don't mind I'd like some quiet time alone,' she adds to hammer home the hint.

Is Bradley smirking? She has the urge to wipe that smile off his face.

As they leave there are hugs and kind words like those given on their arrival. She accepts them graciously but inside she is fuming. She feels betrayed. Does she want to stay in the quartet with these so-called friends?

As she clears away the tea things the thought of quitting the quartet builds momentum. The only other option would be a bit part in some regional orchestra. On the plus side this would end the constant pressure to make their existence known, to chase sponsors, to acquire gigs. Socially it would be less intense with a wider group to befriend. But there would be downsides, more than likely a move out of London for a start. At first it was hard but now the quartet are making a name for themselves, an exciting adventure all down to their own hard work. It would be a pity to waste all that effort when things were looking up. But what happened just now was a disgrace. Where was their loyalty?

She's too tired to think straight; she needs to rest, maybe a nap. She hobbles to the bathroom and eyes the shower. If she fastened a bin liner over her foot and ankle to keep them dry that would be OK, wouldn't it? Nope, she's already ignored one instruction and she isn't going to risk it by disregarding another one.

She collects the remaining Florentines, a glass of water and a couple of painkillers, takes them to her bedroom and collapses onto her bed. Laurie was with her a few hours ago, that's a lovely thought to help her drift off into sleep.

There is no drift though, there's too much on her mind and her ankle aches.

The musicians. Why were they so mistrustful? Maybe joining an orchestra isn't such a bad idea after all.

Her parents. She hasn't told them about her injury yet and they don't know about Laurie either.

A shower. Surely if she's careful the risk of further damage is zero. She does want one ahead of Laurie coming over.

The bedlinen. It needs changing but she might struggle to do it by herself. It would be too weird to get Laurie to help.

The musicians. She can see where they were coming from with such a critical time ahead. Their livelihoods depend on a successful recording and tour. She can forgive them for their stance and regrets her harsh reaction.

Laurie. He's got a lot to deal with. The club, his stepfather, by the sounds of it work, too. She doesn't want to be a burden. Would it be sensible for him to keep away for a few days until her ankle is on the mend?

Bradley. It isn't easy to forgive him. His comment was out of order.

Laurie. No, it would not be better if he stayed away. She wants to see him.

Tomorrow's meal. She mustn't forget to send Laurie a food shopping list. She goes through the ingredients needed. It must be like counting sheep because finally, she sleeps.

21

When Laurie wakes he sees a text from Helen with the list of ingredients she needs for the evening meal. She ends her message with, *I can't wait! XXX + XXX = 2(XXX)!!*

Will get what you need. See you later is his reply. He can't wait either but he's never been one for gushy messages with exclamation marks. Maybe he's wrong about that? He sends a chaser message.

X^3*!*

Helen. *Meaning?*

Laurie. *X cubed.*

Helen. *Oh. Which is more, 2(XXX) or X^3?*

Laurie. *That depends on the value of X.*

Helen. *Oh.*

He hasn't got the time to be texting all morning. He'll start by working on the grant application before the friendly match arranged with a friend. Then it's lunch with Keith, hopefully more work, a quick visit to Dream Café to check on the Mixed C Team's tea, and finally over to Helen. And there's her shopping list for their meal to fit in, too. Somehow it seems like he's been going out with Helen for much longer than a single day.

He's settled down, surrounded by hard copy spreadsheets with his laptop open, when a text from his stepfather comes through. The question he's being asked is a ridiculous one – is it alright to take an additional antidepressant because he's feeling low? *What do you reckon?* the message ends.

Laurie calls immediately. If he didn't know his stepfather so well he might regard this as an attention-seeking ploy. But Keith isn't like that. So more for Laurie to worry about as he endeavours to get Keith to promise that he won't do anything rash.

'I'll be over before one o'clock, after tennis,' he tells Keith, though as he speaks he's wondering whether to abandon playing and get there as soon as possible. He'd feel fully responsible were something bad to happen, a thought that has been ever-present over recent months. But no, he's got to have some relax time and tennis is that outlet.

There's still two hours to go before playing so Laurie returns to his laptop. But he can't concentrate. He shuts down and heads to the mini-supermarket to get Helen's ingredients. Some items turn out to be non-mainstream and he has to trek round a couple of delis, making it a rush to get home, grab his racket and head off to the club. A rush, his whole life is a rush.

The game is not enjoyable. Usually he can switch off from all worries and play without a distraction, but not that morning. His opponent, his close friend Tom, is relentless and fault-free which makes Laurie tense up and snatch at balls. He clocks up an unprecedented number of unforced errors and double faults. Tom shows no mercy.

'Not at your best today, were you?' Tom says as they shake hands.

'No. I've got loads on my mind and I'm knackered.' Although making excuses for his own performance rather than complimenting an opponent is his default stance, Laurie manages to be gracious in defeat. 'You played really well.'

'Thanks.' They are walking past the dismantled clubhouse. 'How's it going with the builders?' Tom asks.

'Not bad.'

'It's hard to spot any progress. There's a lot of chatter going on about it.'

'You mean on WhatsApp?'

'A bit on that but also when people are here playing.'

'There really is no need to worry.'

'OK, but it might be a good idea to send out an email with an update.'

'Yes, I'll do that.'

As Laurie is leaving, the members of the Mixed C Team are gathering in a huddle. Douglas had posted on WhatsApp requesting a female player and has chosen Zadie. She's chatting with Jennifer.

He leaves them to it; he hasn't got time to speak.

After a quick shower he cycles over to Keith. He finds him in calm mode despite the earlier distressing text and subsequent conversation. This is not totally unexpected; his stepfather's mood swings being dramatic and impossible to predict ahead of a visit. Keith has shaved, dressed smartly with jacket and tie, prepared lunch, laid the table and is listening to classical music.

Keith wants to know all about Helen. When Laurie tells him that she's in a string quartet his stepfather is eager to find out more but Laurie has nothing to offer.

Life is a series of tick boxes Laurie is thinking as he cycles across to the café. He'd value an opportunity to enjoy the moment rather than be focusing on what he needs to do next. Not that that was the case yesterday with Helen. He must enjoy every moment alone with her. He's lost girlfriends in the past with accusations of being unemotional, task driven or distracted. That will not happen this time.

The sodding Mixed C Team: how come he's ended up getting involved in their petty goings on? The answer is probably because he fears tension spilling over to threaten the agreement with Bridget and David. That risk should be over now that Ying is out of it. Andras has got his way, Zadie being the only one prepared to play on a cold and gloomy December Sunday leading up to Christmas.

When Laurie steps into the café he hears laughter coming from the tennis club table. The atmosphere is good with everyone chatting away and the plates of sandwiches and cakes are near empty. Andras is the liveliest one, the perfect host as he greets Laurie before dashing to the counter to ask for more tea.

'Everything OK?' Laurie asks Jennifer while Andras is away.

'Well … if you mean did we win, the answer is yeah. Zadie's amazing; she hits the ball so hard.'

'You're hinting there's a but.'

'Zadie did mention a few things while we were on our way here.'

'Like what?'

'Like what a dickhead Andras is and if he touches her again she's gonna thump him.'

'Oh. Touching?'

'Touches on shoulder, hugs at the end of games, that sort of stuff. She can handle it, even see the funny side, but I guess that's beside the point.'

'It is. I'll ask Helen to speak to her, woman to woman. I think that's better than me having that conversation.'

'Yeah, it is.'

'And how did you get on?'

'My best match ever. We won both sets and Douglas couldn't find a thing to tell me off about. I got him back alrighty when I told him to get his second serve in because the opposition weren't good enough to kill a soft one.'

'That's pretty basic.'

'Exactly. He didn't listen, of course. We won both sets 6-2 and guess who was serving when we lost the four games.'

'You're a star, Jennifer.'

'I sure am.'

Andras has returned. 'A fresh pot. Tea everyone. Laurie, you too?'

'No, not for me, I'm in a bit of a hurry.'

'Can I just say that this young lady,' Andras rests a hand on Zadie's shoulder, 'this young lady is an absolute star.'

'Will you please get your hand off me?'

'I'm paying you a compliment, Zadie.'

'I'll count to three then I'll remove it for you.'

'Don't be –'

'One. Two. Thank you.' Zadie stands and lifts up her kit bag. 'I must go. Bye everyone.'

Laurie follows her to the exit. 'Zadie, thanks for playing. Helen will catch up with you for a debrief.'

'Helen's already said she'd speak to me after the match.'

Zadie's exit marks the end of the tea and there are good-natured handshakes all round. Laurie is the last to leave, thanking David for hosting before heading home.

The spreadsheets litter his dining table. He gathers them up and puts them in his holdall ready to take to the office the next day. It's time to prepare to see Helen.

~

In advance of Laurie's arrival, Helen calls her mother. She's been putting it off all day because her injury and dating Laurie have complicated Christmas plans. Her mother has always been odd about her boyfriends. "You have a man – finally. Hopefully one that will last this time," she imagines her saying.

Her mother launches into the preparations for Christmas before Helen has the opportunity to mention her two pieces of news.

Mother. 'Thank God for Ocado; I can't face all that queueing at the supermarket this time of the year.'

Mother. 'I do wish you would eat turkey, just this once and then you can go back to being vegetarian.'

Mother. 'I can't think of anything you might want for a present. I have absolutely no idea what clothes you like nowadays. You're so difficult, though I was thinking about an air fryer.'

Mother. 'Have you decided how long you'll be staying with us.'

Mother. 'Why are you so quiet, Helen?'

'I'm quiet because you haven't stopped talking and I can't get a word in edgeways.'

'Well. I'm all ears now.'

'Mum, a couple of things have happened since we last spoke.'

She tells her about the injury and Laurie, expecting a little more than the "That's a pity" and "That's good" that she picks up.

Irritated by her mother's lack of interest, engulfed as the woman is with her Christmas preparations, Helen reverts to immature petulance.

'So I might not come after all, not if Laurie wants me to be with him and my ankle makes it impossible to travel.' This threat is fictitious; she does intend to go home.

'Well, Helen, there's nothing to stop you bringing your young man with you –'

'His name is Laurie, I just told you that.'

'We'd be delighted to meet him,' her unflappable mother continues, 'and then he could bring you in his car.'

'He hasn't got a car; he has a bicycle.'

Helen envisages her mother's look of horror; she'd love to be witnessing it.

'I see,' the two words oozing judgement. 'Just use a cab then, I'll foot the bill.'

'I need to speak to Laurie first.'

'Quickly please. The final Ocado order has to be in soon.'

'I'm seeing him this evening and we'll decide then.'

'Good. Your ankle, I'm assuming it's nothing serious. You did say it's only a sprain though it might be sensible to go private for a second opinion.'

'No need, it's fine. Look, I'd better go.'

Why did conversations with her mother always end with Helen wishing for better?

She spends the rest of the afternoon playing her cello. Along with tennis it's the activity that allows her to put aside all worries. She's so immersed in practising that the hour she had planned to get ready for Laurie is down to forty minutes.

Helen takes two bin bags out of the kitchen cupboard and uses masking tape to secure a double layer around her ankle. She drags a chair into the bathroom, places it on the shower basin, sits down and turns on the tap.

She could get fully dressed but instead slips on her dressing gown. That will make Laurie laugh – oh and get him turned on, too.

The doorbell chimes.

22

The dressing gown is an immediate success so dinner is on hold.

Afterwards, Laurie insists on helping with the cooking and Helen ends up sitting in the kitchen instructing him what to do next as they discuss their Christmas to New Year plans.

It's too late to amend the Christmas Day arrangement: Laurie will be with his stepfather and Helen will visit her family home. She'll stay overnight with a latish return to London on Boxing Day.

'At least we can have Christmas Eve together,' Helen says, 'and then from Boxing Day right through to after the New Year because I won't be rehearsing.'

'I'm off work, too. That grant application I was telling you about will be on its way by Christmas.'

'Great, a whole week to do stuff together.'

'Hopefully your ankle will be better by then.'

'Maybe, though I might not risk driving to my parents. My mother suggested taking a taxi home but when I told her how much a fare from London to Sussex on Christmas Day was likely to cost she changed her mind. Her plan is to get one of my sisters to pick me up even though it's out of her way and she hates driving through London.'

'I'm lucky, my journey is a five minute cycle to my stepfather.'

'Actually, you were invited to come to mine this year but I know it's impossible.'

'I couldn't abandon my stepdad at short notice. Hopefully next year we can sort something.' The implication of the statement, the assumption that their relationship is long-lasting when this is only the second day, or third depending on how you count, creates a pause for reflection before Helen continues.

'My family will want to meet you well before then.'

'I look forward to that.'

'I don't. When you see how my mother behaves and you think I might end up like her then there goes our relationship.'

'Very funny.'

'Or maybe not funny. Anyway, what will you and your stepfather do on Christmas Day.'

'Nothing exciting. He'll be cooking a traditional Christmas meal, I'll be insisting on a post-lunch walk, and then we'll sit in front of TV. I'll escape late evening before going back for a repeat on Boxing Day.'

'It's not a competition but it does sound like I've got the better deal. But your stepfather, it can't go on with him relying on you for everything, can it? I don't mean that you should stop helping him, I'm more thinking about his welfare. He needs other friendships.'

'I am trying.'

'I'm sure you are. There must be loads of activities for older people – clubs and societies. Isn't there something called the University of the Third Age?'

'He was in that, doing all sorts of things, but he let his membership lapse after Mum died.'

'From what you've said, whatever you do is never enough for him. Something has to change …' Helen stops abruptly. 'Sorry, it's none of my business.'

'No, it's fine. You're saying what I already know but knowing doesn't solve the problem. And on the subject of problems, I have no idea what to get you for Christmas.'

'Honestly, there's no need to get me anything.'

'But I want to. My first idea was jewellery.'

'An engagement ring?'

'No, seriously. I don't see you wear much so I haven't got a clue what style you like.'

'You're right, I don't. I've got heaps of the stuff that I never wear.'

'So, maybe not jewellery then. Another of my possibles is perfume. What's yours called? I like it.'

'*Seduction.*'

'It's worked on me.'

'Hopefully there were other reasons why you wanted a relationship.'

'Nope, it was only the perfume! But is that a good present even though it wouldn't be a surprise.'

'Every time Mum travels abroad she buys me a bottle at duty free. She must think I drink it. I've got enough to open a shop.'

'OK, not perfume. The only other thing I could think of was a day at a spa.'

'That would be fun but here's another idea because I've been thinking about what to get you, too. Why don't we do matching gifts and go somewhere together?'

'Brilliant, I'd love that.' Laurie opens his phone and turns it towards Helen. 'Here are a couple of possibles I was looking at.'

'Why make it a spa day? We could go away somewhere and stay a couple of nights. Only if you want to.'

'Absolutely. Yes.'

'Where would you like to go?'

Laurie is slow to reply.

'I have an idea but I need a bit more time to think this through,' Laurie says at last, showing no inclination to elaborate.

Maybe he wants the location to be a surprise, Helen is thinking. Paris? Venice? Athens? More likely in England though because Laurie's concern about climate change includes a reluctance to fly. She'd be happy wherever they went – a first holiday together.

~

They spend every night at Helen's flat during the week leading up to Christmas and it's remarkable how quickly they're settling into a comfortable routine.

'I'm enjoying this domesticity,' Helen declares as she takes hold of the coffee that Laurie has brought to the bedroom.

There's one day to go before Christmas Eve and the start of their break from work.

'What's on your schedule today?' she asks.

'We're sending off the grant application after a final check. I'm sure it's already as good as it can get but my boss is a stickler for perfection. If there's a comma where there should be a semi-colon he'll be on the case. I'll also fit in a call to Dee today. I want to see if she has any ideas about the club's comms role before I contact the short-listed applicants.'

'Good luck with Dee. I don't think she's great at sharing anything except gossip.'

'At least I'm giving her the opportunity. What's on your list?'

'Ankle exercises and then rehearsal.'

Laurie picks up his phone and glances at the screen. 'I'm late again, I'd better dash.'

To make the travelling cheaper and easier, the quartet schedule their rehearsals after the London rush hour madness. Helen can stay in bed a little longer.

She hears Laurie close the door and moments later unchain his bike and cycle off. Turning and stretching, she's pleased to note the ache in her ankle is lessening.

As he cycles, Laurie is considering how to handle the conversation with Dee; she can be such a brittle character. He'll get it out of the way before tackling anything to do with work rather than keep the task hanging over him for longer than necessary.

'Good morning, Dee,' he begins, as brightly and cheerfully as he can muster. 'I hope you don't mind me calling, but ahead of shortlisting the applicants for the comms role I'd welcome your ideas about the key responsibilities.'

'Why ask me?'

'Obviously because you've been doing the job. With success. You have masses of knowledge and experience to pass on.'

'You do realise that you haven't made contact since our argument.'

'It was hardly an argument. More of a disagreement.'

'You haven't even apologised.'

'I don't see it as something requiring an apology.'

'No, you wouldn't, would you? But now you want my help.'

'It's not to help me, it's helping the tennis club.'

'I hear that you and Helen are an item.'

'News travels fast.'

'Well, it's been trending in the WhatsApp group.'

Laurie clicks the widget and reads the most recent comments.

Tony
Well, I think he's a lucky boy because Helen is a bit of alright.

Shelly

Calling her that is sexist, Tony. You wouldn't call Laurie a bit of alright.

Gus
Here we go again, the f**king woke police are out.

'You should take a look, Laurie,' Dee suggests.
'I might,' he says as he quits the app.
'So is it true?' she asks.
'We are going out if that's what you're asking.'
'An item then.'
Dee is in her sixties and somehow her use of "item" doesn't sound right. Or is thinking that ageist? For all he knows she's a fashion influencer on TikTok with zillions of followers. The immaculately pressed, regulation white Wimbledon gear she wears at the club over the summer months, and her 1980s style shiny tracksuits in winter, suggests not.
'Call it whatever you like.'
'I was thinking though, is it prudent?'
'Is what prudent, Dee?'
'Having our chair and deputy chair in a relationship. What about the potential for conflict of interest?'
'How could that ever be an issue? It's not like I'll be using my power and influence to get Helen a prestigious post with a whacking great salary in the City. Or the lead role in a Hollywood film.'
'There's no need for sarcasm. It's just that the two most influential people at the club are you two.'

'But you haven't explained why that matters. We're part of a committee, any important decisions go through that channel.'

'I've got in touch with the other committee members to see what they think. They need to weigh up the risks.'

'There are no risks. And I'm insulted that you've done that ahead of running it past me and Helen.'

'There you go, you've said it yourself. Expecting something to be run past you two before the others in the committee get to hear about it.'

'That's twisting things.'

'Is it? Anyway, you want to know what your new comms person has to do.'

'It doesn't matter. Happy Christmas, Dee.'

Laurie doesn't give her a chance to respond. Seething, he clicks the red phone icon.

Has Dee made a valid point about conflict of interest and risk though?

No, definitely not.

Laurie is regretting his anger because without Dee's input he'll have to stick with his own selection criteria for the comms job, based on common sense but without in-depth knowledge.

Looking again at the applicants, he identifies two outstanding candidates and another six almost as impressive. All eight have PR, media, marketing or associated experience, more than anything Dee might have picked up in an ad hoc fashion over the years. They won't need Dee to tell them what needs doing.

He looks at his watch, it's not yet nine o'clock. Helen would still be at home.

He calls and provides a sanitised account of the awkward conversation with Dee. 'Of course, I told her that us being in a relationship has no impact on tennis club matters.'

'There are WhatsApp posts about us,' Helen says.

'Are there?' Laurie hasn't told her he's read some, not wanting to bother her with the gossip.

'Take a look,' she continues.

He clicks into the app.

Dee

I can confirm that they are an item and wonder what others think about whether this is an issue for the two controlling our club.

Simon

Issue? What do you mean?

Dee

Only that the deputy chair is hardly going to be challenging the chair on anything important.

Ros

Important? You mean like whether to purchase Wilson or Slazenger tennis balls! Honestly!

Dee

There's no need for sarcasm. It's a fair question, could there be a conflict of interest?

Jimmy
*Effing bollocks, Dee. It's not like they're presidant
and vice presidant of America.*

Ursula
It's president, with an E.

'What's wrong with Dee?' Laurie asks Helen.

'It seems like everyone at the club is thinking the
same. It's nothing we have to bother with. Have you
made any progress sorting out the applicants?'

'Yes. I've narrowed it down to two candidates. I
know both of them from chats at the club and I'm
confident that either would do a great job. I don't
think we need to consult anyone else about the
process. I'd like to interview and select one of them
by the end of the year.'

'Agreed. Just get on with it.'

'So you think it's OK to not involve the other
committee members?'

'Everyone is busy, they'll be delighted it's sorted.'

'But Dee might complain.'

'Let her; no one will take any notice. Hey, fill me
in this evening, I must get going.'

Laurie messages the two candidates, inviting them
for an informal interview at a convenient time over the
next week. By return one drops out, apologising that
his workload has grown significantly since he was
considering taking on the post. The second candidate,

a website and social media guru of national renown, agrees to meet to discuss the role.

Laurie can get straight back to him. *Actually our other shortlisted candidate has withdrawn so if you're happy the post is yours.*

Very happy. I've got loads of ideas to move things along at the club.

I can tell that from our past chats. No need to meet next week but come to the January committee meeting and we can have a one-to-one afterwards.

Fine, See you in January. Happy Christmas.

Sorted. A relieved Laurie can forget the tennis club and concentrate on the grant application. He knows chunks of it off by heart and it seems watertight and ready to go.

That afternoon Laurie and three colleagues stand behind the group leader's monitor and watch him tap the send arrow on his keyboard. The application is on its way and they burst into spontaneous applause. Nothing is certain until approval in writing is received and contracts signed, but the team have been led to believe that the grant is a given. They'll find out for sure within a few weeks.

It's been a good day for Helen, too. Her ankle is on the mend and she can travel without using a crutch. She's still using taxis to travel to the rehearsal room where she's back to enjoying playing with Yvette, Bradley and Sardine having accepted apologies for their behaviour during the visit the day after the accident. They run through the pieces they'll be recording in the studio and reckon that their playing is as good as it can get. There'll be a few days in January to tie up loose ends ahead of making the recording but can look forward to a guilt-free break between Christmas Eve and the New Year.

'Holiday time!' Helen declares as she opens her front door that evening to find Laurie already there.

'I have reason to believe that you are one of an item,' he says, replicating Dee's dour tone.

'With a mission to destroy the tennis club!'

There's a ring of the doorbell.

'I'll go,' Laurie says, returning a minute later with a stack of cardboard boxes.

The food is from the posh South Indian restaurant, the nouveau cuisine one. Even the cartons are posh.

23

Christmas Eve starts with coffee in bed provided by Helen. She's appreciated Laurie's willingness to take on most kitchen duties over the past two weeks and is relieved that she is close to full mobility and able to do her bit.

'Here you go,' she says as she sets down the cup and saucer on the bedside table.

'Mmmm,' he mumbles. He is deep in concentration, catching up with news headlines on his phone, the serious demeanour fixed as he takes on the weight of national and world events.

Laurie doesn't look up which gets Helen imagining them still being together in twenty or more years' time. Would they be like her parents, happy enough to be together, (she thinks so, though you never know), as they sit in comfortable silence, he reading the newspaper, she lost in thoughts? Children would change the dynamics for a while with no lazy mornings during their early years. And then the teenage years, a domestic battleground if anything like it had been for her and her three sisters. And finally the kids would leave home and quietness would descend again. Her mother is often rueing how quiet it is now that all her girls have gone.

Helen smiles, amused to be thinking so far into the future, ridiculously so when they've only been together for such a short while. She isn't into flings though. Every time she's started a relationship she's hoped it will be lasting and has been left disappointed. This one has got off to a great start, nothing more.

She pulls the waistband of Laurie's shorts with their Christmas reindeer design, intent on distracting him. His near nakedness is making her want to jump back into bed. She presses against him; she can feel his body warmth.

'Do you think if we're still together in twenty years' time we'll be wearing winceyette pyjamas, fleecy dressing gowns and plaid slippers?' she asks.

'Twenty years' time? We'd still only be in our forties so probably not.'

'Good,' she says as she lifts up her t-shirt. 'Reindeers off?'

'Definitely,' he says as he yanks them down.

~

'I should be able to get back on a tennis court after the New Year,' Helen announces as she's getting dressed. 'Will you have a hit or two with me before I play anyone else?'

'OK. As long as –'

'I know.'

They've often played in the past and Laurie always wins. Technically she's the better player but he has the power. He's competitive though and she doesn't expect or want concessions just because she's now his girlfriend.

'Are you all set for our Christmas Eve food shops crush?' Helen asks as Laurie zips up his fleece.

'Yep, let's get this over with.'

She's the one who decided on their dinner for that night – a tapas fusion mixing Spanish, Greek, Italian and Japanese taster dishes. The logic behind the choice is that, with nothing else planned for the day, they could have fun messing around in the kitchen making everything from scratch.

'It'll be nice supporting the small delis,' Helen had said in justifying her choice, 'and we can snack for hours while we watch tele or listen to music.'

They get started with the preparation as soon as they're back from the shops with Laurie very much the sous chef, receiving instruction on how to roll sushi and put together a patatas bravas. Everything is ready quicker than expected, leaving several hours to kill ahead of heating up some of the dishes.

'The sun's out for a change so let's go for a walk,' Helen suggests. 'It'll be good exercise for my leg.'

The destination is Alexandra Park which seems to have attracted a sizeable proportion of the local population.

They see a considerable number of the tennis club members out. As they pass several stop to ask how the clubhouse building is going.

'All on schedule,' Laurie repeats.

'Honestly, what's the matter with people?' Helen complains. 'If my dentist walked by, I wouldn't be asking her how many teeth she's extracted this week. Can't they give you some peace?'

'I suppose I can understand their concern.'

'Quick, behind that tree.'

'Why?' Laurie asks as Helen tugs at his jacket and leads him to behind an ancient oak with a broad trunk. 'Could you explain why we're here?'

'It's Dee. She was on the path walking towards us. I'm sure she didn't see us though.'

They remain there for a minute or so.

'Hi guys,' is the greeting as they emerge from their hiding place. 'Wanna explain what you were doing behind a tree?'

It's Jennifer, with Gareth.

'Pulling up this high fashion item,' Helen says, lifting up her trouser leg to expose the thick cream-coloured support sock.

'No crutches. Cool,' Jennifer remarks. 'I guess you'll be on court soon beating everyone.'

'And you're in the Mixed Cs. That's great.'

'Hardly. I think I've plateaued. We're grabbing a tea at the café before heading home. Wanna join us?'

It's one of those awkward moments when telepathy would be useful. Helen doesn't want to.

Good idea,' Laurie says.

They take a table by the window of the almost empty café and Jennifer goes to the counter to order the drinks.

'No David or Bridget today?' she asks David's daughter, Rachel, who helps out during university holidays.

'They knew it would be dead so I got the short straw.' She looks at her phone. 'Only half an hour to closing.'

'Don't worry, we'll be quick. Two teas and two coffees, please.'

'Sorry, I wasn't trying to kick you out.'

When Jennifer returns they talk tennis tactics for a while.

'What are your Christmas plans?' Helen asks Gareth; she doesn't want him to feel left out.

'A holiday, a big one. To the States to visit Jen's mother and stepfather.'

'Sounds brill. My Christmas treat is a return to the family home and I can't even take Laurie with me.'

'Are you left all alone?'

'No, I'll be with my stepdad.'

'Changing the subject,' Jennifer says, 'I've played a couple of times this week and haven't seen any builders around. It's kinda slow going. Will it be finished –'

'I'm sure yes,' Helen interrupts, unwilling to subject Laurie to more tennis club explanations. 'We must get going; there's stuff to cook if we want a meal this evening.'

The farewells are quick.

'Enjoy America.'

'We will.'

'Have a good time with your family.'

'Thanks."

'See you at the club soon.'

'Happy Christmas. Happy New Year, too.'

'Same to both of you.'

'There isn't much left to cook, is there?' Laurie asks when they're out the café.

'I wanted to escape. You deserve time off from interrogation about the tennis club.'

At home, Helen is taking great delight in the presentation of their fusion tapas feast. The maroon tablecloth is covered with an assortment of neatly arranged bowls and plates and there are candles lit.

'If I did social media I'd take a picture and post it,' Laurie says before turning to see Helen take a picture and post it.

The meal is a success, just as they planned, an opportunity to relax and take their time eating as they chat.

'You were going to tell me the destination for our holiday tonight,' she says as she lifts up a mini tortilla. 'What have you come up with?'

'I do have an idea but it's not a given. I need to run it past you first.'

'Fire away.'

'I'd like to take you to Cromer.'

'Cromer? Interesting. It's near Great Yarmouth, isn't it?'

'It is in Norfolk but a bit round the coast from there. It has a totally different atmosphere, too. At least it did have.'

'Oh, so you've been there before?'

'It's where I used to go with my parents when I was a kid, happy times before ... I'm being silly, let's think of somewhere else.'

'Hold on, nothing is silly. What exactly do you mean?'

'My memory is of my mum and dad being as happy as I'd ever seen them while we were there. In love, though I wouldn't have used those words at the time. But it is a place I associated with love, happiness, security. And then Dad got ill and we never went back …'

'That's a lovely story. Sad too. I want to come to Cromer with you.'

'Look, taking the occasional flight is fine by me so let's travel abroad. I was thinking about Budapest.'

'I want to come to Cromer with you.'

'Do you?'

'More than anywhere else in the world.'

'Thank you.' Laurie is feeling tearful. Ridiculous.

'What's it like there mid-winter?' Helen asks.

'No idea, I only visited during summer holidays. Cold and windy I expect.'

'Well, we'll find out, won't we.'

24

Their two Christmases are worlds apart.

Helen's family home is alive with ceaseless chatter, an endless stream of visitors, games with over-excited children, and food, food, food. Drink, too. There's a bit too much interrogation about her new man from her sisters and mother which Helen sidesteps by playing as much as possible with her lovely nieces and nephews.

Laurie's first day with his stepfather begins in the kitchen. He can only observe; he's not allowed to help prepare what turns out to be an uninspiring traditional lunch, but at least the man has something to occupy him. It's no surprise to see Keith gloomy. It was shortly before last Christmas when Jean died so this is not a festive time. Nevertheless, Laurie is making an effort to cheer Keith up.

Unfortunately, getting outdoors for a post-meal walk is impossible because it's bucketing down. That leaves watching TV for the rest of the day.

'So, what would you like to watch, Keith? Either something live or you can choose from iPlayer.'

'I don't mind; whatever you put on is fine.'

'Did you get to see *Shetland*?'

'No, not yet.'

'Want to see it now then?'

'I really don't mind.'

The great frustration and sadness for Laurie is that before his mother died this man was lively and optimistic. Her death has knocked the stuffing out of him. Would he ever recover?

Once, Laurie had reminded him that he was also hurt when his mother died. The comment was not well received. Keith had said something like, "It's not the same because you have your whole life ahead of you but mine is reaching the end."

How do you counter that? But it's in Laurie's nature to try.

'We don't need to watch TV. What about a game, chess or something?'

'No, I don't think I'm up to it.'

'You need to phone your sister to wish her a Happy Christmas.'

'Yes, I should do that.'

'Have you spoken with your son today?'

'He called me first thing this morning. They were on their way to the beach.'

'Christmas in the sunshine, that's nice for them, isn't it?'

'I'm sure it is.'

'Ever thought about visiting them?' (He'd asked this many times).

'It's a long way.'

Laurie manages to escape mid-evening, Keith being tired and wanting an early night.

He's back for a leftovers lunch on Boxing Day and for a while Keith is perkier as he questions Laurie about Helen.

'You're happy, aren't you, being with that Helen? I can see it in your eyes.'

'Yes, I am happy.'

'Is it serious?'

'I hope so, but it's only just started.'

'I hope so, too.'

'You'll meet her soon; I'll bring her over.'

'I'd like that.'

Boxing Day at Helen's Sussex home is mirroring Christmas Day. She plays with her nieces and nephews, chats with the adult members of the family, and greets a further stream of neighbours and friends popping in for a drink, several of them beginning with a version of, "I remember when you were this high" when they see her.

Late afternoon there's an impromptu concert with Helen on piano accompanying a mixed group of performers by age and capability on guitar, recorder, violin or singing. It's fun and she's exhausted by the time her sister is ready to head back to London.

She texts Laurie while on the journey.

Won't speak 'cos I'm in car with sis but hope you had OK time. Shattered and will get home late so let's leave it for tonight. Come over first thing in morning. I might still be in bed! $X^3 + X^2$!!!

Laurie's reply is instant. *Duty completed, at home recovering. See you tomorrow.*

~

'Are you sure that's how you want to spend today?' Laurie asks.

'Like I said, I know fuck all about science beyond that there are things called black holes and that too much carbon dioxide means climate change. Having a top scientist as personal guide has got to be good. If I ever went there by myself I'd be strolling past exhibits without having the slightest idea what the explanations were about.'

'OK, the Science Museum it is then.'

'And when we've had enough we'll only be a short distance from all the South Kensington shops.'

They cycle to the station, her first cycle since the accident, and join a short queue at the ticket office.

A bleep on Laurie's phone signals a message from his stepfather.

'It's OK, read it. I'll get the tickets,' Helen says.

A call comes through as Laurie is reading. He raises an arm to indicate that Helen should delay buying the tickets.

She joins him as he ends the call. 'Is there a problem?' she asks.

'There is. He's having a bad day. I'm worried.'

'Then you must go there now.'

'If I can sort it out quickly we'll still have time for the museum. Perhaps I could meet you there.'

'No, I'll come with you.'

'I'm not sure that's a great idea ...'

223

'You said I should meet him soon. This is the soon.'

'But he's in such a state I'm not sure he'll want you there.'

'Well, we'll see won't we. If he's uncomfortable I'll leave.'

'But –'

'I'm offering to help. I want to.'

Then thank you. I'll text to let him know that you're coming with me.'

'I suggest you don't; we don't want him saying no.'

They cycle back to Muswell Hill and stop at another of those grand Victorian villas, this one with a pointed stone arch at the doorway and lovely ornamental brickwork. The house is set back in a large plot by local standards, enough for a well maintained front garden with mature trees and a gravelled area for cars. There's even a bike stand which they use.

'It's not all his,' Laurie says as Helen stops to admire the property. 'Just the ground floor.'

Helen has been thinking about how to approach this first meeting during the bike ride. She could be bright and cheery as if everything is fine, but that would be an insult to all that Laurie has tried to do over many months to remedy the situation. She'll be polite but restrained, reactive not proactive.

Laurie has a key. He opens the door and calls out. A sprightly elderly man comes bounding into the hallway taking Helen completely by surprise. She'd expected to see a stooping man with a creased face and a deep frown. Instead, he has a broad smile, shows no indication of despondency, and surprisingly displays no astonishment at seeing Helen there.

Helen extends her arm. 'Mr Wilberforce, I'm delighted to meet you.'

'I'm not Mr Wilberforce,' the man says, taking her hand with a firm grip. 'That's Laurie's father's surname. Please call me Keith.'

'I'm Helen.'

'I know. Laurie's told me about you and I can already see he's a lucky man.'

'In that case, we're both lucky.'

'Laurie, why don't you lead Helen into the living room and I'll make us tea.'

'Can I help?' Laurie asks.

'Help make tea? I'm not an invalid.'

'He was in a state when we spoke earlier, I thought it was a crisis,' Laurie explains when they are away from Keith. 'His mood swings do my head in.'

'Let's see how it pans out,' Helen says, turning her attention to the contents of the room. It's a shrine to Laurie's mother, the walls filled with photos of Jean, arty ones, mostly black and white. 'These are wonderful.'

'Keith's the photographer,' Laurie says as he joins Helen by a large portrait of Jean sitting on a sofa looking out into the garden. 'They're all his.'

'I can tell that.' The photographer's love for this woman, as revealed in the images, is so powerful that it has brought Helen close to tears.

'Are you alright?' Laurie asks.

They hear Keith whistling in the kitchen and Helen's deeply emotional response is broken with a smile.

'I'm good. You're mother looks so happy. Beautiful, too.'

'She was.'

Helen inspects more of the room. There is a low glass-topped cabinet housing two cups, a row of medals, and a photo of a much younger though unmistakeable Keith in singlet and shorts.

'Squash,' Laurie informs her. 'He was county champion and playing until well into his seventies.'

They walk across to the french windows and peer into the winter garden. There are covers on a table and chairs. Several tall bushes are wrapped in frost protecting netting. The borders are empty with the soil turned ready for next year's planting or perhaps in advance of the spring flowers bursting through.

Keith has joined them. 'Apologies for the state of the garden. I used to take great care of it but now I just do what I can.'

'I can't see anything more that needs doing.'

'We used to have an allotment, we grew all sorts of vegetables, but I gave it up after Jean died.'

The use of "we", the sad eyes, Helen senses Keith's short burst of zest ebbing away and can understand what Laurie means by unpredictable mood swings.

She is feeling brave; she decides to go for it.

'It must have been terrible losing Jean.'

'It was that, Helen. We were so happy together. There I was, we were, me already in my eighties,

226

making these grand plans for our future. How we chuckled about that. And then it all collapsed.'

'You have Laurie to help you but what about family and friends?' Helen knows the answer regarding family but wants to hear Keith's take on it.

'When you're my age there aren't too many friends left. There are Jean's old buddies, kids compared to me,' he chuckles, 'but I haven't stayed in touch with them.'

'And family?' she probes, surprised that he'd started with friends.

'I have a son working in the Middle East who's going to be out there for a long time. Can't say I blame him really. He comes back with his family for a week or so every summer.'

'Anyone else?'

'A sister. Maggie's older than me. She's never been an active one and I reckon she's suffering for it now. She lives down in Worthing.' Keith chuckles again. 'In warden controlled accommodation, which makes it sound like a prison.'

'Do you ever visit her?'

'Not for quite a while, not since Jean died. I should do, shouldn't I?'

'Yes, you should. You must have loads to talk about.'

'You're right.'

'I've been nagging you to go,' Laurie says. 'You know I'd take you there.'

'Laurie's been fantastic, Helen. He doesn't have to do what he does. After all, I'm only his stepdad, but he's taken on looking out for me.' He turns to face Laurie. 'I can't tell you how grateful I am.' He pauses. 'I know I won't be seeing you as much now you two are together, but that's fine.'

'I won't get in the way. Laurie will be helping you as much as you need. But maybe it is time to think about things differently. Laurie's told me how energetic you were when Jean was alive. I understand that her not being around must be awful. However, you are still living.'

Helen is aware that both men are staring at her. Avoiding eye contact she continues. 'It isn't easy, nothing ever changes overnight, but there are steps you could take, maybe starting with a visit to your sister. Laurie's volunteered to get you there and I'm sure he can sort out a hotel in Worthing. Take up his offer.'

'I wouldn't need a hotel; Maggie has a second bedroom.'

'There you are then. All you need is help to get you there and back.'

Keith stands up. 'I'll just clear away the tea things.'

'Would you like any help?'

'No thank you, Helen, I'm fine. Walking back and forwards to the kitchen is today's exercise.'

With Keith out the room Helen is anticipating a cautioning from Laurie that enough is enough, that there's a risk of Keith panicking. But he remains silent.

'I'll go,' Keith announces when he rejoins them. 'Maggie never seems to have anything planned so I could even try for this week. While I'm working it out Laurie can be making us some lunch.'

25

'I'll go,' Keith had said out of the blue. 'I could even try for this week.'

By the time Laurie returns to the living room carrying a plate of sandwiches, Keith is speaking to his sister, telling her he'll be in Worthing the next day. With the call over and after several "Are you sure?" questions directed at Keith, Laurie phones the warden to check that a visit is doable. He is assured that Maggie is well enough to cope. A disapproving Keith has left the room, considering Laurie's conversation with the warden to be unnecessary. When Helen hears some cluttering she goes out to investigate: Keith is carrying his suitcase, one of those old ones without wheels, to the hallway. He leaves it by the front door.

'I'm not sure whether to hire a car or take the train,' Laurie says to Helen when Keith is in the bathroom sorting toiletries and medications.

'No need for either, you can use my car.'

'Are you sure? That would be a big help.'

'Positive.'

'I can't believe this is happening,' Laurie says, reflecting on past failed attempts to get Keith to visit his sister. Helen has been the catalyst, direct and compelling in her encouragement. 'He's like a new man – thanks to you.'

'Careful,' Helen warns. 'You've been telling me his mood shoots up and down from one minute to the next.'

'I know, but this trip might give him a taste of what life without my mother could be like.'

When Keith returns to the living room, proudly announcing that everything is ready for the trip, he and Helen talk about classical music. His knowledge is impressive and Laurie is happy to sit back, half-listening.

'I used to love going to concerts,' Keith says. 'The proms, now that was something. I got to see Yehudi Menuhin perform once.'

'Lucky you. Well, my quartet have a long way to go but you're welcome to come to our first performance at Wigmore Hall if you'd like.'

'Wigmore Hall! I'd be honoured.'

'Good. That's another thing to look forward to after seeing your sister.'

~

It's the twenty-eighth of December, a Sunday, and Laurie will be taking his stepfather to Worthing to stay with his sister for a few days.

Meanwhile, Jimmy, a member of the tennis club, will be seizing the opportunity to create his first social media posting to go viral.

He is obsessed with social media. He keeps up with gossip and adds to it using several anonymous handles to post provocative comments. Until that day his contributions have only been responses to other people's threads.

Recently the club's WhatsApp group has gone quiet following the avalanche of activity around Oliver and Stephanie's behaviour at the AGM. Apart from a few comments about Ying either leaving or being kicked out of the club and some moaning about conflict of interest from that old witch Dee, there has been nothing of interest.

Jimmy intends to change that because he's discovered a story tucked away on the regional pages of the BBC website.

Jimmy
F**k!ng hell – just read amazing news about the Kilroys!

Simon
You can't leave it at that. What's happened mate?

Jimmy
Just follow this f**k!ng link mate. https:// ...

Dee
You may well have used asterisks and an exclamation mark but it hardly conceals your use of the f word and that is unacceptable on this WhatsApp group.

Jimmy

*What's the difference between what I've written
and you calling it the f word. And anyway, it's got
nothing to do with you because you aren't in charge of
comms anymore.*

Dee
I can still be an upholder of civility and decency.

Jimmy
F**k off, Dee

Beth
What exactly has happened?

Gus
Yes. Give us more info.

The Sunday morning following Boxing Day should
be a time to unwind with the family, possibly sober
up, maybe have a lie in followed by a leisurely
breakfast, perhaps the chance to take the kids or the
dog or both for a walk in the park. Instead, the
WhatsApp group is alive with chatter. Parents, pet
owners and ordinarily selfless partners are forsaking
duties and responsibilities to pass comment on what
they're reading.

~

It had not been a happy Boxing Day for Oliver and
Stephanie. Despite telling friends and associates that
their separation was perfectly amicable with the
divorce imminent, in truth that was anything but the

case. There was bitter argument about the division of assets and added tension because neither of them was willing to vacate Granville Villa since it risked the other party claiming occupancy rights by default. As a result, they continued to share the house, having finally reached agreement on a set of rules that included separate bedrooms, allocated times for use of the kitchen, and no guests allowed, 'guests' the euphemism for sex partners.

Oliver, a defender of the law at work, was a rule breaker at home. He wasn't going to let Stephanie tell him who he could and could not have in the house. There was this pretty little thing working as a clerk in the law courts who Oliver had finally wooed through a combination of bullshit, kudos and expensive restaurants. However, she lived in a shared flat with two friends and insisted that sex at her place would be out of the question. Finding a hotel at short notice during the holiday season was a nightmare unless you were prepared to pay ridiculously over the odds. Oliver could afford it but resented being ripped off. There was no option; to consummate their union for a couple of hours during the afternoon when Stephanie was out visiting a cousin in Chelsea was the answer. Lunch then bed – perfect.

What Oliver didn't know was that Stephanie had a spy in the street, a neighbour who had agreed to inform her if there were any unaccounted for guests. Stephanie had reached her cousin's place and was busy catching up with family news when the text arrived.

He's got a visitor.

There were two choices. One, inform Ollie that she knew what was going on and was on her way back to confront him. Two, surprise and catch him breaking their agreement, and as an aside, find out which foolhardy woman he was with. It was hardly a choice really.

What Stephanie didn't know was that her spy's husband was Oliver's double agent. As soon as his flustered wife grabbed her phone, the man slipped into his study and texted Oliver.

S knows. She's heading back.

'You need to leave, Stephanie's on her way home,' Oliver declared having only just reached his bedroom. The law court clerk was taking off her shoes, sensible winterwear with laces and a low heel.

'You're already separated so I don't see how your wife can stop you having guests.'

'It's complicated but that's how it is. Sorry, you really must go.'

'Then you'll have to take me home.'

'Why?'

She reminded him that it was both a Sunday and an extended holiday, meaning public transport would be useless.

'I'll get you a cab then,' he suggested.

She didn't like cabs she told him; not long ago there had been an incident with a driver.

With little enthusiasm he acquiesced to her request. He was sulking though, such a disappointing afternoon when he'd been all set for fun. His head was in that wonderful, inebriated state – a lightness, a buoyancy, a sensuality.

Slipping on his jacket, he took the flask of whisky out of the inside pocket and took a slug or two to supplement the substantial amount of wine consumed over lunch.

'Actually, are you OK to drive?' she asked on seeing Oliver grab the handrail having lost his balance and slipping on the way downstairs.

'Yes, I'm fine.'

'But drink-driving?'

'I've told you, I'm alright. And anyway, you said you have no other way to get home. Come on, hurry up. Let's go.'

Oliver wasn't sure he wanted to see her again.

Meanwhile, approximately eight miles away across the other side of London, Stephanie was sitting in her car with the engine running, the window open as her cousin challenged her decision to drive.

'Leave your car and let me take you home and then I'll pick you up tomorrow evening after work and bring you back here to collect it.'

'I'm fine. Honestly. I've hardly had anything to drink.'

Stephanie's cousin, a serious and responsible lady, noted the children's water bottle on the passenger seat, a container she had seen many times before. She was fed up hearing Stephanie's jokes about taking it with her into court. That day Stephanie had arrived drunk, the smell of lime on her breath a giveaway. She'd brought a bottle of wine to have with lunch and by the time the text arrived the bottle was near empty.

'Well, I can't stop you but for God's sake drive carefully, Stephanie.'

Seventeen and a half minutes later, Oliver was heading west towards the law court clerk's home, desperate to see the back of her, while Stephanie was dashing eastwards to catch out her husband.

There were two looks of horror and a simultaneous screeching of brakes as the cars veered towards each other. Then the crunch of metal as they collided.

'That's my wife,' Oliver told his passenger.

'It doesn't matter who it is. You're in big trouble because you're drunk,' the female with a sound understanding of the law informed Oliver. 'I'm off,' she added as she opened the door and walked away from the accident scene.

The ensuing public slanging match between Oliver and Stephanie was recorded on phones and immediately posted on social media even though at that stage the gathering had no idea that the adversaries were husband and wife and prominent citizens with a degree of renown.

When the police arrived it was recorded that both cars had crossed the central line on the road. This restarted the public slanging match about who was responsible for the accident. Oliver repeated to the police what he had already told Stephanie, that he was overtaking two cyclists side-by-side, idiots because their headphones prevented them hearing his honk of the horn to get them to move over.

'Surely it's illegal to wear headphones when cycling,' Oliver vented.

'It isn't, sir, but I will get in touch with the Home Secretary right away to get the law changed,' the policewoman responded.

'I don't take kindly to insolence. Do you know who I am?'

'Not yet, sir, but I am about to take down your details. Firstly, I'd like you to blow into this.'

Stephanie was being interviewed by a second policewoman.

'I was trying to get past one of those ridiculously wide trailer bikes they use to carry children in. They might be fine during daylight hours but they're lethal in the dark.'

It was a little after four o'clock. Only now was dusk descending.

'They are only lethal when motorists don't give them the space they need. Fortunately the carriage was empty because it turned over when the cyclist veered to avoid colliding with you. It could have been a disaster.'

'You mean there wasn't even a child in it? Ridiculous! They should not be allowed on our highways if there's no passenger.'

'Madam, has it crossed your mind that the trailer will be empty for half the journeys. You drop a kid off somewhere like school and return home without them.'

Stephanie had expected agreement and sympathy, but instead this policewoman was challenging her. Mind you, she did have a point.

'So, let's take the breathalyser test, shall we?'

Stephanie considered the legal implications of refusing. Could she get away with claiming that the thought of taking the test was inducing panic? She could request a blood test instead in the hope that her alcohol level would have fallen by the time she reached the police station. She was sober enough to accept that using the breathalyser there and then was the best of few bad options.

Oliver and Stephanie eyed each other as they blew into the tubes. The pair of them were way over the limit and a hip flask and a children's water bottle were taken away as evidence.

At the police station, having failed a second test, Oliver and Stephanie were charged. Subdued, with a full awareness of the implications of their folly, they had little option but to head home together in a taxi.

'Idiot,' Stephanie muttered.

'I take it you are referring to yourself.'

'Take it how you like. Idiot.'

26

Helen's phone has been buzzing alerts for WhatsApp messages all morning. She waits until Laurie is in the bathroom before investigating in case it's an attack from Dee for him recruiting a comms person without consultation. It's not that though.

There are fifty-eight tennis club messages following a post by Jimmy. She cursors to the most recent ones.

Abi
Serves them right if they both end up in prison.

Simon
Won't happen. They have too many friends in high places. They'll get off scot-free.

Dee
Well I think British justice will prevail.

Tony
If they fail the brethilizer they won't have a leg to stand on.

Ursula
It's breathalyser, Tony.

'God, look at this, Laurie,' she calls out having accessed the hyperlink for the BBC news feature provided by Jimmy. They read the article, flick through some of the comments underneath it and then return to the tennis club WhatsApp group.

'Honestly, some people,' Laurie says when Helen has put down her phone.

'You mean the Kilroys?'

'Yeah them, but I was thinking about our members wasting their time having a say.'

'It is one hell of a story though. It's hilarious that two upholders of the law can make such a mess of things.'

'But look at the rubbish our members have written, imagining they have the legal expertise to know what the implications will be for Oliver and Stephanie.'

'We do have a fair number of law lecturers and solicitors at the club,' Helen says.

'True. One thing for sure, they'll lose their driving licences and face a fine, though that's probably it since no one was injured.'

'Ha-ha! You're doing exactly what others are doing, predicting the outcome. Why not join in and post a comment?'

'I won't of course, you know what I think about social media, but it does show how easy it is to get dragged into something.'

Helen knows Laurie is right because she's itching to get back to WhatsApp to see what others are saying. She'll do that as soon as Laurie has left. It's just fun, isn't it, even if opinions are worthless?

'I've got about an hour before I collect Keith,' Laurie says.

'OK. You do whatever and I'll get breakfast sorted.'

Helen takes her phone with her to the kitchen for a quick look. The WhatsApp excitement is already dying down.

~

'Two nights, right?' Keith checks as he puts on his seatbelt.

'Yes, two nights.'

'And you will be collecting me.'

'Yep, I'm not going to abandon you there.'

The journey down to Worthing is easy with the traffic light. Keith has pulled a photo album out of his holdall and it's resting on his lap. He intends to share the memories with Maggie.

'Look at this one, Laurie. I must have been about eight at the time. I remember that park well. Look.'

'Keith, do you want us to reach Worthing in one piece? Assuming you do, asking me to look at a photo while I'm driving is not a great idea.'

Keith, oblivious to the warning, continues. 'Oh and look at this one, probably the same day because I'm wearing the same clothes. A brass band played there every Sunday afternoon during summer.'

'Is that when you first got to enjoy music?'

Keith's focus has moved on. 'I do hope we can get to see the coast. We'll need to wrap up warm though, those sea winds will be biting this time of the year.'

'I'm sure if you ask the warden he'll be able to organise something.'

'I want to go shopping; I'd like to get Maggie a memento of the visit. And it is Christmas. Maybe a brooch or a scarf.'

'That's a lovely idea.'

'Perhaps there's something we can see one evening, a concert or a play.'

Given what the warden had said to him about Maggie's condition, Laurie doubts whether an evening out will be possible, but he's not going to say anything to dampen Keith's enthusiasm.

'I wonder whether there's a cafeteria nearby. Of course, I could always cook something for us.'

'There'll be fish and chip places on the sea front. Maybe you could take a taxi down one lunchtime.'

'Yes, I'd like that. Did you see that sign? Eight miles to Worthing.'

'Yep. Not long now.'

'This is my most recent photo of Maggie, with Jean. It must be from three years ago. Best not to look though if you're driving.'

Welcome to Worthing. Twinned with Elztal, Germany and Pays des Olonnes, France.

'See that sign – we've made it. I've not heard of either of those places. Have you?'

'No, I haven't.'

'Do you know where Maggie lives? You can use that satnav.'

'Keith, slow down, take a deep breath because you need to pace yourself. And remember to take it easy with Maggie. She'll be pleased to see you but the warden did say that she's rather frail.'

'I know. I'll be looking after her.'

Laurie smiles. It's great to hear this man in his late eighties say that, it's great to see a new lease of life however short-lived it might be. The warden had assured Laurie that he will keep an eye on the two of them and Laurie has high hopes that this visit will be a success.

The warden greets and leads them to Maggie's flat. Laurie notices Keith's shock on seeing such a fragile woman. He recovers and the younger brother takes hold of Maggie, hugs her gently and tells her that they are going to spend two of the best days ever together.

'You will let me know if there's a problem?' he asks the warden. 'I can come back to collect Keith whenever needed.'

'I've just seen the biggest smile ever from Maggie. This is a tonic that's going to do her the world of good.'

'A tonic for both of them.'

Laurie calls Helen on the way back, reporting on a successful start to the visit.

'Great. Of course I'm delighted for him but for you too. You deserve a break without having to worry. Actually, I'm also pleased for me because I can have you all to myself.'

27

Usually Helen and Laurie are happiest when they're kept busy, but over the next three days, free from worry about Keith, grant applications, tennis club affairs and rehearsals, doing next to nothing is blissful.

They get to discover more about each other as they reminisce about their childhoods – earliest memories, school years, a happy family life for both of them though with Helen's wealth of opportunities far outstripping Laurie's experiences.

Laurie sets up a marathon quiz using Spotify to play tracks from favourite bands from years gone by. The aim of the game is to guess the artist and for a bonus point the name of the song. Helen wins. In addition to knowing vastly more about classical music than Laurie, she outshines him when it comes to pop and rock. Laurie rejects her offer of a quiz covering literature and film, and she declines his suggestion of a science-based competition.

They subscribe to trial offers from a couple of channels and binge watch two series that friends have recommended. Helen tolerates Laurie's interest in sci-fi and in return he sits through hours of an intense family drama.

They eat and drink far too much and spend plenty of time in bed because they're young, the relationship is in its infancy and they are full of lust.

This enjoyable, self-indulgent existence comes to a temporary halt when they travel to Worthing to collect Keith, Laurie taking up Helen's offer to keep him company and do the driving.

'It's not only to be with you; I love the sea,' she tells him.

The arrangement is to collect Keith mid-afternoon but they set off early morning to fit in a few hours by themselves. They head straight for the seafront and Helen parks close to the pier. From there they walk along a promenade lined with palm trees, the leaves swishing madly in the strong wind. The trees seem healthy enough though, despite having to survive English winters. An hour of walking along the promenade is plenty given the inclement weather. They head inland towards the town centre where they discover the Royal Arcade and get lunch at one of the independent cafes.

'It's not a bad place to live,' Helen remarks, 'away from the madness of London.'

'It's for old people though. I doubt whether there's much going on.'

'OK, we'll put it on hold until we're old and grey!'

'On the subject of old and grey, we should collect Keith soon,' Laurie says, signalling to the waitress for the bill.

'I do hope he's had a great time.'

'Well, he hasn't been texting me non-stop which has to be a good sign. Based on the one chat we've had I'd say that it's gone better than we could ever have expected.'

Helen picks up Laurie's use of "we". It's nice, like she's part of the family.

They collect an exuberant Keith who monopolises the conversation all the way back to London.

'It's nice, Worthing, what with the sea air. It's full of old people though.'

'We made it to the pier, I was determined to, but good job I had a hat and scarf with me.'

'There's a lovely promenade for a stroll, lined with palm trees it is. Palm trees in England, I ask you!'

'I'm pleased we could get out and about. I think most of the time Maggie is cooped up in that flat of hers.'

'She can't walk for long though, she's slowed right down. Luckily there are benches all along the promenade so we could have breaks for her to catch her breath.'

'I'm wondering whether she needs a zimmer or even a wheelchair. There's those electric ones, we saw a few of them going up and down the promenade. I did suggest it but Maggie said absolutely not. She's an obstinate one, always has been.'

'To be truthful I'm worried about her being able to cope. I met some friends who help a bit, but there's no one to do the day to day stuff.'

Helen is noting Keith's shift from an upbeat description of what they did together with everything being fine, to concern about his sister's wellbeing.

'What do you mean by day to day stuff, Keith?' she asks.

'The basics really. Shopping, cooking, cleaning. She's not as capable as she used to be, that's for sure. Lunchtime today for example. She was heating up soup in the microwave and it was taking so long I went into the kitchen to see what was what. Good job I did because she'd set the timer for two hours rather than two minutes.'

'God, that is a worry. If independent living is getting difficult maybe she should move to a care home.'

'She'd hate that; wouldn't we all. I don't know though, without someone to regularly check on her that might have to happen. I'll be visiting again but I can hardly pop over to help when there's a problem.'

Helen smiles at the thought of a man close to his nineties seeing himself as the person racing over to support an ageing sister. Laurie is silent; he's sitting in the back so maybe can't hear the conversation.

'You are right to be concerned,' Helen says. 'I liked the warden and I'm sure he'll help as much as possible, but there is a limit to what he can do.'

'Exactly.'

They reach Keith's flat and spend a short amount of time with him, helping to get things sorted.

'Remember, we're here to help whenever needed, including when you're thinking about your sister,' Helen says ahead of a goodbye hug by the front door.

'Thank you, Helen, that's very considerate of you.'

'What do you reckon?' she asks Laurie as they are driving the short distance back to her flat.

'I think the visit was a huge success.'

'But can he handle the new worry, about Maggie?'

'It's given him a purpose I suppose; it could be good.'

'Except that there's nothing practical he can do to help her which might frustrate him.'

'I guess we wait and see. For now I think it's a plus because it's taken his mind off his own situation.'

Laurie has been wondering how Helen has instigated the seismic change. She hasn't said or done much different to what he's been trying over months and months, but a connection between the two of them has sparked Keith's improvement.

Helen likes the way Laurie is always so optimistic, though the downside is his belief that everything will sort itself out in the end. Take the tennis club builders for instance.

Laurie's optimism soon turns out to be right though. When Helen and Laurie visit Keith the next afternoon, he tells them that he's rejoined the University of the Third Age and signed up for three courses that start in early January. He's planning a return visit to Worthing in early March and has already investigated train timetables.

'I want to stay longer this time. Maybe a full week.'

'But why are you looking at train timetables?' Laurie asks.

'I know how busy you are, I don't want to put you to more inconvenience.'

'That's silly, Keith. Of course I'll take you there and back.'

'Anyway, I like train journeys.'

~

Even though it's great to have more free time together, Laurie and Helen can't quite recapture the carefree mood of earlier that week during the remaining days before their return to work.

New Year's Eve is a quiet evening at Helen's place and on a mild first day of January she's up early, impatient to play some tennis.

'Really?' Laurie asks as she prods him playfully to get him out of bed.

'Yes, really. I'm fine to play.'

Presumably everyone else is recovering from the previous evening's festivities because the club is deserted when they arrive. Laurie insists on staying on the side of the court with the slippery corner and he's feeding balls close to her to minimise her need to run.

It's going well but she has the common sense not to overdo it and calls a halt after half an hour.

They linger by the clubhouse building site.

'This is hopeless,' Laurie says.

'Sometimes it's hard to judge how well a new build is going. Getting the foundations and services in place takes ages, but once that's done things move fast.'

Helen says this to stop Laurie worrying but she is dismayed by the lack of progress. There is little over twelve weeks remaining to complete the exterior and tackle the inside which includes installing a kitchen, the bar, the changing rooms and the shop.

As they are leaving they cross paths with members arriving for an afternoon tournament. Happy New Year greetings are chased by comments about the slow progress of the rebuild, leaving Helen and Laurie keen to escape.

Helen flings her arms round Laurie's shoulders and draws him close for a hug as they walk home. 'We're doing our best. And I haven't heard any bright ideas from the critics.'

The return to work after the Bank Holiday is on a Friday. Ahead of going to the university, Laurie cycles to the club to check that the builders are back on site. They aren't. Maybe it wasn't worth starting on a Friday he reasons, but when there's no sign of activity the following Monday, Tuesday or Wednesday, his panic escalates. Texts to Grayling and Grimshaw are unanswered.

Helen alerts him to a new thread on WhatsApp started by Jimmy, possibly intent on recreating his moment of glory with his Kilroy thread.

Jimmy

So where are these builders then? Post your answers.

Gus
They're here but they're fast asleep and I didn't want to wake them.

Dee
Have you really seen them?

Gus
Of course not. I was taking the piss.

Simon
Well, I spotted one of them fast asleep in the cement mixer.

Jimmy
Good one, Si. You should have turned it on.

Dee
You may well joke about this but you won't be laughing in April when there's no clubhouse.

Fortunately, Dee is so unpopular that her comment kills the dialogue. Or is it because two men have turned up on the Thursday. They're back again on Friday to fit roof timbers, so for now Laurie's dread is over even though there's no sign of Lee Grimshaw.

28

'I suggest we don't talk about anything to do with the tennis club this weekend,' Helen says. It's Friday evening and they are sitting in a crowded pub, so noisy with end-of-week excitement that Laurie has to lean forwards to hear Helen. 'What shall we do tomorrow?'

'Sorry, but the Mixed C Team have a home match. I'd better join them at the café after the game to check on things.'

'Oh, I didn't realise that was this weekend. I'll come with you; I promised Zadie I'd be there. One thing for sure, she won't put up with a repeat from Andras.'

'He's learnt his lesson.'

'Has he? I know Andras.'

The next afternoon, as they join the players, they see Andras as voluble as ever, but the others seem subdued.

'He's sick,' Zadie tells Helen, loud enough for everyone to hear. 'Fuckwit,' she hisses.

'There's no need for that,' Andras protests having stopped telling an anecdote mid-sentence.

'Tosser then. I bet that's what you do as soon as you get home.' Zadie stands and picks up her kit. 'I'll call you later, Helen.'

'Sure. I'm around all evening.'

Zadie offers a half-hearted wave. 'Bye everyone. Thanks for the game.'

As soon as she's out of earshot Andras is protesting. 'Can someone please tell me what that was all about? We had a good game and then –'

'Not in front of another team. We can deal with this later,' Laurie says, which the opponents take as a signal to prepare to head off. They're followed by the remaining club players, leaving Laurie and Helen in the café to discuss the situation.

Helen's first thought, admittedly ahead of speaking to Zadie, is that Andras's behaviour is a disciplinary matter. Her phone rings before she can make the point.

'It's Zadie. Best if I take it confidentially,' she says as she steps away from the table.

'It's clear cut,' she tells Laurie on her return moments later. 'Andras was making suggestive comments right through the match, he was touching her, and then when they were on their way to the café he had the nerve to ask if she wanted to join him for drinks this evening. He should be kicked out of the club.'

Laurie's phone rings. 'It's Andras.' He moves away to take the call.

'Well?' Helen asks when he's back.

'He has no idea what Zadie is on about. I did press him over what was said about this evening. Apparently, a group of friends are going out for a few drinks and a meal and when he asked Zadie if she'd like to join them, she was furious. He insists he was only being friendly.'

'Yeah, right. I know which one of them I believe.'

'Maybe, but in the end it's her word against his. I'm not keen on Andras but is it fair to assume that it's always the man who lies about these things?'

'But why would Zadie lie?'

'No idea. I'm just trying to be fair.'

'What do you intend to do then?'

'Well, I'm sure Zadie won't partner Andras again. So the decision is which one of them doesn't get to play in the next match unless Jennifer's prepared to go with Andras.'

'I don't mean what to do about who plays in the next match, that's an irrelevance. What are you going to do about Andras?'

'Do? Nothing.'

'I'm disappointed, Laurie. Can't you see that this is a blatant case of an older man harassing a young woman.'

'You can't turn this into a gender issue.'

'But that's what it is; a man abusing his power.'

'Hang on a minute, it might be rash flirting but that isn't a crime. We both know of older women at the club who are serial flirters with younger men, starting affairs, even responsible for marriage breakups. Isn't that an abuse of power, too?'

'No, it's not the same.'

'What makes you the judge of that? Anyway, I can hardly police the morality of five hundred individuals. It would be impossible.'

'So, you're not going to do anything. You're happy to let Andras coerce a teenager? Go on then, defend the male – as usual.'

'Hang on, Helen, that's unfair. It's not what I'm doing.'

'I'm tired, I think I'll head back to my own place tonight.'

Helen is up and on her way out the café before Laurie has had time to respond.

On her walk home, Helen is wondering whether she's been fair. Where do you draw the line between flirting, pathetic in Andras's case, and unacceptable behaviour. As Laurie said, how could you even begin to pass judgement on the behaviour of every member?

Laurie remains in the café for a while, saddened by their unnecessary argument. He gets it how Helen must feel about Zadie if in the past Andras has chased her too, quite possibly when she was also a teenager. Andras's behaviour may well be poor but is it anything more serious? It certainly doesn't warrant throwing him out of the club which would open a can of worms. Whatever the next step, the argument with Helen needs to be resolved as quickly as possible.

He sends her a text. *Sorry about today, I'm sure we can sort it.*

Thankfully she replies. Quickly. *Yeah, I hated it and there was no need because I know you care about all this. Now that I'm here I'll stay put tonight, I've got stuff to do, but I'll come over after my meeting with the musicians tomorrow.*

There's an audible sigh of relief as Laurie texts back. *Great!*

Helen. *Nite-nite*

Laurie, worried about the absence of a kisses sign off from Helen, texts X^3

Helen. $XXX + XXX = 2(XXX)!!!!$

~

Helen is sure they'll get over their argument but that doesn't prevent another restless night, this time it's gender war thoughts racing back and forth. She's a feminist as are all the strong-minded women in her family: mother, three sisters, cousins, aunts. They'd all have been suffragettes in past times.

She detests Andras's arrogant belief that he's God's gift to women. There's a specific reason why she got so wound up about him flirting with Zadie: she had the same treatment when she was a similar age and he only stopped pestering her when he turned his attention to another young woman.

That's Andras, but can you make sweeping statements based on one man's behaviour? What is acceptable flirting and what goes beyond? Is it their age difference? If it had been a twenty-year old Andras clone doing the chatting up would that have been OK? And Laurie's question deserved consideration: what if Andras had been the young student with Zadie in her forties and doing the seducing, would that be equally inexcusable? It was true what Laurie had said, some women at the tennis club were ruthless flirters. The gossip she'd overheard was shocking.

So, why does she think that the morality codes for men and women are different? She's on the edge of sleep but reawakens with a start when she comes up with *an* answer, if not *the* answer. Imbalance of power is the deciding factor and it's usually men who have the power and the potential to abuse it. The film director and the actress, the teacher and the student, the boss and his subordinate. The list goes on. The politician and the researcher. The priest and members of his congregation.

When she wakes in the morning her first thought is that Laurie was right about Andras. The man was flirting, Zadie told him to get lost and that's the end of it.

Laurie has had a peaceful night's sleep. Based on the exchange of texts, joke kisses included, he's certain that all will be well between them when they meet. Their argument, unpleasant though it was, was largely about semantics. They were more or less in agreement about the incident, the distinction being how they expressed their feelings.

He turns his attention to two potentially awkward conversations. How would the volatile Andras respond when told he couldn't partner Zadie again? How would young Zadie react if he asked her to drop out of the C Team? He'll leave that one to simmer for a while.

When Helen and Laurie meet later that day there's an unspoken truce, with no mention of the Andras-Zadie situation, the wider issue of male-female power imbalance, or the rift caused by their different views on next steps.

'The tennis club …' Laurie begins when they are sitting together on the sofa holding glasses of wine. Helen braces herself for a discussion about their conflict. She really doesn't want this; can't he forget it?

'We have the committee meeting coming up soon and I also have to write an update for the monthly newsletter. I've no idea what to say about the slow progress with the rebuild.'

'For now all you can say is that everything is fine. Mention that it might seem slow going but it always looks that way until the groundwork's done, then after that it flies.'

This is a repeat of what Helen has already told him. Does she actually believe it he wonders.

'So you think I should say that we're on schedule for completion by the start of the new season?'

'Absolutely.'

On hearing Helen's single word of false bravado a sense of doom descends, with Laurie thinking he'll be forever known as the chair of broken promises. The ex-chair.

'Is everything OK? Helen asks.
'Yeah.'

Is he fretting about the row she wonders? She decides that they can't simply ignore what happened. 'I hated yesterday,' she begins.

'Me too.'

'I'm pleased we can move on.'

Laurie smiles. 'We've got too much going to let something like that ruin things.'

'I'm glad you're saying what I've been thinking. Listening more carefully to each other will stop arguments like that ever happening again.'

'It won't happen again,' Laurie states, unsure what careful listening has to do with differences of opinion.

'Good. Can I change the subject?'

'Sure.'

'You know my family want to meet you. Well, I've tentatively agreed to us visiting them next Sunday. Is that OK?'

'Yeah, of course.'

'Great. I'll text Mum to confirm.'

Helen lifts up her phone and is about to begin her message when it rings, a classical tune that Laurie has heard before but can't name.

'It's Zadie.' Helen puts it on speakerphone. 'Hi, Zadie. Everything OK?'

'Yeah, cool, but I've been doing some thinking and I've decided to quit the tennis club.'

'Laurie's with me. Is it alright if we're on speakerphone?'

'Yeah, no probs.'

'Do you want to leave because of Andras?'

'Nah, not really. He is a toss but not a dangerous toss. I can handle him; he isn't as bad as some other tossers I know. Mind you, they're younger so what they get up to is more excusable.'

'OK, lots of tossers out there then. So why leave the club?'

'I'm getting loads of match practice and games at uni, some brill coaching, too. So there's no time to fit in playing at the club.'

'It would be a shame to see you go; the club would miss you.'

'Will miss me 'cos I've decided. But thanks for saying that. Are you cool with me going, Laurie?'

'I remember coaching you when you were a tot and thinking then what a talent you were.'

'Thanks, that's nice to hear. I might come back after uni I suppose.'

'We'll be tracking your progress, Zadie,' Helen says.

There's a little small talk but it's apparent that Zadie wants to end the call.

'It's a shame we'll be losing her, although I can understand her reasoning. At least this has saved the need for a conversation I wasn't looking forward to. Now all that's left is another one I've been dreading – speaking to Andras.'

'Actually you won't need to,' Helen says. 'I called Jennifer earlier today to see if she'd be prepared to partner Andras and the answer is a definite no. So then I spoke to Douglas and he said that since he's the team captain it's up to him to sort it out. He'll tell Andras and then find a partner for him. So we can forget about the club tonight.'

29

It's been a great week, their argument long forgotten. Helen's sessions at the recording studio are going brilliantly well; she's marvelling at the sound quality produced by the team of skilled and patient engineers. Laurie's university group have been sent a list of questions from the grant application assessors, things like "Would it be acceptable to receive the grant in three tranches spread over eighteen months?" and "Would you be willing to provide brief interim reports on a bi-monthly basis?" which surely indicates that the money is all but theirs.

Helen's ankle is completely healed and she's back to her usual high level of tennis. She plays a midweek match for the first team and wins both sets. Laurie has a tournament game against Tom, his closest rival at the club, and comes away victorious after a hard fought battle.

At last there are four walls and a roof up so the clubhouse looks like a proper building. Progress remains slow and there's no sign of Grimshaw the site manager, but at least there are builders there every day. They look close to completing all the outdoor work, so presumably they will soon start working on the inside.

On the Saturday evening a playful Helen fires humorous warnings about what Laurie is about to face on his first visit to her family. He counters with how keen he is to meet that mother of hers who will be able to give away all Helen's childhood secrets. They tumble into bed for a night of clumsy passion, having drunk way too much. The next morning they leave London considerably later than planned.

Laurie prides himself in drawing conclusions based on evidence, and if that's not possible, in deducing what to expect based on logic. From Helen's conversations about her family he's built up a clear idea about what to expect.

Her parents will be living in a detached, sprawling countryside residence crammed full of high value period pieces of furniture – inlaid mahogany cabinets, plush chaise longue sofas, oil portraits of family members – the sort of stuff to be seen in stately homes. Well, maybe not quite as grand but still far more than anything visible in his own family's house.

Being winter, he'll be led to the main sitting room with its roaring fire where the customary cut glass decanters of sherry will be wheeled out on the trolley. He realises that he's replicating what he saw at the Kilroy's dinner party.

And what of Helen's parents, Mr and Mrs Critchley? Immaculately turned out, the mother in tweeds and Liberty silks, the father with blazer and tie. Politely welcoming if rather reserved and definitely inquisitive about the upbringing and prospects for their daughter's new partner.

Laurie's perception has in part been formed through the potentially unreliable evidence provided by Helen, the jovial ridicule of her mother and of her posh upbringing, and more recently an advance warning about the chaotic state of the house.

Helen drives them there, a journey through south London then further southwards. After a little under two hours they pull up outside a red brick, semi-detached house overlooking a common with its small, reeded pond. As they step out of the car they are greeted by the shrill quacking of ducks.

'I have got a key of course, but I'll ring the doorbell because Mum will probably want to be in place to greet you. Are you ready for this?'

'My Spanish Inquisition!'

The front door is opened before Helen has time to ring the bell.

'Come in, come in. It's great to meet you at last, Laurie,' Mrs Critchley says, taking hold of a hand to pull him towards her before flinging her arms round him for a hug. 'I'm Helen's mum Nadia,' she states, adding, 'Helen's told me so much about you.'

'Actually I haven't at all.'

'Well, maybe not exactly, but I could tell what you'd be like based on how happy Helen has been since you've met. It's a nice change to see her like this.'

'Thanks a million, Mum.'

'Welcome, Laurie,' this from Mr Critchley, a broad smile followed by a firm handshake. 'I'm Edward.'

Beyond this warm welcome, a surprise for Laurie is their appearance. No Liberty designer wear, no tweeds or silk. Both are in jeans, slim fitting, tapered to the ankle. Mr Critchley has on the casual striped shirt that Laurie has considered buying at White Stuff. There is a clattering assortment of leather and silver bracelets on his left wrist and a single stud on his right ear lobe. Mrs Critchley is wearing a striking rape seed yellow fleece.

'You must be dying for a tea or coffee. Come into the kitchen. Oh, hang up your coats first.' Helen's mother points to a rack of considerable width crammed full of jackets and coats. 'If there's no space, chuck them onto the bench,' she adds.

The bench and the shelf beneath it are filled with shoes, boots and trainers, most of them caked in mud.

Nadia notices Laurie's indecision. 'Come on Helen, help out.'

Helen's solution is to drop some of the coats onto the floor to create the space to hang theirs. Laurie spins round in expectation of seeing a dissatisfied reaction from her parents but there isn't one. This appears to be a perfectly acceptable way to make room for visitors' coats.

They follow the Critchley parents into the kitchen. Another surprise, this one far outdoing Helen's parents' appearance and the coat rack solution. The kitchen is a disaster area. It looks like there has been a deliberate attempt to maximise disorder. A while back

266

Laurie caught the end of a television programme with someone famous (though not to him) tackling hoarding in volunteers' homes. This room would be an ideal candidate for the show.

None of the base units have the doors that you see in most kitchens to conceal untidiness. Here the low level shelves are stacked with saucepans, pots, pans, bowls and crockery. Further shelves that line the walls contain books, packets and jars of food.

Laurie is immaculately tidy to the point of obsessive and he is finding this kitchen unsettling. As far as he can judge it's unworkable as a venue for cooking.

'You OK?' Helen whispers.

'Sure.'

Somehow the kitchen must be operational because the oven light is on and there's the faint humming of the fan. There's a pleasant aroma, too.

The puzzle broadens. Where will they be able to put whatever they take out of the oven because every worktop space is covered with something or other. And where will they put the plates when serving up? It's not his concern but nevertheless he is worried.

'Are you sure you're OK?' Helen is asking, her look quizzical.

'Yeah, sure,' Laurie says as he puts aside his dystopian analysis of the Critchley kitchen.

Nadia is telling them to adjourn to the living room. She'll bring in the coffees while Edward carries on preparing lunch.

Kitchens are working areas. Living rooms are serene environments for chilling out. On the short walk across the hall, Laurie is therefore anticipating a higher level of orderliness in the latter. Wrong, it's as shambolic as the kitchen. Every surface has stuff on it – magazines piled high on sofas and armchairs, ornaments resting against each other, books precariously stacked, curios filling the mantlepiece, window ledges, coffee table and cabinets. The whole house must be similarly chaotic.

Helen seems oblivious to the chaos as she sweeps a heap of magazines to one side to make room for them to sit on a sofa. Laurie remains standing, surprised by Helen's acceptance or even lack of awareness of this when her own flat is uncluttered and tidy.

'Do you still have your own bedroom here?' he asks.

'I guess so. Sort of.'

'Can I see it?'

'See it? Sure. I suppose we'll be sleeping in there at some stage.' Helen takes hold of Laurie's hand and leads him upstairs. 'Are you sure you're OK? You're acting a bit weird.'

'No, I'm fine. It's nice meeting your parents.'

Helen opens a door at the far end of a long, narrow corridor. 'That's my bed – our bed,' she says as she pulls him onto it and kisses him.

But Laurie isn't focusing on the bed or even the kiss. He is noting a well-ordered room, surprisingly girly with pink floral wallpaper and a One Direction poster.

She catches Laurie looking at it. 'I used to like them. I keep it up as a reminder of the folly of teenagehood.'

'Your room is much … much tidier than downstairs.'

'Yes,' is the single word provided.

Nadia is calling them. 'Coffee's ready.'

Laurie dismisses thinking about the state of the house – it's clearly not a problem for the family – and enjoys a pleasant few hours chatting to Helen's parents. There is no sign of the inquisition that Helen had been joking about ahead of the visit, no probing about his background, job prospects and the like. Nadia and Edward are as happy talking about themselves as they are to find out about Laurie. They cover their own work, their interests and their plans for the future now that all four girls have left home.

'A move?' Helen says when her father mentions the possibility.

'We have lovely memories of almost thirty years here, but perhaps the time is right.'

'I think it could be really exciting; a fresh start for you both,' Helen says.

'You're the first one we've told about the possibility. Do you reckon your sisters will approve?'

Helen pauses to reflect. 'Yes, I do. They'll want whatever you think is best for the future.'

They chat about some of those memories Nadia had referred to and Laurie is an eager listener. It's evident that Helen's moans about her mother are a pretence

269

because the pair of them seem as close as a mother and daughter could be.

Helen's father asks about the recording and the forthcoming concert schedule. 'Are you getting a decent income for those gigs?' he wonders.

'Not bad. Remember it's our first tour of prestigious venues. The organisers need to test ticket sales before paying us loads.'

'All the same, are you managing?' Edward looks across at Laurie. 'Excuse me for talking money, Laurie, but Helen never wants to take anything which is noble but we don't want her to go without.'

'Honestly, I'm OK Dad. Thanks for asking though.'

There's sadness as Laurie thinks about his own family, of how his father died way too soon, too soon to be proud of his son's progress. His parents would have enjoyed meeting Nadia and Edward, Helen too, of course. Keith would like them also.

'We'd better head back,' Helen announces when there's a pause in the conversation. She springs up and Laurie follows suit.

'OK darling,' Nadia says as she gets up. 'When will we see you again? Both of you, I hope.'

'After we get back from Cromer.'

'You never did say why Cromer.'

'It's a long story. I'll tell you after we've been there.'

They are standing in the hallway. As Helen grabs their jackets Laurie stoops to pick up the coats from the floor.

'It's fine, Laurie, just leave them,' Nadia says.

If he did, might they still be on the floor the next time he visits?

'It's OK,' he says as he picks them up and rehangs them. 'It's been great meeting you. And thanks for lunch.'

'A pleasure. I'll invite Helen's sisters next time you visit.'

Helen takes hold of Laurie's hand and edges him towards the door. 'Come on. Time to go.'

'I think your parents are cool,' Laurie says as they drive off.

'Yeah, I suppose so. I knew you'd like them.'

'There's nothing to not like. They're so ... youthful.'

'Immature I'd call it.'

Laurie smiles. He knows her bolshiness is all an act.

—

The following week, ten to go before Easter and the start of the summer season, Laurie is checking the new build each morning on his way to work. There are no builders around, thus ending the brief period of optimism. Helen joins him at the club after work on the Thursday for a game, a dreadful standard of play with both of them distracted by the state of the clubhouse. Yes, there are walls and a roof, but still no windows, no doors, no guttering, no sign of any indoor activity and there are piles of rubble surrounding the site.

'This is absolutely ridiculous,' Helen says, realising as she speaks how pointless her comment is.

Having his voicemails to Grayling and Grimshaw unanswered all week, it's a surprise when Laurie gets a call late on Friday afternoon.

'I know what you're going to say, Laurie, that it's been a quiet week at the club, but there are reasons and I wanted to get things sorted before speaking to you.'

Laurie can't be his usual polite self. 'Sorted? So what exactly needs to be sorted this time? You have a building to complete; you have a deadline. What's the problem, Mr Grayling?'

He's told that Lee Grimshaw, the site manager, has quit the company with no notice, creating short term difficulties. 'The good news is that I've got a new person starting so everything is back on track.'

'Will he be there on Monday?'

'If all goes well.'

'I'm assuming that all *will* go well. Let me have his contact details so I can deal with him directly since you're impossible to get hold of.'

'I don't normally give numbers but as a favour I will. He's called Filip, that's with an F instead of a PH and one L instead of two.'

Laurie adds Filip to his contacts. He'll touch base on Monday.

Grayling is in a hurry to end the call.

'I suppose it might be good news given how hopeless Grimshaw was,' Laurie tells Helen that evening. 'I hope it's OK but I've sent the new person your number as well as mine in case I don't pick up a call. I'll go first thing on Monday to check he's there although I've got no idea what to do if he isn't.'

'We don't have a Plan B do we?'

'No we don't and I'm out of my depth with this. Grayling mentioned something else. Now he wants money in advance to purchase the sanitary ware and kitchen units.'

'No way. Where does he think he's going to store things securely when there aren't even any doors or windows fitted yet?'

'I asked that. He said at his yard.'

'I say no. Before paying him anything I want to actually see the goods on site.'

'Agreed.'

Helen goes to the fridge to collect a couple of beers. She hands Laurie one and slumps down onto the sofa, leaning into him. This worry about the tennis club is draining both of them.

'Fuck, fuck, fuck! What if ...' Laurie begins. 'I'd resign immediately if the clubhouse wasn't ready for the summer season.'

'They still have over nine weeks. It's possible to get it done if they work flat out.'

'It was meant to be a four-month project. It should be finished by now.'

'You're the optimist and you're usually right. Come on, forget about it now. We were going to plan the Cromer trip, so let's do it.'

With less than two weeks to go before they set off, they've barely given it a thought after booking the hotel.

'We need a list of places we might like to visit,' Helen says as she opens her laptop.

30

'Hey, wake up dreamer, we're here,' Helen says as they pull up at the small hotel car park overlooking the sea in Cromer. They wander down to lean against the railings above the promenade and watch as the waves crash against the sea wall.

'What do you reckon?' Laurie asks.

Helen smiles at his boyish enthusiasm. 'Early days but I can't actually tell where the sea ends and the sky begins.'

'It's only mist; it'll blow over before long.'

Helen ponders the distinction between mist and rain; it seems like rain to her. She turns to face their hotel, an impressive structure though it's struggling to maintain its grandeur. Slabs of window lintel have broken off and the exterior paintwork is in desperate need of a redo.

'Come on, let's see what this place is like inside,' Helen says as she takes hold of Laurie's hand.

The furnishings in the reception area are old-fashioned and well-worn. There's no one around to welcome them so Laurie rings the bell on the desk. A young woman steps out of the office. Not a single soul passes through the lobby as Laurie registers, leaving Helen to wonder if the place is deserted because it's winter or whether the hotel has had its glory days and now never fills.

When they reach their bedroom sunshine is streaming through the tall sash window. They abandon their luggage and head outside. The strong wind blowing off the sea has brought in a blanket of dark cloud.

Helen pauses as she looks up. 'It was sunny a minute ago.'

'It's not raining. Let's risk it,' Laurie suggests.

They head for the pier which is down some steps immediately in front of the hotel. From there they turn left and walk along a promenade until they reach a zig-zag flight of white stairs.

'I remember this,' Laurie declares as he starts to climb with Helen chasing after him. At each platform they turn back to face the sea and it's as if, in random order, they are ascending season by season. A harsh dark winter sky. A bitter autumn wind bringing charcoal balls of cloud that race across at speed. A bright blue summer sky with surprising warmth for the time of the year. At this point the sea is looking marvellous with its strips of subdued colour.

As they near the top Laurie's phone rings. 'It's Filip.'

'Don't answer it, he can leave a voicemail. We said we'd forget about the tennis club while we're here.'

Laurie is already talking. 'No problem, Filip, I'll get it sorted for you,' Helen hears him say before he

276

ends the call and drops his phone into his jacket pocket.

'I thought I'd better see what he wanted. The good news is that he's there working, the building is secure and there's been a delivery of kitchen units. He's being hassled by Grayling to pay for the goods. I told him to text the invoice over and I'd sort it out as soon as we're back.'

'OK, but please no more calls. Let's not think about the club for this few days,' Helen says as they manoeuvre the final bend and reach a pretty strip of garden at the top. 'There used to be a posh hotel over there,' Laurie says pointing. Helen looks across at a functional rectangular block of flats, the small windows not doing justice to the view to be had.

'Why did it go?' she asks.

'It was well before my time, but I think it got bombed during the Second World War.'

'Why would anyone want to bomb Cromer?'

'Good question. Apparently Cromer was the last place planes passed on their way back to Germany and they dumped any bombs they had left over to lighten their load.'

Helen intends to check; it doesn't seem plausible though surely Laurie wouldn't be making it up.

They double back into town, strolling through quaint passageways and along a high street that's a mix of attractive old and utilitarian newer buildings. Perhaps the bombing causing destruction is true after all.

The town seems close to deserted. It is winter but had they visited say Brighton or Bournemouth, there would be that all-year buzz. But she's happy because this is Laurie's choice.

He's in childhood reminiscence mode with his 'I don't remember this being here' as they pass a secondhand bookshop and 'I think this might have been here' at a fishmonger with its handwritten boards advertising crabmeat.

That evening they eat at a fish and chips restaurant on the seafront that has awards pinned near the entrance. The praise is justified.

They stay out in search of a lively pub but don't find one. Yes, it is February, but even so.

Helen is happy to give up and head back to their hotel. Going to bed with Laurie that night feels like a dare, somehow illicit, compared to when they're at one of their Muswell Hill flats. Their clothes are scattered across the sage green carpet and the giant oak-framed bed creaks and squeaks as they make love. They laugh; there's always laughter when they're together.

The next morning it's low tide and Helen sees a wide tract of golden sand. The sea is as calm as a pond. They set off along the beach towards Sheringham, passing small scatterings of rocks and pebbles.

'What are they looking for?' Helen asks, gesturing towards those cautiously stepping across rocks close to the water's edge.

'Possibly crabs or maybe fossils.'

'That sounds exciting; the fossils, not the crabs.'

They walk along chatting about this and that, though as agreed, nothing to do with work or the tennis club. With those topics off limit it's like an early date conversation – favourite films, music, books.

Helen stops and looks towards the sea, now glistening in the winter sunshine. 'This is wonderful. I can see why you loved it here.'

'But look! That wasn't here when I was a kid.'

'What am I meant to be looking at?'

He points. 'There.'

'The sea?' she asks, genuinely confused because the angle of his outstretched arm is taking her onto the horizon.

'An offshore windfarm. Brilliant.'

Now she can see the little white sticks protruding from the sea. She hugs Laurie for his excitement.

On reaching Sheringham, which turns out to be a longer trek than Laurie estimated, they have lunch at a pub facing out to sea (and those wind turbines). Helen realises she is totally relaxed, more than is ever the case in London. They saunter through the town and catch a rattling train back to Cromer. She hugs Laurie; she is happy.

The tourist trail over the following days takes them on a boat trip from Blakeney to view a herd of seals packed together on a small strip of land; another beach walk, east to Overstrand; and a visit to a bird hide near Cley next the Sea.

'Why is the "to" missing from the name?' Helen asks Laurie.

'No idea.'

'And why do so many men here wear shorts when it's bloody freezing?'

'No idea.'

More laughter. Always laughter.

'I'm going to pop into the Co-op to pick up a few things for back home,' Helen tells Laurie on their last morning. 'You don't need to come. Finish the packing.'

When they'd walked past the secondhand bookshop on their first day, Helen had peered through the window of the closed shop and noticed old travel posters for Cromer. This is today's destination.

Entering the shop to the tinkle of a little bell above the door, she heads for the display of posters and is drawn to one locked in a glass cabinet. *A gem on the Norfolk Coast* is the text on a stylised view looking inland from the beach towards a cluster of brightly coloured buildings. Their hotel and the vast church are visible, as is the edge of the pier. The sky has white, puffy clouds dotted by seagulls in flight.

'It's an original from the 1950s,' the woman in the shop tells her.

'It's lovely. How much does it cost?'

She hadn't expected to be paying £200 for a poster, but after browsing the others on offer she knows it has to be this one.

'It's an original, not a replica, so you need to keep it out of direct sunlight to prevent fading,' the woman says as she rolls it up and inserts it into a cardboard carton.

Laurie loves it.

'Well, adieu Cromer. Perhaps we'll see you again,' he says as he puts the poster back into the cannister with meticulous care.

'Maybe during summer next time ...' Helen's phone rings. 'It's Filip. Why isn't he calling you?'

'I switched my phone off like you wanted.'

'What should I do?'

'Answer it.'

She puts the call on speaker. ''Hi Filip.'

They listen in stoney silence.

'I'll meet you at the club first thing tomorrow morning,' Laurie says. 'Yes, eight o'clock is fine.'

'What now?' Helen asks.

There is no obvious answer.

31

There are seven and a bit weeks to go before Easter.

'What are our options?' Helen asks after a period of silent reflection in the car on the way back to London.

Filip had called Laurie to let him know that the builders had gone bust, immediately halting any work at the club. A notification that Laurie's phone was out of service explained why he'd called Helen. Filip's command of English wasn't brilliant: could there be a misunderstanding? His desperate tone suggested not. Nevertheless, to make absolutely sure that he'd heard it right, Laurie had arranged the meeting.

'At least I'll be able to see what's left to be done,' he tells Helen, breaking another drawn out silence.

'I think it's a good idea. I'll come with you.'

'There's really no need. As far as I can see it will be a five-minute max conversation. "Are you sure what you told me yesterday is right, Filip?" "Yes, I am sure, Laurie." That'll be about it. You're busy rehearsing for the tour so why waste your time?'

'I won't be able to concentrate on anything until we get this sorted out so I might as well come along.'

Back at home the mood is sombre, the holiday fun already forgotten. Helen gets a pen and sheet of paper and invites Laurie to sit next to her at the table.

'What for?'

'We should write down anything we can think of that might sort this out, however wild an idea.'

Laurie has used brainstorming at work countless times, in his opinion mostly without value, but he goes along with Helen's suggestion.

After five minutes of silence the sheet is still blank because there aren't even wild ideas to put down. Getting the clubhouse ready by the start of the summer season is not going to happen.

Abruptly Laurie grabs the pen and starts writing.

'You've got an idea! What is it?' Helen asks.

'Sorry, nothing. I'm drafting my resignation announcement.'

'Don't be silly; there's got to be a way out.'

'I feel awful. A week ago I was telling David everything was on schedule for us to leave the café.'

'Stop blaming yourself.'

'But it has happened while I'm in charge,' Laurie declares. 'I've not made much of a go of it, have I?'

'You couldn't have done anything differently. Anyway, when you quit so will I.'

'I can just imagine what fun the WhatsApp group will have when they hear the news. There'll be the nasty posters, we know who they are, and then the self-righteous ones like Dee who'll be saying that they knew all along that we lacked the experience to manage the project properly.'

'Yeah, brace yourself for an attack. Or better still, don't read anything.'

'I'll resign as soon as I've spoken to Filip. There's no point dragging it out.'

~

The next morning they are at the club early, ahead of meeting Filip, to see what's been done since they went away and what's left to do. At least there's progress, the outside is finished, the area around the clubhouse paved, and peering through the glass door they can see cables and pipes are being installed and some of the flooring is down.

'They've been working hard,' Helen remarks. 'The obvious thing is to get another builder in to do the finishing off.'

'Which is far easier said than done. We'd need someone with immediate capacity and we probably have to tender; I'm fairly sure that's written into our constitution. That'll take weeks which we don't have.'

'Got a better idea?'

'No, and sorry I was dismissive.'

Their discussion pauses because Filip has arrived early.

The three of them sit on a bench at the side of one of the courts.

'This is poor,' Filip begins. 'I leave a good job to come to Grayling which is a promotion with more money and then a week later he is gone.'

It hits Helen that the difficulties go beyond the tennis club: several men will be losing their jobs as a result of the company going bust. 'I'm sorry for you, this must be awful,' she tells Filip, who acknowledges her sympathy with a nod.

'Lucky I know many in building trade. I am a good worker so will for sure find something else.'

Helen visualises the sheet of blank paper on the table the previous evening. Maybe it didn't have to stay blank after all.

'Tell me, Filip, these other builders you know, are all of them currently working full time?' Helen asks.

'For sure not. Winter is quiet but soon things will pick up fast.'

'So there might be a few weeks when the people you know are looking for work?'

'Yes, I think yes. With my friends that is true.'

'OK. This clubhouse,' she continues. 'Did Mr Grayling give you all the details, things like the surveyors report and the architect's plans?'

'That man, Grayling, he tell me he wants nothing more to do with this work.' He looks across at Laurie. 'He does not like talking to you. So yes, he gives me everything to sort. I know even where I must order supplies for the best price.'

'And you've kept all this paperwork?'

'I only hear yesterday about end of work. No time to chuck them in the bin.'

'Don't.'

'Helen?' Laurie asks. 'What are you thinking?'

'I'm thinking,' Helen continues, looking at Filip rather than Laurie, 'that we could pay what Grayling paid you but you'd finish this job with us managing you rather than him.'

Filip's smile is broad.

'And I mean doing everything,' Helen continues. 'Employ the workmen, plan the schedule, get the supplies, meet deadlines. I suppose we'd pay you extra for that responsibility.'

'I have done projects with teams before. I can do this.'

'We will need to check with the committee,' Laurie tells Helen. 'Perhaps we should run it past a lawyer, too.'

'There's no time for that. What we'd like you to do, Filip, is to complete the building on time using the team you want. How does that sound?'

'It sounds yes.'

'As far as payment goes, we could do that on a weekly basis according to what's been done. Maybe we could meet each Friday afternoon to check on that and then set the schedule for the following week. And regarding suppliers, we'll pay them directly ourselves.'

'Could I have a word, Helen,' Laurie asks. 'In private.'

They move away from Filip.

'I'm assuming you haven't project managed the construction of a building before.'

'Correct.'

'It's a massive responsibility and there's loads you haven't considered. It's not like getting a builder to do a small job at home. We wouldn't have the expertise to ensure that he's complying with the specifications and regulations for a start. And what about legal liability? If there's an accident the club could get sued into extinction.'

'OK, there are things we don't know about so let's get the architect involved. They can join our weekly inspection meetings.'

'And the liability issue?'

'I don't know. Perhaps the architect will be able to help with that or maybe Filip has an idea. Anyway, let's not leave him sitting there.'

'Filip,' Helen begins when they are sitting down together, 'our plan still holds but we have some issues to cover. Laurie has mentioned the importance of understanding the architect's plans fully, like the specifications and the regulations.'

'I understand regulations, I have done work with architect plans. I can do all this.'

'OK, that's good, though we think it's a good idea to have the architect here when we meet.'

'No problem.'

'Our other worry is legal liability.'

'I have my own builder company. It is small, we do little jobs, but we still have to have insurance cover for many millions of pounds. I laugh about this.'

'Great that you've got it,' Laurie says. 'I think we should see a copy of your policy.'

'Also no problem.'

Helen accepts that Laurie is being sensible but he's in danger of sapping Filip's enthusiasm.

'On condition that your insurance is in order and we can get the architect on board, are you happy to go ahead? Or do you need some time to think about it?'

'Not time, no. To get finished there is no time, I need people to start today. My people are good workers, they can do it well, I know this.'

'Get going then!' Helen says.

'Mr Laurie, are you OK with this lady's plans?'

It's a good question, it doesn't take a clairvoyant to sense Laurie's hesitation. He's been taken aback by how quickly things have moved on but it could work. Paying Filip weekly according to what's been done minimises the risk; if the first week turns out to be a disaster they can simply terminate. It is feasible provided they can get the architect on board. 'Yes, I'm in agreement with this lady's plans,' Laurie says, looking across and smiling at Helen.

The three of them shake hands and Filip steps away to make phone calls.

'Surely you're at least slightly worried about the responsibility,' Laurie asks Helen.

'I'm terrified!'

'That's good to know.'

'The first thing I'll do is contact the architect to explain what's happened and our solution. I suppose we'll have to pay them for joining us at meetings but we do need them here. We have a contingency fund, don't we?'

'Yes,' Laurie says, 'and not paying directly to Grayling will boost funds.'

'Good. Give me his number and I'll make the call.'

'Actually the architect is female.'

Helen is dismayed by her presumption.

'But look Helen,' Laurie continues. 'How are we going to fit this in? You're up to your eyeballs with rehearsals and I'm working flat out.'

'Let me lead and I'll make it happen. As Filip said, "I can do this". Well, so can I.'

'What about your rehearsals though?'

'They start mid-morning so I can get here early each day to check on things and I can keep Friday afternoons free for our meetings. The tour isn't until after Easter, by which time the building will be completed. Easy!'

The plan does hinge on the architect's cooperation and Helen calls as soon as she gets the number from Laurie.

Caroline Cusack is brilliant. 'I've gone down to a four-day week and Fridays are my day off so that fits perfectly,' she tells Helen.

'But if it's your day off it doesn't fit.'

'I've been at a loose end since making the change. This will be great to fill some time.'

'Are you sure?'

'Positive.'

'And can I ask how much it will cost the club?'

'Nothing. The practice got enough of a fee first time round. Anyway, this will be in my own time and I've been searching for something to do to help the community. It's the perfect start.'

'It's all systems go,' she tells Laurie. 'We should let members know what's happening though.'

Laurie sends out an email and Helen posts on WhatsApp.

Helen

The original clubhouse builders have quit but we've got a great new team up and running in their place. We're on schedule to finish on time with a great project manager overseeing it – me! Seriously, although I am the club person who'll be keeping a check on things, there's a site manager and our architect has agreed to assist.

Players start seeing Helen at the club not in her usual tennis gear, but with an orange hard hat, a yellow visibility jacket and heavy boots. For now, the doubters and chauvinists keep quiet, but Helen knows that can change in the blink of an eye if anything goes wrong.

She inspects progress daily, perfectly at ease as she chats with Filip and his colleagues. Caroline, the architect, is dropping in more frequently than the initially agreed Friday afternoons to help Helen. She checks the adherence to the specifications and the quality of the work.

Laurie is engaged but in a backroom capacity, paying invoices and handing over the cash each week for Filip to pay the builders. He'd much prefer to make bank transfers but accepts Filip's reasoning.

'My men have no bank accounts so I need cash to pay them,' Filip had explained ahead of the first Friday.

'Everything is on schedule,' Laurie is able to report at the next committee meeting, 'in fact ahead of it.'

32

'I haven't seen much of Helen lately,' Keith tells Laurie. It is five-thirty and they are sitting in Keith's living room during one of Laurie's brief, regular visits after finishing work and before joining Helen.

There are six weeks to go until the Easter break.

'I told you, she's extremely busy what with rehearsals and looking after the clubhouse build. She sends her love.'

'It is a shame though because I want to tell her about my U3A courses.'

'You can tell me,' a marginally peeved Laurie suggests.

'I could do but I wanted to let Helen know which composers we're listening to.' One of the three courses Keith has signed up for is *The Great Romantic Composers*.

'Is she coming over?'

'Keith, I've just told you, she's too busy.'

'Literature isn't your thing, is it? Helen's interested in it; I imagine she's heard of Camus. I wonder what she makes of him.' Another of Keith's courses is *French Literature*.

'Have you made this?' Laurie asks, looking at the three-dimensional paper bird that's resting on the coffee table. It looks delicate so Laurie decides not to pick it up although he'd like to work out how it was folded. Keith's third course is *Introduction to Origami.*

'Yes, I did. Do you like it?'

'I think it's amazing.'

'Thank you. I hope Helen can come over tomorrow.' His stepfather has developed one hell of a soft spot for his girlfriend.

'Maybe she can although I think she's arranged a midweek meeting with the builder and the architect. Anyway, I have to go now.'

'I must make more of an effort to see him,' Helen says when Laurie reports back on his stepfather's infatuation. 'He must think I've abandoned him. And on the subject of seeing people, we need to set a date for you to meet my sisters.'

Her eldest sister Holly's nagging has been relentless.

'Saying you're busy doesn't hold, Helen,' Holly had complained during their telephone conversation earlier that afternoon. 'Before you were going out with Laurie you managed to fit in visits all the time. Don't you want us to meet him; don't you want to see our children?'

'Of course I do, but I've told you, the clubhouse rebuild plus rehearsals is taking up all my time.'

'I'm assuming you don't have weekend rehearsals and I'm also assuming that those builders of yours don't work then either. So a Saturday or Sunday visit must be possible.'

'We've got tennis matches most weekends.'

'On both days?'

'Usually yes, one of us is playing on a Saturday and the other on a Sunday. Look, I'll see if we can sort out a free day.'

'So,' she's telling Laurie when they're together that evening, 'how would you feel about meeting my sisters during a weekend?'

'I'm fine with that. You're the one with the impossible schedule. If you find a good day, I'll slot in.'

They check their diaries and pick a free Saturday. Holly is quick to confirm that the selected date works for everyone.

The next morning, ahead of rehearsals, Helen is back at the club with flapjacks for the workmen: she's often bringing them treats. She doesn't need a tour of the site every day, she can see that things are going well, but Filip is keen to point out what they've been doing. At the outset he was honest enough to tell her that he was unsure whether the clubhouse would be finished in time but that he would do everything possible to make it work. Increasingly he is confident it will be completed.

Helen is loving her hectic routine with a surge of energy to deal with the dual pressures of managing the build and rehearsals ahead of their prestigious live performances. And then there's the joy of being with Laurie; her sex drive has gone through the roof.

When she arrives at the rehearsal room the three musicians are in an animated huddle.

'What's up, guys?'

'Our album is out and the first reviews are stellar,' Bradley says. He hands her his iPad and she jumps from one review to the next, for now focusing on the headlines and the ratings.

'And I've spoken to our agent this morning,' Sardine says. 'Tour tickets are flying; some venues are already sold out.'

'And if they aren't yet, with reviews like this they soon will be,' Yvette adds.

'We'll be able to pay off our student debts,' Bradley says. Perhaps this is a joke, it's hard to tell with Bradley, but it is true that each of them has the burden of a hefty debt carrying a cruel interest charge. It would be a relief to clear at least some of it.

The practice is a disaster, they're too distracted to play. At each break Bradley checks for new reviews, ending up with the breaks lasting longer than the playing. Helen can't remember who is the one who suggests they abandon, but consensus is instant and they have lunch together in an upmarket restaurant.

The meal includes wine, quite a lot of wine, and she returns home a bit the worse for wear. It's her turn to cook tonight but she can't be bothered. Maybe they can get a takeaway.

There's a message from Laurie on her phone. It was sent mid-morning but she hasn't been checking notifications.

Don't bother cooking anything, I'll book a restaurant. Home around five-thirty.

Was Laurie telepathic, though it would have been a takeaway rather than a restaurant that she was set to propose? But a restaurant is a great idea because the wonderful reviews and high ticket sales are events to celebrate. It will be her treat.

She takes a shower, puts on a dress for a change, streams some Mendelssohn, makes a sobering double espresso and waits for Laurie.

His news had come through soon after arriving at work. He'd switched on his laptop and the email popped up: their grant application had been accepted. They'd been hoping, they'd been optimistic, but competition for grants is intense so nothing was certain – until now.

He hears cheering and joins the rest of the team gathered in his supervisor's office.

'Well, the man says, 'this is excellent news indeed. We can now begin planning how to take our research forward.'

'What, now? Today?' the youngest in the team asks, a young female graduate with a reputation for being a bit of a party animal.

'Yes now. We are here to work, that's what we're paid to do.'

'Well, I think we should have the day off to soak up our success.'

All eyes are on the supervisor whose behaviour has never been predictable. He could be a harsh critic one day and fun-lovingly flippant the next.

'Fair enough. I declare this an official celebration day.' The supervisor opens a filing cabinet and pulls out a bottle of scotch. Laurie collects paper cups from the water dispenser and they toast their achievement, the subsequent coughing suggesting that scotch is not the usual tipple for all but the supervisor.

Laurie is unsure who suggests abandoning the university's staff restaurant, but there is unanimous agreement and they end up at a rather exclusive restaurant close by. Any thought of a return to the university to work that afternoon is ditched: drinking fine wines and then constructing complex spreadsheets would be impossible.

Laurie sits in his office swishing down a couple of paracetamol with a strong latte to supress a hangover.

He texts Helen. *Don't bother cooking anything, I'll book a restaurant. Home around five-thirty.*

She is quick to reply; her rehearsal must be over. *Good idea, I've got things to celebrate. Tell you when you're here.*

Laurie leaves his bike at the university and takes a taxi to Helen's.

She can hear jangling as Laurie struggles to fit his key into the keyhole. 'I'm just a bit drunk,' he says as he greets her with a hug that is perhaps more of a collapse onto her for support. 'I've got some great news.'

'Me, too. And I'm as drunk as you.'

There are congratulatory kisses as each item of good news is announced. The kissing becomes more intense and one thing leads to another, specifically, clothes are removed. A meal at a restaurant is forgotten as they head for the bedroom, their love making paused mid-evening with the arrival of the takeaway.

33

How could everything have fallen apart so quickly?

Wednesday night had been bliss, both of them on a high with their respective news.

On the Thursday morning Laurie is the first to wake. With a mug of tea by his side, he sits in the kitchen streaming the news from several sources, this his usual start to a working day.

Helen joins him and they share an unhurried breakfast together before leaving for work. After the euphoria of the previous day it will be back to their regular routine, in the laboratory for Laurie, and after a quick visit to see Filip, at the rehearsal room for Helen. There's a kiss at the front door. Laurie watches her stride towards the club, the cello case strapped to her back.

Without turning round, she raises an arm and waves as if she can sense his gaze and is acknowledging it.

Laurie had left his bike at university the previous afternoon so he'll need to take a bus. The journey is quicker than anticipated and he arrives with half an hour to kill ahead of his first meeting. He makes his way to the staff café and orders a coffee.

He opens his phone and resumes catching up with the news. The internet is his source of information and commentary on world affairs: that's fine, of course. It's the random unsubstantiated comments at the end of the news articles that get to him, this along with gossipy social media posts. He doesn't have an Instagram account. He rarely posts on Facebook. He abandoned twitter when it was renamed. No way will he ever waste time by clicking into TikTok. He rarely looks at threads on the tennis club's WhatsApp group, leaving it to Helen to alert him if anything of concern crops up.

On his way out of the café, purely by chance, he catches sight of the headline in a Metro that someone has left lying around. Metro is the free daily London newspaper, a tabloid with little journalistic merit, crammed full of ads. Under the title *Kilroy killjoys* he spots a photo of Oliver and Stephanie, probably an AI generated one because they're facing away from each other with the backdrop of an empty courtroom, their countenances furious. He picks up the paper and reads about the two prominent lawyers who are in court charged with drink-driving offences. They'd crashed into each other and they're husband and wife.

There is a rack with daily newspapers by the café entrance. Laurie takes all of them out. The tabloids are having a field day and even the broadsheets are featuring the story. By all accounts a vicious slanging match followed the accident, witnessed by an army of bystanders who are now prepared to tell their story.

Is this really news, Laurie is thinking as he reads on? He could be delighted that the pair are having a hard time but he finds himself feeling sorry for them.

He replaces the newspapers tidily and makes his way to his office at the side of one of the labs.

When he logs on there's an email from Dee waiting for him.

Laurie, I'm emailing you because I know you don't use WhatsApp much. However, as chair you have a duty to see what is being written. The comments directed at Oliver and Stephanie are unacceptable and you must intervene. Best wishes, Dee.

'Give me five minutes,' he tells the three team members standing by his door ready for their meeting.

Dee is right, the club's WhatsApp group is buzzing and the comments are unacceptable. A disgrace.

Jimmy
Here we go again, our ex-chair (not allowed to say chairman) showing himself up.

Gus
He's a sitting duck!

Jimmy
Don't get what you're on about.

Gus
Chair? Sitting?

Jimmy
Still don't get it.

Brian
More to the point, the corrupt establishment will close ranks and those f**kers will get off lightly.

Tony
I was wondering how long we'd have to wait for you to go on about unfair class bias, you commie c**t.

Brian
Better than being a racist c**t.

Dee
We do not want such abusive language in this group.

Brian
Who says? Anyway, we're only having fun aren't we Tony.

Abi
I think this whole being in court thing is such a laugh. It serves the f**kers right.

Frank
This will ruin their reputation in the judicery.

Ursula

It's judiciary, Frank.

Douglas
Excuse me for stepping in. You might have heard that Zadie is leaving the club and I'm looking for a replacement to play the remaining Mixed C Team matches. Contact me directly if interested.

The comments are still rolling in but Laurie has seen enough. Why does social media bring out the worst in people – and it's usually men?

Laurie
I want this thread to end now please. This is the official club group and not a forum for nastiness.

Dee
Agreed. Well done for making the point Laurie.

Jimmy
What's it got to do with you, you're always interfering?

Laurie receives an email from Dee insisting that the offensive miscreants are removed from the group. She names Jimmy as the first to be struck off.

Laurie's team are back outside the office. 'Sorry, another five please, guys.'

Laurie

Enough personal stuff, please take note of my previous request.

He hates being involved in this meaningless exchange but the attacks on Stephanie, Oliver and now Dee are continuing.

Laurie
This is no longer a polite request. Further vicious posts risk disqualification from our WhatsApp group.

The usual suspects are ignoring what Laurie had hoped would be his final warning.

Laurie
I will not tolerate this. Remember that our juniors can access this site. Continued rudeness and I'll be terminating club memberships.

The wave of antagonistic posts comes to an end, though it's likely that Oliver and Stephanie's posts rather than Laurie's threat is the reason.

Oliver
There is no need for any further slanderous gossip. Since I am no longer made to feel welcome at this club, I hereby resign my membership.

Stephanie
No need to feel sorry for Ollie who is again being economical with the truth. He's leaving because he's

moving to Mayfair to live with a new girlfriend. The poor woman. But yes, the personal attacks on me have hurt so I, too, am resigning my membership.

Laurie fills Helen in with the details that evening. She has no idea what's been going on, being too preoccupied with rehearsals to follow up on WhatsApp notifications. She skim reads the group's thread before googling to glance at some newspaper headlines about the court case.

'You know what,' she says, 'the Kilroys quitting is the best possible outcome.'

'Are you ready to go?' Laurie asks. Having abandoned the idea of eating out the night before they've booked an upmarket restaurant to celebrate their successes at work.

'Give me a minute, I'm nearly done with Instagram.'

Laurie sees red, inexplicably so. Yes, he's wasted hours during the day dealing with valueless and vicious social media, but even so, this doesn't explain his wave of anger. His sigh is weary and drawn out. 'Honestly, I don't see what you get from all of this.'

'I'm letting fans know that performance tickets are running out fast.'

'Isn't there a better way to do that?'

'No, there isn't.'

'Well there should be. Something that bypasses the social media nastiness that's out there.'

'Instagram isn't too bad, but yes, it can be nasty, even a harmless post to promote a concert. I'm told how ugly I am or how sexy I am, I've been sent photos of dicks, today someone suggested that playing cello with my legs spread apart must be fun and could I post a pic with me naked!'

'Exactly. Doesn't that make you feel sick?'

'If I let it, but Yvette and I try to laugh it off. I don't want to sound dismissive though because I'm not; it's appalling. Thankfully, the disgusting comments are more than outweighed by the nice ones. I know you hate it all and I can appreciate why.'

'At work it's been a nightmare, as damaging as any personal attack. When we announced the news of our grant within minutes there were comments about bias and bribes. Apparently we're controlled by a cabal, we're interfering with God's work, we're AI creations rather than real people. Those wild conspiracy theories go viral; it's disgraceful.'

Helen has never seen Laurie so worked up. She takes hold of his hand. 'It's OK Laurie. Sensible people, the ones who matter, believe you.'

He continues his outpouring. 'Something that we've proved beyond doubt is called fake news, the easiest two words to use when you don't like it. What some dickhead is discrediting could well have followed decades of rigorous scientific progress, but call it fake news and suddenly everyone's a world expert and it *is* fake news.'

'But I'm agreeing with you. It's appalling.'

'Have I told you that the science faculty at university has to spend tens of thousands for a team to monitor social media and step in to discredit the morons? What a waste of resource.'

'Laurie, please calm down. Let's go to the restaurant, I'm starving.'

'I am calm but one more thing – what's going on is deadly serious. Social media is threatening humankind.'

'That's dramatic.'

'Is it? Elections are already being twisted through social media campaigns and there are conspiracy theories about everything. I mean it Helen, if it isn't controlled soon, social media will bring an end to civilisation as we know it. Why would anyone ever want to bring children into this world?'

No children? The conversation has taken a dramatic turn and Helen is shocked into silence. She does want children. She wants to get excited as they grow up. She wants the joy of listening to a first concert with her child performing on piano or flute or violin or clarinet or even cello. She wants the joy of her child beating her for the first time on the tennis court. Of course, it hasn't been a topic for discussion with Laurie – they've only been going out for a few months – but now that she's thinking about it, this child that she's envisioning is a boy, a boy the spitting image of Laurie.

Laurie softens his categorical declaration. 'Children, no children. It's not a big deal.'

'But it is. Wanting children or not is a pretty fundamental question. A binary choice, isn't that what you scientists call it? There's no middle way, no scope for a compromise.'

'The thing is –'

Helen realises that she is still holding Laurie's hand. She lets go and stands up. 'I definitely do want children.'

'Let's just drop it, Helen.'

'I'm not sure I can. I'm going home now.'

'But we've booked the restaurant.'

'That's not the key issue here!'

As soon as she steps out of Laurie's flat she's in floods of tears. Their relationship is new and decisions about children are miles away, but she feels somehow deceived.

Texts from Laurie are pinging across but she isn't going to read them.

34

Laurie sits in his living room at a loss about what to do. He waits for a while, half-expecting to hear the key in the lock and a shout of "Hi, I'm back." Or maybe a call or a text with, *I'll meet you at the restaurant.*

Fifteen minutes pass. Half an hour. There isn't going to be a return or a call or a text.

The obvious first need is to cancel the restaurant booking which he does online, aware as he types that this should have been way down his list of priorities. The most important thing is to speak to Helen.

He calls. He texts. She isn't responding.

Yes, she was angry, upset too, but how had a perfectly ordinary conversation about the negative impact of social media brought that on? The trigger seemed to be when he'd questioned bringing children into such a world, a casual remark with no pre-thought. Having children might be nice or it might not be.

The fundamental issue, the misuse of social media, was true enough. It had reached a crisis point that afternoon at work. His team had received death threats, sent to their personal email addresses. *We know where you live so there's no peaceful sleep for you anymore.* One female colleague, already dealing with a daughter refusing to go to school because of online bullying, was particularly distraught. All this when his university department's mission was to improve the quality of healthcare worldwide.

If he had told Helen specifically about the threat, might she have understood his comments about social media, humanity and children?

Since she wasn't replying to messages should he go round to apologise? If she let him in, and that was a big if, and she asked whether he meant what he'd said about never wanting kids, he'd have to say he didn't know. That was hardly going to solve matters. Perhaps the best thing was to let the dust settle overnight. Helen joked about how he was always putting problems to the side with the expectation that things would sort themselves out, and that that usually was the case. Soon she'd realise that his comment had been offhand and she'd make contact. Or was that the strategy of a coward?

~

Helen's anger and dismay do not subside during another one of her sleepless nights. She wants children, he doesn't, so that's it for their relationship because there can be no room for compromise. She reflects on losing the man she loves and having to return to the dating sites junkyard. She really doesn't want this. She doesn't want to end it with Laurie.

No way is she going to make contact though, that's up to him, and sending texts and leaving voicemails are not good enough.

She has little enthusiasm to visit the tennis club to see how Filip is getting on; she feels like ditching involvement, but without her input they'd be struggling. Laurie or not, she can't let the club down so she does go. There are under five weeks remaining to complete the building and she comes away from the meeting confident.

Laurie's stepfather calls late that evening.

'Hello Keith.'

'Laurie's told me what happened. He's desperately upset and I know you well enough to believe you are too.'

'Do you know the reason?'

'I do.'

'It's pretty fundamental.'

'It is, but you need to consider whether Laurie meant what he said.'

'I see him as someone who's always careful with words, in fact obsessed with accuracy. He never says anything without thinking it through.'

'In his rational world yes, but not in his emotional one. He's hopeless at dealing with emotions, has been all the time I've known him. I think you're changing that for him but he's not there yet.'

'Maybe, but …'

'So the trick is to give him time to process anything about feelings.'

'But wanting children is a basic yes or no. I wish it had never come up because we're a million miles from thinking about having a family together. This whole thing is mad.'

'I can tell you that as far as kids go he's never given it a thought. It's a maybe, definitely not a no.'

'What are you suggesting I do then? Tell him it's all fine and we can sort out kids later.'

'Exactly that – assuming you still want to be in a relationship with him.'

She does.

'Helen,' Keith continues. 'You know all that "You're the only one for me" tosh. I'm not sure I believe it but I will say that you two together is something special. Don't lose it. Laurie is desperate to speak with you but you haven't been answering his calls. Will you do that if he tries again tonight?'

'Shouldn't he be banging on my door?'

'He'd like to but thinks you'll turn him away.'

'He's probably right.'

'Courage is not his strongest point when dealing with such matters.'

'OK, tell him I will speak.'

'A wise choice.'

'And thank you, Keith,' Helen says despite wondering whether she has been duped into making contact when it's Laurie who should be working out what to do. She's crying. Angrily, she brushes away the tears as her phone rings.

She presses the green telephone icon below the photo of a smiling Laurie and takes a deep breath.

'Helen, it's me. Laurie.'

This redundant first statement makes her smile: it's so Laurie! She's looking at the photo of him on her screen, there's the recognisable voice, Keith has just said he'd be calling, and yet he sees the need to announce who it is.

'I'm sorry. I hate this. I wasn't thinking straight, I wasn't thinking at all. I'd had an awful day and well, OK, maybe nominally there was a reason for saying what I said but it doesn't indicate that I meant it because I don't, in fact I've never really given much thought to whether –'

'Stop! Slow down will you, you're gabbling.'

'The thing is, I miss you.'

'That's a good starting point.'

'Stuff is going on at work that's doing my head in.'

'Then share it, Laurie. If you'd done that then we might not be where we are now.' As she speaks she realises that a man being open about confronting a difficulty had never been evident in her past relationships.

'I want to see you. Please can I come over tonight?'

She knows they will be back together but can't quite reach telling him so during this conversation. 'No. Let's leave it until tomorrow and see what's what then, shall we? I'll call you.'

She misses him. They've spent nearly every night together since the relationship started, nights curled up against each other, the passion, the ecstasy. Life is too short and all that stuff.

312

She walks over to Laurie's flat, climbs into bed with him and wraps herself round his warm body.

~

Helen decides to put aside any conversation about children; it's not as if they would be thinking of starting a family in the near future. They are happy together, that's what matters.

On their way to visit her sister, while Laurie is listening to some current affairs comedy on the radio, she is reflecting on how well things are working out. Top of the list is being back to how it was with Laurie, then there's the exciting build up to the tour, plus the challenge of project managing the clubhouse rebuild. There's something else though, something intangible. When she's on a bus on her way to rehearsals and hears people nattering and laughing; when she's in a café and sees a couple smiling as they hold hands; when she watches a jogger's determination in a London park, these everyday occurrences for ordinary people are helping to make her happy.

'You know what,' she tells Laurie, having turned down the volume as his programme comes to an end. 'The world is a wonderful place because of the commonplace things that people say and do.'

'Where did that come from?'

'I was just thinking. I can understand you loathing the state of the world including some of the stuff on the internet, but away from that there's so much love and happiness. And we all need to do everything we can to keep it that way.'

He looks across and smiles. She's crying. 'Helen?'

Her emotions have got the better of her for no obvious reason. Maybe there is a reason though, the fear that a small number of sick bastards out there are intent on ruining the lives of ordinary people. 'It's OK, Laurie, I'm fine. More than that, I'm so lucky.'

Poor Laurie, he does struggle to deal with feelings because he's moved on to a completely different topic. 'What made your parents chose four girls' names beginning with H?'

Having travelled across London from north to south, they have stopped outside a large house in a location once considered a poor neighbourhood but now decidedly affluent. Laurie has been told that Holly works in marketing, her husband Martin does something in the City, they have three children and a cat called Wallpaper.

'I did ask once but my mother's answer was along the lines of why not.'

Hazel, a couple of years younger than Helen, lives with her partner nearby her parents in Surrey. She's at the late stage of pregnancy for her second child. Heidi, the youngest by several years, lives in Brighton and has recently got engaged. Heidi and Hazel will be popping in during the afternoon; Helen and Laurie have been invited to lunch.

After introductions, Helen joins Holly in the kitchen and Laurie remains with Martin, who is tasked with looking after the children.

Holly comes rushing into the living room. 'Martin, a disaster. I know I've got chilli flakes somewhere but I can't find them. Would you pop out and get me some, please.' She turns to face Laurie. 'Can you sit with Bennie for a few minutes? He won't be a problem if we put on Octonauts. Sandy's doing something upstairs and Dawn is still asleep, so it's only him.'

'Sure,' says Laurie as four-year old Bennie takes hold of two remotes and manages to switch on the TV and find the right channel.

Laurie thinks he should be reading a story or playing Duplo rather than have the child fixated on a TV screen. Another failure of modern society.

Bennie climbs onto the couch and snuggles against Laurie. 'Ready?' he asks as if he's the grown up and Laurie the child. Laurie nods and Bennie presses the remote. 'That one,' Bennie continues. *'Aunt Killygasro.'*

Laurie smiles. 'OK, *Mount Kilimanjaro* it is.'

The cartoon characters look odd but Laurie is surprised that the science included in the story as the team undertake an expedition on the volcano is impressive, using simple language to get across complex ideas about microclimates.

When the team reach the subzero zone at the top of the mountain, Bennie cries out. 'Oh no, Kwazii too high too quick. Help him.'

One of the characters is suffering from altitude sickness and this four-year old is learning about the danger of gaining altitude too rapidly without acclimatising.

Bennie's sister Sandy is standing by the door as the expedition reaches the summit of the mountain. Clouds of gas are pouring from vents.

'They're fumaroles,' Sandy says.

'How do you know that?' Laurie asks ahead of one of the characters naming them.

'I already knew. We've done volcanoes at school.'

As Bennie continues watching, Sandy tells Laurie about magma, lava flows and volcanic ash. He's impressed by the ten-year old's grasp and she's the one digging deeper than her parents into the exact nature of Laurie's work when they're sitting together at lunch.

'I love science,' Sandy says. 'I'm going to be a scientist – just like Laurie.' She monopolises him for the rest of the visit, deflecting the probing by Heidi and Hazel later that afternoon.

'Well, that's my family,' Helen says as they head home.

'They're all great. Sandy's a star and Bennie is hilarious.'

Helen notes, of course she does, that he's mentioned the children first. She wants to let him know that he was a huge hit with Holly's kids, in fact the whole family loved him.

She won't say this, of course, because there's no need. As Keith had pointed out during their chat after the argument, Laurie processes events like this in his own time and in his own way. She places a hand on his thigh and squeezes. He takes hold of it and returns it to the steering wheel.

There was no hidden agenda for the visit but it was clear that Laurie had bonded with the children and enjoyed his time with them.

So, maybe ...?

35

'Can we stop at the club for a minute? I want to double check the list of jobs for next week,' Helen asks as they approach Muswell Hill. 'Filip said he'd leave a note inside the building.'

There are four weeks to go until Easter.

'We could grab some kit first and have a hit while we're there.'

'Great idea. I need to burn off some of that lunch and tea.'

They stop at both flats to get changed and collect their rackets.

The club is deserted and they realise why when they read a note on the clubhouse door: the electricity supply is disconnected so the floodlights are out of use.

Helen unlocks the building, now firmly secured to safeguard the equipment and supplies stored inside. She accesses the flashlight on her phone and is delighted to note that the kitchenette units are installed and the bar area is under construction.

They must have been in today to get this finished. Working on a Saturday: brilliant,' Helen declares.

'Yes, you are!'

'Let's play tomorrow,' Helen says, using the club app to reserve a court. 'Done, eleven o'clock so we don't have to rush in the morning.'

Seventeen hours later and Helen has beaten Laurie decisively. This is a first and it's not because he's eased up while playing her. He never does that and he's a bad loser.

'You only won because I'm shattered. I hardly slept last night,' he says.

'Hang on, I was in bed with you. I'm just as shattered.'

'I don't think so. I was still awake when you were definitely asleep.'

'It is OK to lose, Laurie.'

He frowns. 'Come on, let's go.'

They're stopped in their tracks by Jennifer who is at the club to play the final Mixed C Team winter league match.

'All set?' Helen asks her.

'You bet. My new tactic when playing with Douglas will be a winner.'

'What is it?'

'I've told him that if there's a single word of criticism I'll be walking off the court.'

'Would you do that?'

'No, but he won't risk it. Hey, project manager, the clubhouse is coming along swell.'

'I'm happy with it,' Helen says. Over the past couple of weeks comments about lack of progress have been replaced by compliments.

'Actually, I was gonna catch up with you guys after the match to invite you over for dinner next Friday. Gareth and I have something to celebrate.'

'Is it …?'

'No, I don't think it's what you're thinking. You'll find out. Better go, he's here. 'Hi, Douglas.' Jennifer turns back. 'Is Friday OK though?'

'Yes, lovely thanks.'

'A dinner party; just like grown-ups!' Helen jokes when Jennifer has left them. 'It's because we're now in the couples category.'

'We did get an invite to the Kilroys.'

'That was different, for scheming rather than genuine. If you've got over losing you can come back with me for lunch.'

'I accept. Then later this afternoon I suppose a final check on our nightmare team's tea at the café.'

'Why bother? Ying and Zadie are sorted.'

'Did you know that Dee is the one partnering Andras. I almost feel sorry for him.'

'Shit, I didn't. That will be fun! I won't be joining you though.'

When Laurie arrives at Dream Café late afternoon the atmosphere seems fine with friendly chatting.

'Good game?' he asks nobody in particular.

'We lost,' Douglas says, 'but it's OK to lose when it's a great match. Jennifer played well.'

Laurie looks across at her. She's heard Douglas's praise and is grinning.

Laurie sticks around for tea, it will be one of the last opportunities to enjoy club-funded cakes at the café. He takes hold of a small square of pastry topped with custard and raspberries and watches Dee carry the teapot over to the counter for a refill.

'She's a battleaxe,' Andras whispers to Laurie, 'and she can't play tennis. I won't partner her again.'

'You won't have to; everything changes for the summer league matches.'

'Maybe so, but today was a waste of a good afternoon,' Andras says before getting up and crossing paths with Dee on his way to the toilets. They don't make eye contact.

'What an arrogant man he is,' Dee whispers to Laurie. 'I'm doing the club a favour this afternoon but I won't be playing with him again. Most unpleasant.'

'Should we kick him out of the club.'

'No, I don't think … are you making fun of me, Laurie?'

'A gentle tease, but anyway, it all changes for the summer matches.'

'I don't appreciate your humour.'

Andras has returned and the conversation is congenial with Andras and Dee participating as if they are the best of friends.

'I'll be off,' Laurie says, happy to leave them to it.

He thanks Bridget on the way out.

~

It's a short walk from Helen's flat to the dinner party venue. In affluent Muswell Hill houses range from rather nice to out of this world. Jennifer place, set in another of those tree-lined streets where

Victorian villas have been constructed with quirky beauty, fits into the latter category.

They ring the intercom to gain admission to the lobby and ascend a sweeping staircase to Jennifer's top floor apartment.

When Gareth greets them they can hear voices coming from the room to their right. This is where they are led. Jennifer springs up and introduces them to Kelly and Darren, a couple they've seen around but have never spoken to.

'And this is Lily,' Daren says. Cradled in his arms is a toddler with straw-coloured hair and a podgy face. 'She should be fast asleep by now but Lily makes her own mind up about that.'

Darren places the child onto the rug. 'She won't stay there for long; she's started crawling,' he says. As if on cue off she goes, heading straight for Laurie who crouches and hands her one of the soft toys scattered across the room. She starts a nonsense conversation which Laurie tries to replicate. Lily's parents are smiling and Helen is inwardly elated.

'Enough,' Darren says as he takes hold of Lily. 'Bedtime.' There is success this time round; he returns ten or so minutes later to announce that Lily is fast asleep in the spare bedroom.

Darren is quite some character and before long everyone is laughing at his seemingly endless collection of tales about being a security alarm fitter.

'So there I am in what you'd call a mansion and this woman is shouting, "Darren, could you come up and help me decide where to put the sensors?" (He's imitating a posh, whiny female voice). I tell her I'll do that after I've got downstairs sorted. You see, I have to do it that way to run the circuit properly, but she's insisting. "Only for a minute." Well, you know what they say, the customer is always right, so up I go. "In here," she says so I'm in her bedroom and she's on the bed, stark bloody naked. So I says –'

'Darren, I really don't think anyone wants to hear more,' Kelly interrupts.

'Can I just add that nothing happened. Kelly knows I never would.'

'Can I just add,' Kelly says, replicating her husband's tone, 'that the story is mere fantasy.'

'And can I just add, fantasy or not, thank you Darren because I haven't laughed so much for ages,' Helen says.

'And can I just add,' Jennifer begins, 'that Gareth and I have something to celebrate and we want to share it with you. It's about this place.'

'Just a minute.' Gareth leaves the room, returning with a bottle of champagne and six glasses.

'This apartment has come on the market and we're buying it.' Jennifer's announcement is met by the pop of the cork. 'We didn't think we had a chance when we put in an offer but the landlord wanted a quick sale. And so ...'

Helen is dying to know what they paid for it, but of course won't ask. Laurie is estimating the cost. Probably over a million, over a million for a top floor flat.

'We're so lucky,' Jennifer continues as if she's picked up Helen and Laurie's thoughts. 'Money's gonna be tight but my job at the hotel is going great –'

'And for some reason they're promoting me to Head of Science at school,' Gareth adds.

'Brilliant,' Darren says. 'I did notice the place isn't alarmed. Maybe –'

'You just wanna see me naked in the bedroom, don't ya, Darren!'

This, Laurie and Helen's second dinner party together, is as far removed as can be from the one at the Kilroys.

'That was a great night,' Laurie says on their way back to Helen's flat. 'Darren is so funny and I love the way Kelly teases him and he plays up to it. He's great with Lily.'

'I thought that, too. But Jeez, Jennifer must be doing well at the hotel to be able to afford that place.'

'When you're famous with your music we'll be able to live somewhere like that.'

'We? What makes you think I'd want you in my château?'

'Oh, it's in France, is it? Seriously though, tonight has made me think about what our lives might be like.'

Helen stops. What exactly is Laurie referring to? Moving in together? Marriage? Owning a property? Children!

'Yeah,' is all she can think of saying.

They walk on.

'How long do you think it takes before you know someone well enough to be sure they're the one you want to marry?' Laurie asks.

'Are you asking me to marry you?'

'No, of course not. It's a hypothetical question.'

'Good, because I don't know the answer.'

36

It's the first night of the tour. Helen's quartet are playing at Wigmore Hall to a full house which is hardly surprising given the rave reviews for their first album.

Keith has been in seventh heaven since Laurie arrived earlier that evening. He'd insisted they leave home ridiculously early in case of heavy traffic.

'But we're taking the train,' Laurie reminded him.

'Even so, let's get going.'

On the Underground into Central London, Keith provides detailed information about the pieces to be performed. Apparently Debussy's *String Quartet in G Minor* and Schubert's *D Minor Death of a Maiden* are brave choices, extremely difficult to play. Laurie makes a point of remembering the titles and composers but the rest of what Keith says goes in one ear and out the other.

They are the first to enter the auditorium.

'I'm glad we're here ahead of the crowd,' he tells Laurie. 'We can admire the cupola in peace.'

'The what?'

Keith points to the painted dome above the stage and proceeds to explain the symbolism of every ray of light, tangled thorn and naked or semi-naked individual depicted on it. He pauses his instruction when Helen's family arrive, hugging them as if they are long lost friends. They have front row seats and join the rapturous applause as the four musicians take to the stage. Laurie knows in advance that the musicians intend to dress to shock, discarding the conventional black tie and black gown dress code. There are a few gasps and murmurings around them as the group prepare to play.

'We want to make a statement,' Helen had told Laurie as she held up a short orange sequined dress when they were in her flat one morning. 'We want to be sassy and sexy.'

She had jumped out of bed and was slipping the dress over her naked body.

'What do you reckon?'

'Want to come back into bed?'

'No, seriously?'

'You will wear underwear on the night?' he joked.

'I'll think about it.'

Now, seeing her up on stage, he can't dismiss the image of Helen in that dress without underwear. It's very short, shorter than he remembers, with a side slit running up to near the top of her thigh. Yvette's lookalike dress is yellow and the two men are clownlike in their baggy yellow trousers and orange shirts.

He looks across at Keith to gauge his reaction, but the music has started and he's nodding to the beat, his mouth agape and his eyes shut.

Laurie's attention returns to the stage. He watches as Helen's right arm sways back and forth, the fingers of her left hand racing up and down the fretboard. He appreciates that what he's hearing is an incredible feat and is trying to take in the music, but he's struggling to concentrate. To him it's jumbled and unmemorable.

'Don't worry,' she had told him one late afternoon during an at-home practice after he admitted to his struggle. 'There's no rush. It will grow on you over time.'

For the sake of their relationship he will delve into the mysteries of classical music, he will learn to enjoy it, but for the moment he feels out of his depth as he glances up to the cupola steeped in its Greek mythology, and then across to an audience that seems universally enraptured by the performance.

Finally, he joins the tumultuous applause as the concert comes to an end, his thoughts divided between pride for Helen and relief that it's over.

The four musicians come to the front of the stage and bow, and again Laurie is remembering the morning when Helen tried on the dress without underwear. God, what a shallow pleb I am, he thinks.

'Magnificent,' Keith says and Laurie snaps out of his reverie.

There is a reception in a smallish room behind the stage, with the quartet joined by a select group of friends and family. Helen and the other musicians circulate amongst those identifying themselves as reviewers or journalists. Drinks and canapés are served.

Finally, with numbers dwindling, Helen is by his side.

'What do you reckon?' she asks.

There's no time to answer because Keith has stepped in front of him to lavish praise.

~

With further concerts at Wigmore Hall over the next two evenings, this opening night reception is a sedate affair with an early end. There will be two performances at The Barbican before the UK tour outside of London starts, two hectic weeks with the first stop a concert at Bath Assembly Hall.

Helen will be away for most of that time with Laurie taking over the management of the clubhouse. There are less than three weeks to go before Easter but his job will be straightforward because Filip and his team are ahead of schedule and little more than snagging is left to do. A date for the official opening has been set and Helen will be back for that.

On their final morning together before Helen sets off to Bath, she presents Laurie with a reminder of his tasks.

'Oh, and you won't forget to water my plants, will you?'

'Nope, it's on my list.'

'And dustbins go out on Tuesday evenings.'

'Yep, got that.'

'And you're sure you're OK with Filip?'

'Helen. Chill. There's hardly anything left to do and I'll still be checking every morning.'

'I know, I know. I think I'm a bit nervous about the tour.'

'What's to worry about? You've had five brilliant nights in London; the reviews have been amazing. It's just a case of a repeat performance.'

'It isn't as simple as that though, is it? If you play a great game of tennis one day it doesn't mean you'll be equally brilliant the next day.'

'No, true enough.'

Finally, Sardine arrives in the hired minibus and Helen seems bursting with excitement and confidence as she leaves. Laurie knows she will be fine and when he googles reviews each morning his belief is confirmed.

A refreshing take on these well-worn works.

These youngsters have a bright future.

Dazzling – the performers and their music.

His morning visits to the club to see Filip are short and straightforward though he senses the man and his team's disappointment that it's him rather than Helen meeting them.

Helen's absence will give him more time to spend with Keith. His stepfather is a changed man since those dire, depressing days of only a few months ago. A short while after Helen's departure, Keith surprises Laurie by asking if he would take him to Worthing for a short stay with his sister. Laurie is happy to oblige and uses Helen's car to bring him there and back.

Keith is quiet on the way back to London.

'Is everything alright?' Laurie asks.

'Yes, fine. It was a good visit.'

Laurie talks about the brilliant reviews Helen's group are receiving; Keith remains subdued.

'Are you sure you're OK?' he asks as they approach Muswell Hill. 'Shall I stay on a bit and cook dinner for us?'

'That would be good because there's something I'd like to talk through with you.'

That something is one hell of a surprise. 'I'm going to move to Worthing so that I can be near Maggie,' Keith announces.

It soon becomes clear that this is more than a tentative plan for some stage in the future. Keith has been plotting while in Worthing. An estate agent is visiting later in the week to value the London home before putting it on the market and his offer for a flat in a new complex close to Maggie has been accepted.

'I might need some help from you, Laurie. Getting a solicitor and a removals company and the like. Will you do that?'

'I can, but could we take one step back? Are you sure about this?'

'Yes, certain. The easy option in life is to keep everything as it is, even when the right thing to do is staring you in the face. This is the right thing and at my age there isn't much time to deliberate about it, is there?'

'No, there isn't, Keith. I think you're amazing. Give us a hug.'

Hugging has never come naturally to Laurie and as they embrace he's wondering whether he has ever hugged Keith before. Perhaps he did after his mother died; he can't remember.

The men pull apart and there are tears in Keith's eyes. 'What a softie I am,' he says as he brushes his face dry with the arm of his cardigan. 'I'll tell you something, I'm looking forward to being with Maggie and by the sea but I won't half miss seeing you two. You saved me you know, you and that wonderful girl of yours.'

'You haven't got rid of us. We'll be down to visit.'

Of course there will be visits, but as they look at each other with affection both know that there won't be many of them.

Later that evening, during their regular WhatsApp video call, Laurie tells Helen about Keith's plans.

'I'm flabbergasted that he's got things done so quickly. I looked up the details of his flat in Worthing and it's lovely.'

'Send me the link.'

'Will do. He's going to have plenty left over once he's sold his flat so there won't be any financial worries.'

'I think he's made a good decision. I'm happy for him and we'll have an excuse to go to the seaside.'

'Did tonight go well?'

'Yes, but I'm absolutely shattered. I've had enough; I'm glad the tour's almost over.'

'You've got me to look forward to!'

'Exactly. Hey, changing the subject, are we free on the Saturday evening after I get back?'

'That's the evening before the clubhouse opening.'

'I know. It's not brilliant timing but there's no choice.'

'Yeah, it's free. You'll only have just got back so I haven't planned anything. I reckoned you'd want to unwind.'

'That'll have to wait. I've got something nice for us to do.'

~

The final days until the end of the tour drag on as Laurie waits for her return. He's expecting to see an exhausted Helen desperate to relax, but she arrives buzzing with excitement, looking great and full of energy.

'Here, take this,' she says, handing him a well-worn envelope. 'Go on, open it.'

Inside are two tickets to see Closed at the iconic Koko venue in Camden.

'They're one of my all-time favourite bands. How did you know that?'

'You have mentioned it once – or twice or a million times – and I've seen their albums in the box where you keep your old CDs.'

'But how have you managed to get tickets? When they announced that this was absolutely their last reunion tour, every venue sold out on the first day.'

'They always hold a few tickets back for special guests.'

'Very funny. I'm hardly a special guest.'

'Not you. Me. Google their album from three years ago, the *Double Standards* one.'

Laurie takes out his phone and searches. 'OK, found it. Now what?'

'Look at the backing musicians.'

'YOU! It's you.' True enough, on a couple of tracks Helen Critchley on cello is listed. 'You never told me.'

'The secret life of a classical musician. After college I took on all sorts of session work before the quartet. And I'll be doing more of the same unless we get hugely successful.'

Laurie is schoolboy excited on the bus during the short journey between home and the venue. They join the noisy and rowdy queue to get in. The waiting crowd are singing Closed anthems.

'Aren't you going to join in?' Helen teases. 'And why haven't you got the tee-shirt,' she adds, looking at the unofficial uniform worn by the fans.

'Can we queue jump?' Laurie asks.

'I'm important, but not that important.'

There's a roar as the band appear on stage. As they play, Helen is watching Laurie as much as the band: he's in la-la land. She loves him and she can see that whenever girls are becoming women, boys are still boys for quite a while longer before becoming men.

Closed perform one of the tracks she played on, her part now covered by a synthesiser. It's not nearly as good but it would have cost a fortune to have a string section up there with them.

Laurie's treat continues because Helen has got passes for the post-concert party. It's already rowdy by the time they arrive, the noise deafening with vast volumes of alcohol and who knows what else being consumed to the beat of loud music. There are no canapés here, no triangles of toast with mushroom pâté or puff pastries filled with blue cheese like at the Wigmore Hall reception. It's different and that's great, Helen is thinking.

Laurie meets his heroes and is lost for words as an amused Helen looks on.

'I really like your music,' he manages to utter like an awestruck teenager.

Helen laughs as the ageing rock guitarist turns to face her. 'She's a cool chick, this one.'

'I know.'

She's laughing all the way back to his flat because Laurie can't stop talking about the experience, reminiscing about favourite tracks. 'Mind you,' he concludes, 'I'm glad tonight was their final gig. I think you reach an age when it's probably sensible to stop.'

'I intend to carry on playing until I'm a hundred!'

'Yeah, but you're not rock and roll.'

37

The clubhouse is looking great. Caroline's design is both functional and attractive with its wooden floors, bifold doors overlooking the courts, cosy lounge area and sleek bar.

A good-sized audience has gathered to celebrate the opening. Some are in kit having played social tennis, others have come to get a first look at the new facility.

With unpleasant memories of the alcohol-fuelled pandemonium at the Dream Café during the AGM still with him, Laurie has insisted that the bar shutters remain firmly down during this event, despite the club's social rep grumbling about loss of revenue.

Speeches in front of large groups are not one of Laurie's strong points and he's nervous as he calls for quiet.

The loud chatter continues.

'Will you be quiet everyone!'

'Thank you, Dee. Welcome, and I promise I won't take up much of your time.'

'Good,' he hears, then from someone else, 'Why is the bar closed?'

'Because I remember what happened last time a bar was open during a tennis club meeting.'

'Open the bar,' someone calls out and a few others pick up the chant.

'Show some manners!' Dee shouts. This petite middle-aged woman with her booming voice has always managed to generate fear and compliance and the chanting stops as quickly as it had begun.

'Thank you, Dee.'

The two lead chanters leave the building, tutting as they go, and their absence is enough to improve the atmosphere in the clubhouse.

Laurie continues. 'This place is amazing. You'll know there have been difficulties delivering on time, what with the original builders pulling out. I want to thank Filip and his team for taking on the job and working incredibly hard to get it finished. That's Filip over there. Filip, please come over to accept our thanks.'

There is cheering as Filip stands next to Laurie, raising his hand in acknowledgement of the thanks. Only Laurie and Helen, possibly Jennifer too, know the extent of gratitude that Filip deserves.

'Next, I'd like to thank Helen for overseeing the project after the builders quit.'

There is a round of applause and Helen takes a dramatic bow.

'OK, I declare the clubhouse open.'

'Wait!' Dee says as she steps up to Laurie and Helen's side. 'I think that Laurie deserves praise too.'

There is further cheering and applause.

'It hasn't been easy given his inexperience,' Dee continues, 'and I admit that there have been times when …'

Dee is still talking but no one is listening. Some are rushing to the bar, the social rep unwilling to delay the opportunity to generate income for a moment longer. Others are chatting with friends and acquaintances. Several are heading outside to play more tennis. A few of the more considerate members come up to Helen and Laurie to thank them for their hard work, but before long the two of them are left alone.

'Well, we made it,' Helen says. 'A close call but we got there.'

'That may well turn out to be the most stressful few months of my life.'

'Nah, there'll be worse,' Helen jokes before abruptly breaking off because caring for a newborn is the first thing that comes to mind.

'My speech didn't go brilliantly well.'

'It was fine, Laurie. I spotted that journalist from the local paper so we might get a mention next week.'

'Which means we'll have a rush of new applications. I'd better check the waiting list. I also need to make sure that the captains have sorted out their teams for the summer.'

'We have a membership secretary, a committee member responsible for social events and we have team captains. Let them do their jobs. You deserve a rest. We both do.'

'I suppose so.'

'I'll get us some beers. After that, I'll buy the most expensive bottle of wine the club has to offer and after that, it's shots. And then we'll stagger home together and I'll drag you into bed with me. Is that a deal?'

'Tempting, though I do have a match tomorrow.'

'I'll get the beers.'

~

Laurie isn't joking. The last Men's A Team match of the winter season is the following day. Although the clubhouse is open, the agreement with Bridget and David was to hold all winter league post-match teas at their café and this will be the final one.

Laurie is seriously hungover the next afternoon and struggles to reach anywhere near his usual standard of play.

He's discussing backhand grips with members of the opposing team when Helen enters the café.

She sits down and grabs a cake. 'I'll miss these.'

David comes across with eight beers and sets them onto the table. 'Hi Helen. Want one?'

'Isn't this meant to be a post-match *tea*?' she asks.

'It's the final game so we're celebrating,' Laurie says, presumably having forgotten that a few hours earlier he'd announced that he was never going to have another drink.

'OK, in that case I will, thanks.' She has a lingering headache, but what the hell.

'Here, take mine,' Laurie says and he follows David to the counter. Their conversation to collect another beer is lasting longer than expected.

'What was that about?' Helen asks when he's back.

'I'll tell you later. It's not a problem though.'

Helen and Laurie stay behind to chat with David when the others have left.

'This is it, David, our final use of your café. We made it, our clubhouse is open, and being here has been brilliant.'

'It's been a pleasure.'

'You might not have thought that on the first night,' Helen says.

'A distant memory. Has Laurie mentioned the invite?'

'Not yet.' Laurie turns to Helen. 'David and Bridget have invited us over for a meal next Saturday.'

'To mark the end of your time here. We're grateful for how well you two have managed everything. Talk about old heads on young shoulders, you've been tremendous.'

'We'd love to come,' Helen says.

'Then we'll see you next Saturday. Around seven.'

Laurie is sighing as they start walking back to his flat.

'What's up?'

'I should never have played today, last night's drinking did me in.'

'I take it you lost.'

'Yes, but how do you know?'

'Let's just call it intuition.'

They walk on.

'I like them,' Helen says.

'Like who?'

340

'Bridget and David. They're cool. I got to know Bridget a bit at that awful Kilroy dinner party.'

'I'm sure we won't be seeing Oliver and Stephanie there next Saturday.'

'No way, but I suppose there'll be other guests. It looks like we've made it onto the Muswell Hill Couples Dinner Parties circuit.'

'Is that good or bad?'

'It just is.'

38

'I never drink this much,' Bridget claims as she tops up her own glass and unsteadily drops the bottle back onto the table. 'What a lovely colour.' The pink fizz has mixed with the dregs of red. 'Andy's at the café all weekend so we can unwind a bit.'

Andy is Bridget's son, in his second year studying Computing at the University of Oxford and currently on Easter vacation.

The six of them are sitting round the dining table, the meal over.

'Bridget, you were telling us how come you and David set up the café,' Helen says.

'So, yes ... that crazy man over there,' Bridget says pointing at David, 'he tells me he's done with accountancy and working for the local government and he wants to open an arts café.'

'Crazy? Didn't you think he meant it?'

'Saying you want to do something and making it happen are two quite different things. I'd seen this fantasy of his written on one of his outrageous lists, David is a list person, but I didn't think there was a hope in hell of him going through with it.'

'I only succeeded when you agreed to help,' David says.

'Yes, I did agree, it was one of those spur of the moment decisions. I had an OK job at an art gallery – secure, well-paid – but then one day I decided I'd had enough. So I chucked it all in to help set up the café.'

'Which has worked out brilliantly,' Helen says. 'That's such a lovely story. I can see why you called it Dream Café.'

'Actually, I had two dreams,' David says, looking across at Bridget. 'To open the café and to be with this gorgeous woman.'

Helen is enjoying hearing about their hosts' lives. 'And you have the hotel, too. On the Hill.' She turns to face Jennifer. 'Which is where you work, of course.'

Jennifer reddens. She and Gareth are the other two guests that evening.

'Is it OK to say, Jennifer?' David asks. 'Well,' he continues without waiting for her permission, 'we've been working flat out since taking on a share of the hotel. This is our first weekend off this year, which can't be healthy. We decided to do something about it and fortunately it was an easy decision because we have a brilliant deputy manager.'

All eyes are upon Jennifer who looks down and inspects her table mat.

'Are you sure it's alright for me to say?' David asks, again continuing without having a response. 'We're reducing our stake in the hotel and stepping away from all management. Jennifer and Gareth are now part-owners with Jennifer running the place along with Melissa, the original owner.'

'I'm hugely grateful to Bridget and David,' Jennifer says. 'I guess I'm kinda like David with his café dream. I've always worked in hospitality, I started off as a waitress, and my dream has been to run a hotel. There couldn't be a more perfect place than On the Hill.' Her voice tapers off as tears well up. 'I love it there.'

'You'll be brilliant, which is pointless to say because you already are.'

'Thanks, David.'

'Will you be involved, Gareth?' Helen asks.

'No, it's Jennifer's baby. I'm enjoying the teaching and I've got loads to learn about heading a department. I need to keep on top of the new technologies too, it's all moving so fast and I want my students to have the most up to date stuff.'

'He's a brilliant teacher,' Jennifer says.

'On the subject of dreams, mine was to be with Jennifer but then stupidly I lost her. That won't happen again.' Gareth turns to look at Jennifer. 'I promise.'

'So, that's us oldies owning up to our dreams. What about you two?' Bridget asks, looking from Laurie to Helen and back to Laurie again.

Now the others are looking at Laurie who isn't rushing to answer.

It's Helen who is the first to address the question. 'I want to be part of one of the best string quartets, I want to play at the Royal Albert Hall, I want to have top hit albums, I want to regularly feature on Classic FM and BBC3. I used to think that travelling around the world performing was what I most wanted. I started that way back with the National Youth Orchestra and I am looking forward to our European tour this summer. But you know what? They're all great dreams but … but …' tears are rolling down Helen's cheeks, 'but I know there's something much more important than any of that: spending time with the person you most care about. Sorry,' she adds with a watery smile. 'Too much wine.'

Laurie takes hold of Helen's hand. He's been quiet for much of the evening, happy to listen to everyone else's stories.

'Well, that leaves me. Being with you, Helen, that was my dream from the first time I saw you at the tennis club. There is something else though. I'm involved in research that could lead to my team developing cures for the world's most serious illnesses. And that isn't pie in the sky; it's possible in our lifetime.'

'Wow,' David says. 'That beats everything.'

'You know what I'm thinking,' Bridget says. 'Perhaps in our different ways – through science, teaching, music, the café – we're all helping to make the world a nicer place.'

The quiet reflection around the table is broken by Bridget. 'Let's celebrate the realisation of our dreams. A toast to us!' She's topping up glasses as she speaks.

Jennifer and Gareth are beaming as they clink glasses, excited about the purchase of the flat,

Jennifer's new role at the hotel and Gareth's progress at his school.

David and Bridget are all smiles in the knowledge that they will have the time to do fun stuff at last. As part of their rethink about the future they have decided to move in together. No one knows that yet, not even their children.

As Helen holds up her glass she's watching the others, thinking about the mysteries of relationships. How complex they are, how they can swing in an instant from deep affection to petty bickering and back to … back to love. That word, at times chucked around like confetti, at other times left unsaid, and always so elusive to comprehend. A magic word that can restore trust, bring an intense rush of warmth, create confusion, cement a bond.

'I love you,' she hears Laurie say.

It's unplanned, a surprise to him as he says it because he's never uttered those words to anyone before.

Helen has overused the word in the past. It's let her down and she's been careful to avoid it with Laurie.

Until now.

She touches his glass with her own.

'And I love you, Laurie.'

Printed in Great Britain
by Amazon